A Friend in Need

"You're going to have to find out who killed Roy, you know," Carolyn said.

"Absolutely not," Phyllis said. "You heard what Mike said. I think I'd be risking his career if I were to get mixed up in this investigation."

"But you know good and well they think Eve did it, and once they get an idea like that in their heads, they stop looking for anybody else! You saw what happened in those other cases. If you hadn't stepped in and uncovered the real killers, innocent people would have gone to jail . . . probably including me!"

"Those were isolated cases," Phyllis insisted. "Most of the time, the police and the sheriff's department are very good about finding out what really happened—"

"Are you prepared to risk Eve's life on that?" Carolyn broke in. "Because that's what you'll be doing if you turn your back on this, you know. Do you honestly believe she could survive being sent to prison? Do you want to have to go to Huntsville to visit her and see her wasting away to nothing in there behind those iron bars?"

"I think they send most of the female convicts to Gatesville instead of Huntsville," Sam said, then when Carolyn gave him an angry look hurried on, "Anyway, it doesn't matter, because Eve's not gonna be convicted of anything, and she's not gonna be convicted of anything because she's innocent. We all saw her with Roy the past couple of months. There's no way she would ever hurt him, let alone kill him."

Phyllis knew that was true. The conventional wisdom was that anybody was capable of anything under the right circumstances, but she didn't believe that. Maybe it was true in most cases, but some things were so far beyond the pale that they simply were impossible.

She turned toward the phone, and Carolyn asked, "What are you going to do?"

continued . . .

Other Fresh-Baked Mysteries by Livia J. Washburn

The Pumpkin Muffin Murder

Killer Crab Cakes

The Christmas Cookie Killer

Murder by the Slice

A Peach of a Murder

The Gingerbread Bump-off

Wedding Cake Killer

A Fresh-Baked Mystery

LIVIA J. WASHBURN

AN OBSIDIAN MYSTERY

OBSIDIAN

Published by New American Library,
a division of Penguin Group (USA) Inc.,
375 Hudson Street, New York, New York 10014, USA
Penguin Group (Canada), 90 Eglinton Avenue East, Suite 700, Toronto,
Ontario M4P 2Y3, Canada (a division of Pearson Penguin Canada Inc.)
Penguin Books Ltd., 80 Strand, London WC2R 0RL, England
Penguin Ireland, 25 St. Stephen's Green, Dublin 2,
Ireland (a division of Penguin Books Ltd.)
Penguin Group (Australia), 250 Camberwell Road, Camberwell,
Victoria 3124, Australia (a division of Pearson Australia Group Pty. Ltd.)
Penguin Books India Pvt. Ltd., 11 Community Centre,
Panchsheel Park, New Delhi - 110 017, India
Penguin Group (NZ), 67 Apollo Drive, Rosedale, Auckland 0632,
New Zealand (a division of Pearson New Zealand Ltd.)
Penguin Books (South Africa) (Pty.) Ltd., 24 Sturdee Avenue,
Rosebank, Johannesburg 2196, South Africa

Penguin Books Ltd., Registered Offices:
80 Strand, London WC2R 0RL, England

First published by Obsidian, an imprint of New American Library,
a division of Penguin Group (USA) Inc.

ISBN 978-1-62090-850-1

Set in New Caledonia · *Designed by Elke Sigal*

Printed in the United States of America

PUBLISHER'S NOTE

This is a work of fiction. Names, characters, places, and incidents either are the
product of the author's imagination or are used fictitiously, and any resemblance to
actual persons, living or dead, business establishments, events, or locales is entirely
coincidental.

The publisher does not have any control over and does not assume any responsibility for author or third-party Web sites or their content.

*This book is dedicated to my husband, James Reasoner,
and my two daughters, Shayna and Joanna,
who have to sample even when the recipe
turns out to be a real loser.*

*I*t was the silliest thing. As she sat there on the metal bunk with its thin, hard mattress, her back against a cinder-block wall painted a hideous shade of institutional green, Phyllis Newsom felt like she ought to be singing a song.

"Nobody Knows the Trouble I've Seen," to be specific. As far as she could remember, although she had heard that song a number of times, usually in a movie or TV show, she had never actually sung it before.

But that made sense, because she'd never been locked up in jail before, either.

Phyllis sighed, closed her eyes, and lifted a hand to massage her temples. She wasn't going to sing. The only reason such silly thoughts even occurred to her, she realized, was that she was trying to take her mind off the fact that she'd been arrested.

A woman her age, who had never been in trouble with the law in her life—well, not real trouble, anyway, if you didn't count annoying a police detective every now and then—and she'd been arrested, locked up, thrown in the hoosegow, checked in at the old gray-bar hotel . . .

She was doing it again. Trying to distract herself. And it wasn't working.

"Shoot," she whispered.

She was in the county jail, just off Fort Worth Highway near the railroad tracks, not far from the eastern edge of downtown Weatherford, Texas. She'd been here before. Not in the jail itself, of course, but in the building, since it also housed the Parker County Sheriff's Department, and her son, Mike, was a deputy.

Thinking about Mike made Phyllis squeeze her eyes even more tightly closed. This was going to be so humiliating for him, having a mother who'd been arrested. She wondered if he had heard about it yet. If there was any way to keep him from ever finding out, it would be worth it.

Of course, the best way would have been not to interfere in a murder investigation in the first place—District Attorney Timothy Sullivan had warned her that he wasn't going to put up with it anymore—but if she had done that, it would have meant leaving one of her best friends at the mercy of a legal system that was already convinced she was guilty. Phyllis couldn't do that.

Anyway, what she had done wasn't really that bad. Technically it might be considered obstruction of justice and interfering with a police investigation, but as far as Phyllis was concerned, she had just been trying to get to the truth.

Life in the jail went on around her. Doors slammed. People, mostly men, talked to one another, but occasionally she heard a woman's voice, too. Footsteps sounded on the tile and cement floors. A buzzer of some sort went off. A phone rang.

Phyllis opened her eyes and studied the holding cell. The wall behind her was an exterior one; that was why it was made of cinder blocks. The interior walls were metal painted the same noxious shade of green. The steel door had a small window covered with metal mesh in it. That was the only window of any sort in the small room. The floor was cement and had a drain with a metal grate over it in the center of the cell. She didn't want to think about why the cell had a drain in it. There was . . . something . . . built into one wall that she thought was a toilet, but she wasn't sure. If it was, it was bound to be extremely uncomfortable. A built-in fluorescent light and a vent in the ceiling for the heating and air-conditioning system completed the room's furnishings.

Phyllis felt a scream trying to well up in her throat. She crossed her arms and stiffened her resolve. She was not going to give in to the emotions she felt right now. She was going to remain cool and collected. She really hadn't been here that long, and surely she wouldn't be here much longer. Her lawyer, Juliette Yorke, had promised to be here right away.

In fact, footsteps were coming along the corridor outside the holding cells right now, she realized. When they stopped on the other side of the door, she heaved a sigh of relief. They would be taking her to a bail hearing now, and soon she could start trying to figure out what to do about this travesty of justice.

But when the electronic lock buzzed and the door swung open, it wasn't Juliette who stood there; it was Mike in his sheriff's department uniform, and he looked angry, upset, and scared all at the same time.

So much for the futile hope that he wouldn't find out about it.

"Mike . . . ," Phyllis said.

"Mom," he said, "what the hell have you done?"

Phyllis felt some anger of her own. "I don't like you taking that tone with me, Mike, and as for what I've done, I didn't have any choice. I have to prove that Eve isn't a murderer. You know good and well that Eve Turner never killed anyone in her life!"

Chapter 1

Christmas Eve, several weeks earlier

"Oh, my, look at all the cars," Phyllis said as Sam Fletcher drove his pickup along the block where they lived. "I didn't think people would start showing up this early. They've blocked off the driveway, Sam."

"Yeah, I see that," Sam said. "Tell you what. I'll stop in front of the house and you can get out and go on in. I'll find a place to park down the street and walk back."

"That's not fair. You live here, and these people don't."

"Yeah, but that means they won't be stayin'. They'll all leave when the shower's over. I can bring the pickup back down then."

"Well, I suppose so," Phyllis said. "I just hate to put you to any more trouble after everything that's already happened today."

"You mean that killer we caught?" Sam asked with a smile.

"Or that you caught, is more like it. Heck, I'm gettin' used to that. How many times does this make?"

"Don't even think about it," Phyllis told him as a tiny shudder went through her. "I want to put all that behind us. This is Christmas Eve, after all, and it's Eve's bridal shower, too. I think that's plenty to keep us busy the rest of the day, don't you?"

"If you say so." Sam brought the pickup to a smooth stop in front of the big old two-story house he shared with Phyllis, Carolyn Wilbarger, and Eve Turner, two more retired teachers.

They wouldn't be sharing it with Eve for much longer, though. Another week and she and Roy Porter would be married. Eve and Roy planned to come back here to the house after their honeymoon and stay temporarily while they continued looking for a place of their own, but that wouldn't be the same.

But then, nothing ever stayed the same, Phyllis mused as she got out of the pickup. Like it or not, life-altering changes came along every few years. She had become a teacher, gotten married to Kenny, given birth to their son, Mike, continued teaching while they raised him into a fine young man, seen him marry and have a son of his own, retired . . .

And then Kenny had died, leaving her to rattle around alone in that big old house. Dolly Williamson, the former superintendent and a longtime friend, had suggested that Phyllis rent out the extra bedrooms to other retired teachers who were on their own, and once Phyllis had done that, she'd believed that from then on, life would settle down into a serene existence without the upheavals of youth.

Well, *that* hadn't worked out, had it?

People had come and gone in the house. Mattie Harris,

one of Phyllis's oldest friends, had passed away. Sam Fletcher had moved in. Now Eve was getting married and moving out. That was inevitable, Phyllis supposed. Although she didn't know the details because Eve hadn't lived in Weatherford at the time, she was aware that her friend had been married several times. Really, Eve had been without a man in her life for longer than Phyllis had expected.

Then there were the murders . . .

But as she'd told Sam, she didn't want to think about that, so she didn't. As she stepped up onto the porch, she didn't allow herself to remember the body she had literally stumbled over there not that long ago. She didn't glance at the house next door, where she had found another body a few years earlier. And as she stepped into the house and saw all the people crowding into the living room, she told herself sternly that nobody was going to try to poison her guests at this get-together.

They'd better not, anyway.

Carolyn Wilbarger spotted Phyllis and quickly came over to her, smiling and nodding to some of the ladies along the way. Still smiling as she reached Phyllis, she said in a tight-lipped whisper, "Oh, my word. I didn't expect this many people."

Smiling as well, Phyllis replied, "Neither did I."

"When you called from the police station and said you didn't know how long you'd be, nobody had shown up yet. But then . . ." Carolyn shook her head. "That other business . . . ?"

"All settled," Phyllis told her. "I'll fill you in on the details later. Right now . . . well, this is Eve's day."

Eve certainly appeared to be enjoying it, too. She sat in the big armchair, beaming at the guests and the pile of presents that surrounded her. There had been some talk about how she shouldn't expect a bridal shower at her age and with numerous marriages in her past, but it was true that she had been living here with Phyllis for several years and didn't really have all the things she would need to set up housekeeping again. From the looks of it, after today she would.

The house was extravagantly decorated for Christmas because it had been part of the annual Jingle Bell Tour of Homes a couple of weeks earlier. Phyllis and Carolyn had added a few things to celebrate the upcoming wedding, including tables for the gifts covered in blue tablecloths with silver trim. They had decided to go with white roses since the cloths were blue and they looked great in the silver vases. Still, the theme remained overwhelmingly Christmasy. In a couple of days, when Christmas was over, they would take down all those decorations and start getting ready for the wedding, which would take place here on New Year's Eve.

Eve, Eve, Eve, Phyllis thought. There was no getting away from it.

"Phyllis!" Eve said, seeming to notice her for the first time. "Come here, dear."

Phyllis kept the smile on her face as she made her way across the crowded room to Eve, who stood up and hugged her.

"Thank you so much for this," Eve said. "I know you've had a lot of other things on your mind, but despite that you've given me the best bridal shower a girl could ever want!"

Phyllis patted her lightly on the back and said, "You're very welcome. I'm glad we were able to do this for you. We're all going to miss you once you've moved out."

"And I'm going to miss you, too," Eve said. She lowered her voice. "I didn't expect this many people to be here. I put everyone I could think of on the guest list because I thought a lot of them wouldn't be able to come, what with it being Christmas Eve and all. But it looks like practically everyone showed up!"

"Yes," Phyllis said, "it does."

In fact, there were so many ladies in the room that it was starting to seem a little claustrophobic to her, as if they were sucking down all the air and she couldn't breathe. She knew that feeling was all in her head, but that didn't make it seem any less real.

"I think I should go out to the kitchen and check on things," she went on. "You just sit down and have a good time."

"Thank you, dear." Eve leaned closer and added, "I owe you. Big time."

Phyllis waved that off and headed for the kitchen, motioning with a slight movement of her head for Carolyn to follow her.

When they were in the kitchen by themselves, with the door closed, both of them said, "Whew!" at the same time, then laughed at the identical expression.

"Refresh my memory," Phyllis said quietly. "Did even half of those people out there RSVP to let us know they were coming?"

"They most certainly did not," Carolyn said. "And it certainly would have helped if they had."

"But all too typical these days," Phyllis muttered as she looked at the trays of snacks spread out across the kitchen counters.

There were warm sweet bacon crackers fresh out of the oven, nutty caramel pretzels, and cheddar garlic palmiers.

Phyllis knew from the smell in the air that the stuffed mushrooms were warming in the oven. There was a zesty cheese ball softening on a decorative silver plate with a matching knife. And in the refrigerator, waiting to be brought out, was a tray filled with mini curried turkey croissant sandwiches. Enough food to feed an army, as Sam might say, but that was good because they practically had an army in the living room.

The back door opened, and Sam walked into the kitchen. "Hope it's all right I came around this way," he said. "I didn't particularly want to run the gauntlet out there."

"I don't blame you," Phyllis said. She frowned. "I just remembered . . . Weren't you and Roy supposed to go bowling this afternoon?"

Sam's eyes widened. He slapped himself lightly on the forehead and said, "D'oh! I forgot all about it, what with catchin' killers and all." He took his cell phone out of his pocket. "I'll call him right now and tell him I'm on my way."

"Yes, that would tend to distract a person," Carolyn said.

Sam grinned and waved as he went back out the door with his cell phone held to his ear.

"I'm glad Sam and Roy have become friends," Phyllis said. "I'm sure it's been tough on him, being in a strange town where he doesn't have any friends or family."

"He didn't put a single person on the guest list for the shower or the wedding," Carolyn said.

"I know. But he seems to be all right with it. As long as he's got Eve, I think he's happy."

"He should be. She's a fine woman. He's lucky to have her."

Phyllis smiled. Carolyn and Eve had squabbled quite a bit over the years, but Phyllis knew that they really cared for each other. Carolyn could be a little on the prickly side sometimes. It had taken her more than a year to get used to the idea of Sam living in the house.

"What still needs to be done?" Phyllis asked, putting her mind back on the matters at hand.

"The chocolate chocolate chip cupcakes are already on the table along with some cookies and the vegetable and fruit tray, and the punch is in the punch bowl. Eve suggested that we spike it, but I vetoed that. The last thing we want in the living room is a bunch of tipsy teachers."

Phyllis laughed. She had to agree with that sentiment.

"Everything seems to be under control," she said. "We'll wait a while before we bring the rest of the food out. Eve wanted to play some games first and then open presents, so it'll be a while before anyone's ready to eat."

Carolyn's eyes narrowed. "I swear, if anyone brought any of those perverted gag gifts—"

"I'm sure everyone will be the soul of decorum," Phyllis said.

Actually, she wasn't sure of that. The retired teachers, the ones from the generation she and Carolyn and Eve belonged to, were all ladies, raised to observe the proprieties. But some of the younger ones, the ones who were still teaching . . . well, you couldn't ever be a hundred percent sure of what they might do.

But even so, the last thing she would have expected to hear as she and Carolyn started along the hall toward the living room was voices raised in anger.

Chapter 2

"At least you never caught me changing grades because those football players are morons," one of the women was saying as Phyllis hurried into the living room. She was standing in the middle of the room facing an equally angry woman, while the rest of the guests sat there looking distressed or embarrassed.

"I never changed a grade for anyone," the second woman insisted. "And I didn't have to keep a *mouthwash* bottle filled with vodka in my desk just to get through the day, either." She made air quotes as she said the word *mouthwash*.

"That's a despicable lie! Those slutty little dullards only started that rumor because I expected them to actually do their work."

Phyllis saw Eve wince at the split infinitive. Once an English teacher, always an English teacher, she supposed. She was the same way whenever someone got facts from American history blatantly wrong.

Contrary to what Phyllis had been thinking a few moments earlier, it wasn't two of the younger teachers who were arguing. Rather, it was a couple of the retired teachers, women approximately the same age as Phyllis, Carolyn, and Eve. Phyllis knew them only slightly, and it took her a few seconds to come up with their names.

Loretta Harbor and Velma Nickson—that was it. Both of them had taught at the high school with Eve. Loretta had taught some sort of advanced math—calculus, maybe—and Velma was home ec. Phyllis didn't think she had ever exchanged more than a dozen words with either of them.

Now, though, she said, "Ladies, ladies, there's no need for this. And you don't want to ruin Eve's special day, do you? Besides, it's Christmas Eve! We should all be filled with the holiday spirit."

Loretta said, "If you want to talk about spirits, you should ask Velma about her mouthwash bottle!"

"That does it," Velma said. She was a tiny, gray-haired, birdlike woman, but just then she looked like she was ready to tackle Loretta and drag her to the floor.

Carolyn moved past Phyllis and said, "If you two are going to squabble like a couple of third graders on the playground, the least you can do is take it outside!"

Eve finally stood up. "Everyone, please. This is a glorious, happy occasion. Loretta, Velma, for my sake, can't you put those old grudges aside for a little while?"

The two women continued to glare at each other, but after a moment Velma shrugged and said, "I suppose I can ignore her. For you, Eve."

"And I certainly have more willpower than she does," Loretta said. She made a tippling motion.

"Just no backbone or integrity," Velma shot back. "Or maybe it was just that your eyesight was bad and you couldn't tell a B from an F."

Carolyn got between them and said, "Sit down, both of you. Now."

Grudgingly, Loretta and Velma retreated to the chairs where they had been sitting, on opposite sides of the room. Still glaring at each other but not saying anything, they sat down.

"Fine," Carolyn said. "Now, let's all just pretend like this never happened."

Yes, Phyllis thought, that's what ladies of their generation did. They pretended that anything unpleasant had never happened, unless they were forced to admit otherwise.

Carolyn put a hand on Eve's shoulder and said, "Just go on with whatever you were doing, dear."

"Well . . . we were playing Truth," Eve said. "I'm not sure that's a good idea anymore."

"What about the Dare part?" Carolyn asked.

"Oh, goodness, most of us are too old for dares."

"Well, then, uh . . . we can open presents."

Eve's face lit up. "Now, that's an excellent idea."

All the chairs in the room were full, including the extra ones Carolyn had dragged in from other rooms when the crowd began to grow beyond expectations, so she and Phyllis had to stand while Eve opened the presents. Phyllis had a notebook and pen ready so she could write down each gift and who had brought it; this way, Eve could send thank-you cards after the wedding. She supposed that if some of the younger women had that job, they would type the list into their smart phones and e-mail it to themselves and send thank-you texts, but she wasn't that technologically advanced. She could make calls on her phone, and if she had time to stop and think about what she was doing, she could take a picture with it, but that was about all.

Loretta and Velma seemed to get caught up in seeing what gifts Eve had gotten, like everybody else, so after a few minutes they stopped glaring and really did ignore each other. Phyllis was glad. She was sorry the party had been marred even for a few minutes, but she was confident the disturbance hadn't been bad enough to ruin Eve's memories of the day.

Her own memories of this Christmas Eve already included uncovering the identity of a murderer. She didn't need a geriatric catfight to go along with that.

She looked around the room and realized that she only really knew about half of the women. Most of the others were familiar to her, and she even recalled the names of some of them. But there were a few she didn't remember ever seeing before.

There had been names on the guest list that Phyllis didn't know at all, too. These were women who had taught at the high school with Eve for a year or two, at the end of her career. By that time Phyllis had already been retired, and she'd never had any contact with those younger teachers. Everybody liked Eve, though. It was just a natural reaction to her personality. So Phyllis wasn't surprised that those women had come to the shower.

As the pile of gifts dwindled almost to nothing, Carolyn said quietly to Phyllis, "I'll go take the mushrooms out of the oven and set the rest of the food on the table."

"I can come help—," Phyllis began.

"I can manage just fine," Carolyn said. "You're keeping the list, remember?"

Phyllis nodded. "All right. I'll be there in a minute, though, as soon as we're finished here."

Eve opened the last few gifts, and Phyllis made note of them. Later she would type up the list on her computer, but since she couldn't get to the desk in the corner of the living room very easily because of all the guests, she took the notebook with her and stuck it in a drawer in the kitchen.

Carolyn had already gotten the other snacks set out on plates and trays. Phyllis put the ice cream balls on top of the punch and gave it a light stir. It turned a pretty light blue color. She put her hands under the bowl and said, "I'll take this into the dining room. You can bring one of the snack trays."

They spent the next few minutes transferring the punch and all the food to the table in the dining room, where napkins, plasticware, and festive paper plates were already set out so that the guests could help themselves buffet-style.

The table was covered with an elegant white tablecloth, and there were two blue candles and two silver hearts intertwined. Carolyn had already put the buttercream chocolate cupcakes in a couple of wire trees. She had left the top center spots on both wire trees empty and had put small vases of flowers in them. Silver plates of assorted cookies surrounded the trees. There was also a big fruit tray with a sweet creamy dip and a matching tray of vegetables with a veggie dip. She had obviously been very busy while Phyllis was gone. When everything was ready, Phyllis went to the living room and said, "All right, ladies, we have refreshments in the dining room."

She was glad to see that everyone seemed to be smiling and talking and laughing. The brief unpleasantness between Loretta Harbor and Velma Nickson appeared to be forgotten. Loretta and Velma were both huddled with separate groups of friends and weren't paying any attention to each other anymore.

Phyllis's announcement started a migration to the dining room. It was still early enough in the afternoon that the guests could eat without spoiling their supper. The noise level in the house went up even more as everyone chatted happily.

Eve lingered in the living room as everyone else went into the dining room. She came over to Phyllis and squeezed her arm.

"I can't tell you how happy this has made me, Phyllis," she said. "You know me—I'm not a sentimental old softie, but I could almost cry, having all my friends around me like this."

"You deserve all the happiness you get," Phyllis told her. She slipped an arm around Eve's shoulders and hugged her.

"Carolyn told me you solved that awful murder."

"I was lucky," Phyllis said. "I figured it out before it was too late."

"You always do, dear." Eve laughed. "My goodness, I'm glad Loretta and Velma didn't murder each other right here in the living room! But then you wouldn't have had to solve that one, would you, since we'd all know who did it."

"Don't even talk about it," Phyllis said. "No more murders, especially not here." She paused. Since Eve didn't seem to mind discussing the incident, she went on, "Those things they were accusing each other of . . ."

"Changing grades and nipping from a bottle of vodka during class?" Eve smiled. "Oh, my, yes. Loretta wasn't just about to let any of her precious football players fail her class and get booted off the team, and as for Velma . . . she'd be snockered by the time the dismissal bell rang on the first day of school, and I'm not sure she sobered up until the last day in the spring! She was one of those high-performance boozers, though, who could always get her work done, drunk or sober."

"Good to know," Phyllis muttered.

Eve linked arms with her and said, "Let's go sample those delicious appetizers of yours. Do you know if Carolyn spiked the punch like I suggested?"

"I'm pretty sure she didn't."

"Good, then we don't have to worry about Velma diving headfirst into the punch bowl."

Phyllis couldn't do anything but laugh as Eve led her toward the dining room.

For the next half hour or so, everyone spread out through the dining room and living room, eating snacks off the paper plates and drinking punch from plastic cups. They all seemed to be having a good time, and Phyllis was glad. She liked being a hostess and seeing her guests enjoying themselves.

But she was glad to see them go, too, drifting out by twos and threes after hugging Eve and offering her their best wishes on her upcoming wedding and marriage. Having company was fine, but the aftermath of having company was better. Phyllis didn't even mind the cleaning up that much, especially when she had Carolyn and Eve to help her.

"What were Sam and Roy doing this afternoon?" Eve asked as they put away the leftover food.

"Sam said they were going to go bowling," Phyllis replied. "I don't know when they'll be back."

"It doesn't matter. Roy and I have a quiet evening planned. I've had enough excitement for the day, I think. And it *is* Christmas Eve."

"I'll be going over to Sandra's house," Carolyn said. She and her daughter spent a lot of holidays together. Some years, Phyllis would have gone to Mike and Sarah's house for Christmas Eve, or they would have come here and brought her grandson, Bobby, but this year, with the added distraction of the bridal shower, they had decided to wait until Christmas Day to come over.

That was fine, Phyllis thought. Families needed to have their own holiday traditions that weren't tied to what the parents or grandparents had always done. That was all part of the inevitable process of change she had been thinking about earlier.

"What about you and Sam?" Carolyn went on.

"*It's a Wonderful Life*, of course," Phyllis said. "Maybe *White Christmas*, if there's time." She never tired of watching those classic movies, even though she had seen them so many times she practically knew all the dialogue by heart.

"No other plans?" Eve said.

Phyllis shook her head. "Nope."

What more could she want than to curl up on the sofa with Sam and watch some good movies? Especially after the day she'd had.

To be honest, right now that sounded pretty much like heaven to her.

Chapter 3

"**I** saw the cutest cake topper in a magazine the other day," Carolyn said a couple of days later as she sat at the kitchen table with Phyllis and Sam. The three of them were lingering over their breakfast coffee. "It had the bride dragging the groom, as if he were trying desperately to get away. Do you think we should try to find one like that for Eve's cake, Phyllis?"

With an effort, Phyllis managed not to frown as she said, "Well, I'm not sure." She knew that Carolyn had a pretty low opinion of marriage in general because of the way her own had worked out, but she didn't think a cake topper like that would send a very good message. It wasn't really appropriate, either, since Eve was hardly having to drag Roy to the altar. "I thought the topper we'd picked out already was pretty good . . ."

"I think Carolyn's jokin'," Sam said with a smile.

"Of course I am!" Carolyn said. "That would be ridiculous. You didn't think I was serious, did you, Phyllis?"

"No, of course not," Phyllis said.

It bothered her that she hadn't realized Carolyn was joking. Although to be fair, Carolyn had never been known for her witticisms. She was the one who always took things deadly serious. Maybe her own sense of humor just wasn't up to par these days because she'd been overwhelmed by everything that was happening.

At least Christmas Day had passed in a peaceful, pleasant manner. She and Sam had spent the day here with Mike, Sarah, and Bobby. She hadn't prepared a big meal. Instead they had feasted on the leftovers from the shower. Even though more guests had shown up than expected, Phyllis's tendency to have more food on hand than was really necessary had come in handy. There had been plenty left to feed all five of them on Christmas, which made it an easy day for her.

Now that was behind them, and she could turn all her attention to preparing for Eve's wedding.

"So what's on the agenda for today?" Sam asked.

"We have to get all the Christmas lights and decorations taken down, boxed up, and put away," Phyllis said.

"Some folks leave 'em up until after New Year's, you know."

"Yes, but most people don't have a wedding in their house on New Year's Eve."

"You've got a point there," Sam admitted. "We had help from half the neighborhood puttin' 'em up. With just us, it's liable to take a while to get them all back down."

"All the more reason to get started," Phyllis said as she stood up.

Sam's prediction proved to be true. The three of them worked all day getting the lights and decorations back in the boxes they had come from. Some of those boxes were stored in various closets, while the boxes of white lights were left out for the wedding decorations. Sam had to carry others up a ladder and into the attic that could be accessed through the garage. At least they had good weather for it. Christmas Eve and Christmas Day had been cloudy and blustery, but this day after Christmas was crisp, cool, and sunny, a perfect winter day in Texas.

"Is it the British or the Canadians who call this Boxin' Day?" Sam asked as he carried a box of lights up the ladder in the garage.

"Goodness, I don't know," Phyllis said. She was holding the ladder to make sure it didn't slip. "I think it's the British. Or maybe it is the Canadians. Or both. I mean, Canada was part of the British Empire."

"Could be," Sam said as he slid the box through the opening under the rafters. "Whoever it is, I think they've got the right idea."

"I'm not sure it has to do with boxing up Christmas decorations."

"You could Google it and find out," Sam suggested.

"I could," Phyllis said, "if there was any reason to do that."

Sam disappeared through the opening. She heard him moving around up there in the storage space. He emerged a few moments later and started down the ladder. She stepped back to give him room when he reached the bottom.

"You're getting all dusty," she said. She brushed at his thick salt-and-pepper hair. "And cobwebby."

He grinned. "That's all right. Anybody as old as I am ought to be a little dusty."

Phyllis didn't point out that they were practically the same age. And she certainly wasn't gathering dust.

By late afternoon, all the lights and decorations were boxed up, although quite a few of the boxes still had to be carried up into the attic. They were stacked in a corner of the garage, out of the way, and Sam said, "I'll take those up there tomorrow. You ladies can get on with your plans for the wedding. I know you've still got a lot to do."

"The cake is the main thing," Carolyn said. "We've never attempted anything quite that big before."

"It's going to be interesting," Phyllis agreed.

After much discussion, they had decided it would be best to keep the cake as simple as possible, in the hope that there would be less of a chance for anything to go wrong. The plan was that it would be a layered white cake with smooth white icing sitting on a floating-tiers cake stand. Those layers would be wrapped with see-through silver snowflake ribbon with a smaller blue satin ribbon behind it that would show through. In the original design, the cake topper would have sat on a nice blue bow. They had planned on putting plastic snowflakes on the top and second layers, leaving the bottom layer plain but sitting artfully on some tulle and scattering more snowflakes on the table around the cake. This had seemed like an appropriate touch since the wedding was taking place during the winter, but Eve had bought a cake topper just a few hours earlier that required them to rethink the cake plans. This cake topper had a twisted glass heart with doves, flowers, and a bride and groom. After much more discussion, they decided to keep the simple smooth frosting, but they would put touches of hearts and flowers with the frosting to match the topper.

"I think we should have a cake tasting," Phyllis continued. "I'll bake some cakes tomorrow morning, and we can get together with Eve and Roy tomorrow afternoon."

"Why do we need to do that?" Carolyn asked. "Cake is cake."

She had made that same comment several times while they were making up their minds what to do, and Phyllis supposed it was true, at least to a certain extent.

"I know, but I still think it would be a good idea to let Eve and Roy know exactly what they'll be getting."

"I don't think they're really worried all that much about the cake." Carolyn shrugged. "But it doesn't matter to me."

Sam said, "And any excuse to eat cake is a good one, as far as I'm concerned." They had left the garage and come into the kitchen while they were talking, and now he leaned a hip against one of the counters. "I don't think Roy is worried about much of anything. He's about as calm as any fella I've ever seen who was gettin' married in less than a week."

"Well, why shouldn't he be calm?" Carolyn asked. "He's getting a fine woman in Eve."

"Oh, no argument about that," Sam said. "But any time a fella's fixin' to settle down, certain thoughts have to be goin' through his mind."

"Like giving up his freedom?"

"Well, yeah."

Carolyn sniffed. "Yes, like the freedom to scratch himself and throw his dirty clothes on the floor is so important and will be such a sacrifice for poor Roy."

"That's not exactly what I meant . . ."

"No, what you meant is that all men are allergic to commitment, even at Roy's age. Good grief, it's not like he's tying himself down for the next thirty or forty years. He's not going to live that long!"

"I suppose not," Sam said, looking like he wished he had never brought up the subject.

Phyllis took pity on him and said, "From what I can tell, they're both very happy and looking forward to being married, and I'm glad for them. So, cake tasting tomorrow afternoon at two o'clock?"

"I'll be there," Sam promised with a grin.

Eve and Roy ate supper with the three of them at the house that night. Roy tended to like eating out—he had gotten used to it during all those years when he'd been single, he said—but he seemed to enjoy these home-cooked meals, too.

"I hope you don't think I'll be able to feed you like this," Eve commented during the meal. "My cooking skills don't even come close to matching up with Phyllis's and Carolyn's."

"You know I'm not worried about that," Roy told her. He smiled. "I'm marrying the total package."

With his silver hair, easy smile, and casual good looks, Roy was an attractive man, no doubt about that. He was semiretired from a company in Houston that did consulting work for the oil and gas industry. Since the jobs he did now were all on the computer, he was able to keep his hand in, as he put it, and work from anywhere, including Weatherford. All he had to do was log in to the company's network.

Sam had found out all of that by talking to Roy, who hadn't been very forthcoming about his past with any of the others. Sam had also discovered that Roy had been married once before, to a real estate agent who had passed away following a short illness. It was good that he wasn't a lifelong bachelor.

Being married to Eve might have been a big adjustment for him. To Eve, of course, with several husbands in her past, being married was a normal state of affairs.

"We're going to have a cake tasting tomorrow afternoon," Phyllis said. "If that's all right with the two of you, naturally."

"I don't think we have any plans in the works," Roy said. "Do we, Eve?"

She shook her head. "No. At this point we're just waiting for New Year's Eve. All our arrangements have been made."

"Where are y'all goin' on your honeymoon?" Sam asked.

"The Bahamas," Eve said. "I'm really looking forward to it. I've never been there."

"How about you, Roy?"

"Oh, yes, I've been there," Roy replied. "The place is beautiful this time of year. Actually, it's beautiful any time of year."

"You don't have to fly through that triangle to get there, do you?" Carolyn asked with a frown.

Eve said, "You're thinking of the Bermuda Triangle, dear. They're totally different places."

Carolyn shook her head. "Oh, well, Bermuda, Bahama, I always get those two mixed up."

"What about the Virgin Islands?" Sam asked.

"Oh, I think we'd all be out of place there," Eve said. She wiggled her eyebrows like Groucho Marx and made both Sam and Roy burst out in laughter. Phyllis smiled. Carolyn was the only one who didn't seem amused.

Phyllis picked up her glass of iced tea and said, "Here's to your honeymoon. May it be a wonderful trip that you never forget."

"I'll drink to that," Roy said.

Chapter 4

The delicious aroma of cake baking filled the house the next morning. Phyllis didn't have just one cake in the oven, though. She had three baking, each a little different from the others. She used a basic sour cream cake recipe and split the batter evenly into three bowls, adding almond extract in one, coconut in another, and lemon extract in the last. She thought Eve and Roy ought to have the final say.

Sam came in from the garage where he had been working, carrying the remaining boxes up to the attic. He had assured Phyllis that he didn't need her to hold the ladder and had promised that he would make sure it was steady and well braced before he started up it. She had been a little worried about him despite those assurances, and while she was working in the kitchen she'd been half listening with one ear for the sound of any trouble.

"That's done," he reported, brushing dust off his hands. "And I got to tell you, with those cakes cookin' and the smell risin', that attic has never smelled better."

"You'll have to wait for this afternoon to try them," Phyllis said. "They'll be cooled off by then, and I'll have some frosting on them. Anyway, we can't very well sneak a taste before Eve and Roy. It'll be their cake, after all."

"You're right. I'll just enjoy the smell between now and then."

Phyllis laughed. "Help yourself to that."

"I put up the ladder. Any more chores you need done?"

"Not right now."

"All right. Holler if there's anything I can help you with."

She couldn't have asked for a better tenant, Phyllis thought as Sam left the kitchen. He was always helpful and invariably friendly. He got in a bad mood from time to time—who didn't?—but they never lasted for very long. Yes, he had been a good tenant, a good friend . . . and sometimes more. With all this wedding talk, the possibility couldn't help but crop up in her mind every now and then . . .

But no. After Kenny's death, Phyllis had been convinced that she would never marry again, and nothing had changed her mind on that point. Did she love Sam? Probably. She certainly enjoyed spending time with him and having him around, and she could no longer imagine this house, and her life, without him in it. But she couldn't help but think that being married might change things.

No *might* about it, she told herself. Being married *would* change things between them, and there was no guarantee that the change would be for the better. She was happy the way things were. Why risk that?

Carolyn came into the kitchen and broke into Phyllis's train of thought. "That's certainly a wonderful smell," she said as she bent down to look through the window in the oven door. "What do you have in there?"

"I just used a plain vanilla sour cream cake and added different extracts," Phyllis replied. "It's a fairly dense cake and should be easy to frost. We'll let Eve pick which flavor she likes best. And Roy, of course."

"Roy's going to go along with whatever Eve says, and you know it. He's just like all the other men in the world—no real opinion about anything."

Phyllis wasn't so sure about that generality, but she figured Carolyn was right about Roy agreeing with whatever Eve decided. He had gone along with her decision to come back here to Phyllis's house after their honeymoon, even though originally he had wanted them to rent an apartment until they could find a place of their own. It was important to Eve to be in a house, though, and in the end Roy hadn't been stubborn about it.

Later, Phyllis took the cakes out of the oven and used a wooden toothpick to check each of them, pushing the toothpick down into the center of the cake and then pulling it out to see if any batter clung to it. When the toothpick emerged cleanly from all three cakes, she knew they were done and now just needed to cool before she put the frosting on them. She had already mixed up the buttercream frosting and had it in the refrigerator waiting to be spread on the cakes.

As Eve and Roy left to go to lunch and do some shopping, Phyllis reminded them, "We'll have the cake tasting around two, so don't eat too much. Leave plenty of room for cake."

Roy patted his stomach and grinned. "Won't be a problem," he assured her.

While they waited for the cakes to cool and cleaned the living room, Phyllis and Carolyn talked about the other decorations they planned to put up for the wedding. Eve had found some pretty blue-and-white curtains to replace the ones in the living room. They went ahead and took down the old curtains, cleaned the windows, and put up the new curtains after ironing all the wrinkles out.

Later they would move most of the furniture out of the living room and put it in the garage. White lights and tulle tied with ribbon would go up the banister. Bows would be placed on the backs of the rented chairs at the end of each row along the center aisle. Flowers and candles would finish the decorating. They could use most of the decorations from the shower in the dining room to set up for the reception.

Roy's prediction proved to be accurate. He had no trouble sampling all three cakes, and neither did any of the others. And Carolyn was a prophet as well, because when Eve pointed to the coconut-flavored cake and said, "That's my pick," Roy nodded without hesitation.

"That's the one I liked the best as well," he said. "Proving once again that great minds think alike."

Standing where only Phyllis could see her, Carolyn rolled her eyes and nodded as if to say, *I told you so.* That really wasn't necessary, because Phyllis had never doubted it.

There was a short discussion about the punch, and it was decided that a piña colada punch would go well with the cake, and the groom's cake would be the same batter as the cupcakes at the shower, with a chocolate buttercream icing. Roy had had one of the cupcakes when he and Sam came back from bowling and really liked it.

That was the last real decision that had to be made. The flowers were already ordered and would be delivered on the morning of the wedding. Phyllis would bake the cake that morning; then she and Carolyn would frost it and decorate it during the afternoon, so it would be ready for the wedding, which was scheduled for five o'clock. The dresses that Eve, Phyllis, and Carolyn would wear to the ceremony were upstairs, hanging in their closets. As Phyllis cleaned up after the cake tasting, she took a deep breath, both physically and mentally.

They weren't ready yet . . . but they would be. She had absolutely no doubt of it.

On the evening of December 30, Phyllis had baked the chocolate chocolate chip groom's cake, and it was cooling in the refrigerator. She would bake the wedding cake first thing in the morning. Now she was relaxing, sitting in the living room reading a nice thick historical novel set in medieval times . . . the era, not the theme restaurant, as she had told Sam earlier when he asked what she was reading. He was in one of the other armchairs with a Western paperback. Phyllis liked the fact that they could sit there, each reading quietly but aware of the other's presence, without feeling the need to talk. Every relationship needed that sort of comfort zone, she thought.

Carolyn was upstairs, and Eve and Roy had gone out for dinner. They had been gone for quite a while, and Phyllis expected them back soon. Then for the last time, Roy would kiss Eve good night and go back to the motel where he had been staying for the past few weeks. Phyllis didn't know where they intended to spend their wedding night, and it was none of her business.

For now she was happy to just sit in the same room with Sam and read, but a few minutes later, that changed. She heard car doors outside and looked up from her book, saying, "That must be Eve and Roy."

"I reckon so," Sam said, still engrossed in the tale of the Old West he was reading.

His concentration was broken, too, though, when the front door was thrown open and Eve hurried in.

"Turn on the television," she said with a note of alarm in her voice. "I need to see the weather forecast."

Phyllis had been so busy for the past few days that she hadn't paid any attention to the forecast, which could be a mistake in a state known for its changeable weather. The remote control was on the small table beside her chair. She picked it up and turned on the TV set, switching quickly to the cable station that carried the satellite radar feed and the forecast from the National Weather Service.

"Uh-oh," Sam said. "That doesn't look too good."

Roy came into the house behind Eve, who obviously had hurried ahead of him. "What about it?" he asked. "Is it going to snow?"

"Shh," Phyllis said as she looked at the radar image on the screen with its broad bands of pink signifying frozen precipitation stretching across Oklahoma.

"—spread southward across the Red River overnight," the disembodied voice on the TV was saying. "The atmospheric disturbance now located over New Mexico will move eastward and combine with the overrunning of warm air aloft over cold air at the surface to produce widespread areas of freezing rain, sleet, and snow during the day tomorrow. This mix of frozen precipitation will extend from the I-35 corridor into East Texas with an expected accumulation of one to three inches. Accumulations will be lighter and scattered west of the I-35 corridor."

"There you go," Sam said. "We're west of I-35, so we probably won't get anything."

"That's not what he said," Eve replied, still visibly upset. "He said it would be scattered. That means we could still get snow and ice here."

"Even if we do, it probably won't be very bad," Phyllis said. "It might keep some people from coming to the wedding, but I'm sure most of the guests who said they were attending will be here."

"What about the airport?" Roy said. "We're supposed to catch a flight out for the Bahamas on New Year's Day."

Sam said, "The airport hardly ever shuts down. It'd have to be a lot worse than the way they make it sound to keep the planes from getting in and out. You might be delayed awhile; that's all."

Roy nodded and sighed. "I think you're right. See, Eve, we panicked for nothing. Someone at the restaurant was talking about how there was a big snowstorm coming, so we wanted to find out."

"Well, I don't blame you," Phyllis said. "But I really don't think there's anything to worry about."

"I'll believe it when I see it," Eve said. "If anything goes wrong now—"

"It won't," Roy told her as he put an arm around her shoulders. "We've waited all our lives to find each other, and nothing's going to keep us apart now. I believe that with all my heart, Eve."

She turned toward him, leaned against him, and rested her head on his shoulder as he hugged her.

"I hope you're right, Roy."

"Of course I am," he said, his voice brimming with confidence. "By this time tomorrow evening, you and I are going to be husband and wife, Eve. Just you wait and see."

Chapter 5

*T*he first thing Phyllis did when she got up the next morning was check the sky.

"What are you doing?" Carolyn asked as she came out onto the back porch and found Phyllis standing there peering up intently at the gray clouds.

Phyllis didn't answer the question. Instead she said, "Do those look like snow clouds to you?"

Carolyn squinted at the sky. "Not really. But don't go by me. I'm not a meteorologist."

"Neither am I. But Eve came in last night worried because the area's supposed to get some snow and ice."

"That shouldn't stop her from getting married. Unless the roads got really bad and the preacher couldn't get here."

Phyllis looked at her and said, "Oh, goodness, don't even say that where she can hear it!"

"Have you checked the forecast on TV this morning?"

"Not yet." Phyllis turned toward the door, shivering in her

thick robe as a vagrant gust of cold air blew across the back-yard. "I wanted to take a look at the sky first."

They went into the kitchen, and Carolyn said, "You go see what they're saying on TV, and I'll start the coffee."

Phyllis went into the living room and turned on the weather station again. There was still an awful lot of that frozen-precipitation pink extending down across the Red River from Oklahoma now. Most of it did appear to be aimed at Dallas and points eastward, but one finger of the storm stretched westward toward Denton and Decatur. If it kept coming in that direction, it could brush across Parker County and hit Weatherford.

The temperature down in the bottom corner of the screen read 38 degrees. So it was above freezing right now, she thought, but that could change. At this time of year when a front came through, the temperature often dropped during the day, rather than going up as it normally would.

"Fingers crossed," she whispered to herself. There were a lot of factors at play here, as the meteorologists liked to say, and as always in the face of the weather, all the puny humans could do was wait and hope.

Sam came into the living room. "How's it lookin'?"

"Iffy," Phyllis said. "We might not get anything."

"That's what my gut's tellin' me." He smiled. "No way the weather wants to mess with Eve Turner."

Phyllis had to laugh. "I hope you're right," she said. She hadn't sat down while she was watching TV. She switched it off now and put the remote back on the table. "I'll get started on breakfast. We still have a cake to bake."

"You and Carolyn have a cake to bake," Sam said. "My job is just eatin' it."

"Actually, Mike is going to be over in a little bit, and the two of you will need to move the furniture out of the living room and set up the folding chairs. Also you'll be in charge of traffic control this afternoon when people start showing up." Phyllis added under her breath, "Assuming they do," then felt bad about doubting that things were going to work out.

Carolyn had already started cooking some pancakes. Phyllis began scrambling eggs and frying bacon. Those aromas mixed with that of the coffee to create a delicious smell that filled the house. It was enough to bring Eve downstairs . . . but not enough to distract her from her worries about the weather.

"How does it look?" she asked.

"Good," Phyllis said with as much heartiness as she could muster. "I think it's going to miss us."

"I'm going to go look at the radar," Eve said. She hurried out of the kitchen.

When she came back a few minutes later, she seemed somewhat relieved. "I think it's going to go east of us," she said. "But I'm going to be keeping an eye on the sky all day anyway."

"You don't want to spend your wedding day doing that," Sam told her. "Tell you what—you let me watch the weather for you. I see as much as one snowflake, I'll come tell you right away."

"You promise?"

Carolyn said, "Oh, good grief, what does it matter? It's not like you can *do* anything about it."

Eve glared at her for a second, then said, "Thank you, Sam. I appreciate that, and I'm glad someone around here cares about my special day."

Carolyn opened her mouth to say something else, but Phyllis made a warning gesture and mouthed, *Let it go.*

"Breakfast is almost ready," Phyllis said. "Let's sit down and enjoy it."

They did, and the brief moment of friction was soon forgotten. Phyllis didn't blame Eve for being nervous. Even under the absolute best of circumstances, a wedding was a stressful affair.

Sam kept his promise, checking the weather forecast frequently during the morning and also going outside to study the sky. After Mike arrived and they had moved the big television out of the living room, he checked the one in his bedroom. By noon all the furniture had been moved, the floor was clean, and chairs were set up. Although the overcast continued, no precipitation had fallen in Weatherford as far as Phyllis knew. It had been sleeting in Dallas for a couple of hours, and that big city would soon be paralyzed by icy roads.

"The airport's still okay," Sam reported to Phyllis after a check online. "No cancellations, no delays. Looks like the slick stuff just missed it, and by tomorrow this storm system will be gone. Things are gonna work out for Eve and Roy."

"That's good news. Every time I looked out the window I was afraid I'd see snow falling."

Sam grinned. "Well, earlier I saw a snowflake here and there, but it only lasted for a few minutes."

"And you didn't tell her?" Phyllis asked, her eyes widening.

"Didn't see any point in it. They were so few and far between that they didn't amount to anything. And they melted as soon as they hit the ground." Sam shook his head. "We're not gonna have a white New Year's, which is fine with me."

"Me, too."

"How's the cake?"

"In the freezer. That'll make it easier to frost, but it's perfect so far."

"That's just what I figured," Sam said.

Mike had left as soon as they had gotten all of the heavy furniture out, so Phyllis, Carolyn, and Sam cleaned and decorated the living room. After cutting a piece off, Carolyn gave Sam a roll of white tulle and some lights and told him to go decorate the staircase banister. He looked a bit worried but took the roll and lights and headed toward the staircase.

Phyllis used the smaller piece to decorate the mantel by draping the nylon tulle and weaving white lights through the tulle along the length of the fireplace. She pinned it in place with pushpins and double-stick tape. Carolyn placed votive candles in holders across the mantel as Phyllis put an arrangement of flowers at one end of the mantel and tapers in holders at the other end.

They created an altar by covering a rectangular table with a white tablecloth. In the center they placed a flower arrangement like the one on the mantel, and tapers in holders sat at each end.

As they were putting bows on the backs of the chairs, Carolyn commented that maybe she should have given this chore to Sam. After they finished, they went to check on his progress.

He had draped the tulle tied with ribbon up the banister with the lights inside the material and was just checking the lights as they came up. He smiled when Carolyn looked at his work and gave him a nod of approval. They added a bow at the end for a finishing touch.

Eve had retreated to her room on the second floor and didn't want to eat lunch. Phyllis tried to persuade her that she ought to eat, but she didn't work very hard at it. If Eve was too nervous to eat, it was best not to push her. As soon as the cake had sat in the freezer long enough, Phyllis and Carolyn went to work frosting and decorating it. Phyllis worked on the groom's cake while Carolyn worked on the wedding cake. Carolyn was a little more skilled with the decorating tips, so Phyllis was happy to let her do most of the finishing touches. By the time they were finished, the cakes were a thing of beauty, Sam declared.

The wedding cake had three tiers and sat on a floating cake stand that had white tulle and white lights powered by a battery along the back support. The little battery pack was hidden with a bow. The cake was a creamy white with hearts iced on the sides to match Eve's topper. The groom's cake had chocolate frosting with matching hearts on it.

Carefully, Sam carried the wedding cake into the dining room. "If you drop it," Carolyn warned, "don't even pack your bags. Just leave and never come back."

"Don't worry," Sam told her. "I won't drop it. But if I did, the door wouldn't even have a chance to hit me in the backside before I was gone."

The punch was made and sitting in the refrigerator ready to be poured into the bowl. The decorations were up. The flowers had been delivered, expensive at this time of year but beautiful to look at as well as filling the air with their fragrance. All the preparations were made. The only thing left now was for everyone to get dressed. Phyllis and Carolyn got into their dresses. Phyllis really did like her dress. The sapphire blue was a good color for her, and the trumpet skirt was slimming and created curves in all the right places. The ice blue one Carolyn had was nice, too, but she liked the darker blue. Carolyn commented that she was glad they had gotten the bows to match the dresses fixed. They added some simple jewelry, did their hair and makeup, and then went to help Eve.

Eve had decided to go with a sleeveless white lace floor-length dress, but she added a pretty three-quarter-sleeved white lace bolero. She also didn't want to spend the morning at the beauty shop, so Phyllis and Carolyn helped her with her hair and makeup.

Sam put on his suit and stepped outside again, even though the storm front had moved on past the area and the chances of bad weather now were small. While he was standing on the porch, Roy drove up and parked in the driveway. He was very dapper and handsome in his suit as he got out of his car.

"None of the guests have arrived yet?" he asked.

"Nope," Sam replied. "They ought to start showin' up soon, though. We sort of dodged a bullet on the weather, so more than likely we'll have a full house." Before they went in, he paused and put a hand on Roy's arm. "I don't know if I've said this before, but Eve means a whole lot to all of us, and we're glad she found a good fella like you, Roy. If anything was to make her unhappy, well, none of us would be happy, either."

Roy chuckled and asked, "Is that a veiled warning to treat her right or else?"

"The thought that you might not never entered my mind, old son," Sam drawled. "I'm just sayin'; that's all."

Roy clapped a hand on his shoulder. "Don't worry. I intend to devote the rest of my life to making that woman happy."

The first guests began to arrive a few minutes later. Phyllis and Carolyn were putting the finishing touches on Eve's makeup when Sam tapped on the door and called through it, "Roy's here and folks are startin' to show up."

"Is the minister here yet?" Eve asked.

"Not yet. I'll keep you posted."

"Don't worry, Eve," Carolyn said. "Everything's going to go off without a hitch . . . so to speak."

"I'll hold you to that," Eve said.

"Right now, just hold still," Phyllis said, "so we can get this right . . ."

By a little before five o'clock, the driveway and the curbs along both sides of the street were full of cars, and the living room of Phyllis's house was full of people. Fewer guests had shown up for the wedding than for the shower, which was a good thing, because the room wasn't as uncomfortably crowded as it had been a week earlier.

Phyllis stood at the top of the stairs and looked down at what she could see of the living room. Everything seemed to be perfect. Maybe if she held her mouth right it would stay that way, she thought, an old saying she had heard frequently when she was a child.

Sam walked past the bottom of the stairs with the minister who would perform the service. He gave Phyllis a thumbs-up. She crooked a finger at him, and he said something to the minister, then came up the stairs.

"Did he bring the music?" Phyllis asked.

"Yep. Got it loaded in the CD player."

"How's Roy holding up?"

Sam grinned. "He hasn't bolted for the exit, if that's what you mean. Seriously, he's fine. Lookin' forward to bein' married to Eve."

"All right." Phyllis glanced at her watch. "I think we're about ready to start, then."

"I'll tell the preacher. You'll hear the music and know when it's time to come down."

Phyllis took a deep breath and nodded.

"Let's get these two married," she said.

Chapter 6

"It was a beautiful ceremony, wasn't it?"

"Yep."

"Eve was so lovely."

"She sure was."

"And the music and the flowers and the cake . . . oh, the cake . . ."

"All perfect," Sam said. "Couldn't have asked for everything to be any better."

Phyllis lifted her head from his shoulder, where she'd been resting it as they sat together on the sofa, which had been moved back into the living room along with the other furniture after the ceremony with the help of some of the guests. "It was, wasn't it?"

Then she kissed him.

Sam's arm tightened around her shoulders where he had draped it casually when they sat down. When Phyllis broke the kiss, he smiled and asked, "What was that for? Not that I'm complainin', mind you."

"I just want you to know how much I appreciate every-thing you do, Sam. Having you around just makes everything easier."

"I'm always glad to help out; you know that."

"I know. And I don't think any of us thank you enough."

"So that kiss was just gratitude?"

Phyllis smiled. "Well . . . not completely."

"Good to know."

He leaned down and did the kissing this time.

The sound of Carolyn coming down the stairs made them sit up straighter, although Sam didn't remove his arm from Phyllis's shoulders. Carolyn came into the living room and sank into one of the armchairs.

"If you two are as worn out as I am, you probably don't want to do anything for a week," she said.

"It's been a pretty stressful couple of months," Phyllis ad-mitted, thinking back to the Harvest Festival at Holland Lake Park, then Thanksgiving and everything that had come after that in December.

"It'll be midnight after a while," Sam said. "A whole new year. We can put this one in the books. Out with the old, in with the new."

"Good riddance," Carolyn said.

"I wouldn't go that far," Phyllis said. "Some good things happened this year, too. Eve and Roy finding each other, for example."

Carolyn said, "The jury is still out on that one."

"Are we gonna stay up and watch the ball drop at mid-night?" Sam asked.

"It doesn't drop at midnight our time," Carolyn pointed out. "When it's midnight in Times Square, it's only eleven o'clock here, and what do I care if it's the New Year in New York already? The TV stations used to have the decency to delay the broadcast so that they showed the ball dropping when it was midnight here, but they don't go to that much trouble anymore. Anyway, the whole celebration's never been the same since Guy Lombardo died."

"I dunno. I miss Dick Clark," Sam said.

"He was all right on *American Bandstand*, I suppose." Carolyn shrugged. "And he was better than that boy who's on there now."

"You mean Ryan Seacrest?" Phyllis asked.

"I don't know these people's names. Anyway, they could bring back the ghost of Guy Lombardo and every one of his Royal Canadians, and I wouldn't stay up until midnight to watch it. I'm tired. I'm going to bed."

"I agree," Phyllis said. "They can ring in the New Year without us."

"I might stay up and watch," Sam said. "There's somethin' about sendin' the old year off into history and welcomin' the new one that appeals to me. Maybe it's the old hope-springs-eternal thing."

"I hope the New Year is more peaceful than the last one," Carolyn said as she stood up.

Phyllis certainly couldn't argue with that.

The New Year started off peacefully enough. The first two weeks passed without anything major or exciting happening in the big old house on the tree-lined street a few blocks southwest of the courthouse square in Weatherford. There had been a small snowstorm, not much more than a dusting of white on the lawns and cars and bushes, which was nothing unusual. Upheavals, political and otherwise, continued elsewhere in the world, but not here. Sam came down with a cold but shook it quickly. Phyllis started thinking about recipes she might use in the cooking contest that was held in conjunction with the annual Peach Festival. That was a long time off yet—July—but it never hurt to start thinking about these things early. She knew that Carolyn would already be considering options for her own entry in the contest.

And they got a couple of old-fashioned postcards from Eve and Roy in the Bahamas, not saying much except that they were having a fine time on their honeymoon. According to the second postcard, they expected to be back in Weatherford on January 15, assuming the weather in Texas cooperated and their flight wasn't delayed.

Eve had written the postcards, but both she and Roy had signed them. Phyllis propped them up on the mantel in the living room. All the decorations were gone now, taken down and put away. It was unlikely there would ever be another wedding here, Phyllis knew, but if there was, they would be ready.

The weather was nice on the fifteenth, so it seemed that there would be nothing to keep Eve and Roy from arriving on schedule. Phyllis was eager to see her old friend again. She had a roast cooking and intended to welcome the newlyweds back with a big supper. She and Carolyn had also made a hearts-and-flowers banner that read WELCOME HOME EVE AND ROY, and Sam had hung it over the fireplace.

Eve called on her cell phone at about three o'clock. "We're

back!" she said. "Our flight just landed. And we had a wonderful time!"

Phyllis had taken the call. She said, "We can't wait to see the two of you and hear all about it."

"I don't know how long it'll take us to get there. I suppose it'll depend on the traffic."

Phyllis knew how terrible the traffic could be on all the roads leading in and out of the giant airport. "Just be careful," she said, "and you'll be here whenever you can."

"That's right. And Phyllis . . . we have a surprise for everybody, too."

Eve wouldn't say anything else about that. She said goodbye, leaving Phyllis to pass along the part of the conversation Sam and Carolyn hadn't been able to hear.

"A surprise?" Carolyn repeated. "What in the world do you suppose she means by that?"

"Maybe she's expectin' already," Sam said with a grin.

Carolyn gave him a withering look. "You have *got* to stop saying things like that. You think you're funny, but you're not."

Sam appealed to Phyllis. "Am I funny?"

"Not in this case," she said. "Sometimes, though, you can be fairly droll."

"I reckon I'll take it," he said with a shake of his head. "Looks like all I'm gonna get."

Carolyn said, "I can't imagine what the surprise could be, unless they brought us presents of some sort from the Bahamas. You don't think they'd bring us some of those ridiculous grass skirts, do you?"

"Those are from Hawaii," Phyllis pointed out.

"Yes, I suppose you're right, but they're still tacky."

"And with these knobby knees of mine, I'd look downright foolish in one of 'em," Sam said. He held up both hands in a gesture of surrender. "I know, there I go again. I'll stop."

Eve had sounded excited about the surprise, whatever it was, Phyllis thought, but at the same time, she had detected a slightly forced note in her friend's voice, as if Eve had been trying to be happy about it but not completely succeeding. That worried Phyllis. She didn't think anything major had happened, or Eve would have just gone ahead and told her about it. But it would certainly ease her mind to find out what Eve had been talking about.

That slight worry Phyllis was experiencing made the time seem to pass more slowly, and after a couple of hours had gone by, the minutes really dragged.

Carolyn seemed to be concerned, too. "I thought they would be here by now," she said.

"They're probably sittin' in a traffic jam somewhere," Sam said. "At this time of day, you've got to expect that. I'm not sure there even is a good time of day to come or go from that airport."

Phyllis knew he was right about that, but it didn't make her feel any better. Finally, more than three hours after Eve's call, headlights pulled into the driveway and car doors slammed outside.

"It's about time," Carolyn said. "Supper's ready."

That was true. The pot roast was done, but it could continue simmering in the Crock-Pot with the potatoes and carrots for a while without being hurt by it. Phyllis went to the front door and opened it as she turned on the porch light. Eve and Roy smiled up at her as they came along the walk. Both of them had tans that it would have been difficult to get in Texas at this time of year.

"Come in!" Phyllis said as she held the door open. "My goodness, it's wonderful to see you both!"

The reunion in the hallway was an effusive one. Phyllis hugged Eve, and then, after only a second's hesitation, hugged Roy as well. Sam pumped Roy's hand and slapped him on the back. Carolyn hugged Eve but shook Roy's hand. Everybody was talking at once.

After things had settled down a little, Roy took a deep breath and said, "That smells wonderful! Roast, isn't it?"

"That's right," Phyllis said. "Supper's ready, but it can wait for a few minutes. Let's all go into the living room and sit down and catch our breath."

"That's a good idea," Eve said. "That'll give us a chance to talk to you."

"About that big surprise of yours, I imagine," Carolyn said.

"Actually, that's right. I think we should get that out of the way first."

"Well, come on," Phyllis said. "Goodness knows, we're all curious."

When they went into the living room, Eve saw the banner over the fireplace and exclaimed, "Oh, my! That was so sweet and thoughtful of you." She grew solemn. "I'm afraid this is just going to make things harder."

That feeling of unease cropped up inside Phyllis again. She said, "What do you mean by that?"

"Well . . . the banner, and the way you were all so happy to see us, and the lovely dinner that you obviously fixed to welcome us home . . . that's going to make it more difficult to tell you what we have to tell you."

"What in the world are you talking about?" Carolyn asked.

Roy put a hand on Eve's shoulder and said, "Would you like me to explain things to them, dear? It was my idea, after all."

Eve shook her head. "No, that's very nice of you, but these are my friends—"

"My friends, too, now," Roy said with a smile.

"Of course, but this is something I should do." Eve faced Phyllis, Carolyn, and Sam and went on, "I know you were expecting us to move back in here for the time being, but I'm afraid we're not going to be living here after all."

Chapter 7

A moment of surprised silence passed; then Carolyn said, "Not living here? What are you talking about? Where are you going to live if not here?"

"I thought you were going to stay here while you look for a house of your own," Phyllis said.

Eve nodded. "I know that was the plan, but Roy found this charming bed-and-breakfast in the country outside of town, and the owners have agreed to let us stay there on a longer-term basis than usual. It'll be sort of like renting an apartment, but not exactly."

Roy said, "I think it's important in the early stages of a marriage for a couple to spend as much time together as they can."

"But . . . but you won't have any more privacy in a bed-and-breakfast than you would here," Carolyn objected. "There'll be people coming and going all the time."

"Yes, but there they'll be strangers," Eve said. "I won't feel any desire to spend time with them, and they won't be interested in us. I can devote all my attention to Roy and to our search for a house of our own."

What Eve was saying actually made sense in a way, Phyllis thought. The anonymity of the other people staying at the bed-and-breakfast would make it seem like they had more privacy, whether they really did or not. But that didn't mean Phyllis wanted things to happen that way.

"We'll support your decision, whatever it is," she said, "but we were really looking forward to having the two of you here with us."

She gestured toward the banner over the fireplace to support her words.

"Oh, I know!" Eve said. She came over to Phyllis and hugged her. "And everything you've done means so much to me. But this is the right thing for us. I know it is."

Once again, Phyllis thought she heard the tiniest forced note in her friend's voice. But maybe that was because she wanted to hear it, she told herself. She wanted to believe that Eve could be persuaded to abandon the bed-and-breakfast . . . when she knew that they didn't really have the right to try to persuade Eve to do any such thing. Being friends meant what she had just said: accepting and supporting their decisions.

"All right," Phyllis said, "on one condition."

"What's that?" Eve asked.

"That the two of you will come over here for dinner at least once a week."

Roy grinned and said, "I think we can guarantee that, Phyllis. We'll probably still be around so much you'll get sick of us and boot us out."

"That will never happen," Phyllis said.

Sam said, "It's all settled, then. Why don't we all sit down to dinner now, and you two can tell us all about your trip?"

They headed toward the dining room, and while they were in the hall, Eve said quietly to Phyllis, "I'm sorry about springing this on you that way. I would have told you on the phone, or written to you about it, but I just couldn't figure out how to tell you. I decided it would be better to do it face-to-face."

"It's all right, Eve, really," Phyllis said as she took her friend's hand and squeezed it. "We'll miss you, but it's not like you're leaving forever. You'll still be around."

"You can count on that," Eve said.

Over dinner, in addition to telling Phyllis, Sam, and Carolyn about their trip to the Bahamas, Eve and Roy also explained more about the bed-and-breakfast.

"We went by there on the way from the airport so I could take a look at it," Eve said. "That's why it took us longer to get here. Roy told me about it while we were on our trip, but I couldn't agree until I had seen it for myself. I had just about made up my mind, since I knew it was what he wanted, but I had to see it, just to be sure."

"Which is certainly fair," Roy put in. "I wouldn't have expected otherwise. Nobody wants to buy a pig in a poke."

"You think kids still say that these days?" Sam asked. "They'd know what a pig is, but I'm not sure they'd know what a poke is."

"Never mind that," Carolyn said. "Tell us about the bed-and-breakfast, Eve."

"Oh, it's utterly charming! It's in the hills southwest of town and has a beautiful view of the Brazos River."

"It was originally a farmhouse," Roy added, "but it's been remodeled and brought completely up to date. And it's in the middle of twenty or thirty acres, so even though it's only a few minutes from town, it's so quiet and peaceful, you feel like you're in the middle of nowhere."

"It sounds lovely," Phyllis said.

"And you sound like a sales pitch, Roy," Carolyn said.

He laughed. "I don't mean to. But as soon as I saw it, I knew I wanted to spend some time there with Eve while we look for a home of our own."

"I think that was a good idea," Phyllis said. She was determined to be supportive of what Eve was doing.

"After Roy had shown the place to me, I knew it would be all right, so we went ahead and left our bags there," Eve said.

"So you're moving in there tonight?" Carolyn asked.

"I didn't see any reason to wait."

"What about all the things in your room?"

"Well, I was hoping that Phyllis would let me leave some of them here until we find a house," Eve said. "Is that all right, Phyllis?"

"Why wouldn't it be?" Phyllis asked.

"Well . . . I assume that eventually you'll want to rent that room to someone else."

Phyllis, Sam, and Carolyn looked at each other in surprise. At first when Eve had told them that she and Roy were getting married, Phyllis had hoped that Roy would just move into their home and things would go on roughly as they had before. Then, when it was established that Eve would be moving out, at least eventually, the question of what to do with the room had crossed Phyllis's mind, but only briefly. She'd been much too busy, what with the holidays, the bridal shower, the wedding—and the murder—to even think about it all that much. And since she'd believed that Eve and Roy were coming back here to stay temporarily, it had been easier to just put the whole thing out of her mind. She suspected that Sam and Carolyn felt the same way.

It had been several years since Sam had moved in, and during that time they had all settled into a comfortable routine. If someone new came into the house, it would be more than just a change. It would be an upheaval. Phyllis wasn't sure she wanted that. Financially, she didn't *need* another boarder, although the extra money certainly came in handy. She just wasn't sure it was worth getting used to all the changes that might come about.

For now, though, she was noncommittal as she said to Eve, "We'll worry about that later. Of course you can leave some of your things in the room, for as long as you need to."

"Thank you, dear. You're always so sweet."

After dinner, they took coffee and dessert—slices of s'more pie, which was a cross between a pie and a brownie, that Phyllis had made earlier that day—into the living room.

"How'd you happen to find that place, Roy?" Sam asked when they had all settled down on the sofa and in armchairs.

"I was out just driving around one day when I saw it and decided to investigate," Roy said. "You know, I've never spent much time in this area, so I like to explore and find my way around. When I saw this house sitting on top of a hill, something about it just drew me. I felt like that was where I wanted to spend some time with Eve."

"He has such good instincts," Eve said with a smile.

"Ever given any thought to owning a place like that?" Sam asked.

"Oh, now, don't give him any ideas," Eve said before Roy could reply. "Remember when we went down to Rockport and took care of that bed-and-breakfast for Phyllis's cousin? There's a lot of work involved in something like that."

"Not to mention the dead man on the dock," Carolyn added.

Roy's eyebrows rose. "Another murder?" he asked.

"That was just an isolated incident," Phyllis said quickly.

"Hmmph," Carolyn said.

"Anyway," Roy said, "I don't have any experience at running a bed-and-breakfast or any other sort of business like that, and since I'm semiretired, I don't particularly want to learn. I'm fine with just staying there and enjoying it."

"I don't blame you," Sam said. "When you've worked hard for as long as we have, you deserve to take it easy."

They continued to chat amiably while they finished their coffee and pie, until finally Roy said, "Well, it's getting late. I suppose we'd better be getting home, dear."

Eve was sitting next to him on the sofa. She leaned closer and embraced his arm as she said, "Home . . . I like the sound of that. Even though it's not really our home."

"It is for now," he told her with a smile. "Anywhere you are, that's home for me."

Phyllis saw Carolyn look away so the newlyweds wouldn't notice her eyes rolling slightly. The affection between Eve and Roy did seem a little overdone, especially for people their age, but Phyllis had no doubt it was genuine.

There were hugs and handshakes all around again. When

they were saying good night at the front door, Phyllis quietly told Eve, "If there's anything you need, don't hesitate to call on me. I'd do anything for you—you know that."

"I know, dear." Eve leaned in and kissed Phyllis on the cheek. "Thank you for everything you've already done."

"It was my pleasure," Phyllis assured her.

The three of them stood on the porch and waved while Eve and Roy got back into Roy's car and left. As they watched the taillights recede along the street, Carolyn said, "Well, that certainly didn't turn out the way I expected it to."

"No," Phyllis said, "but I'm sure it'll be fine."

"I'd feel better if they were staying here."

"They would have left sometime," Phyllis pointed out.

Sam said, "That's what these kids do. They grow up and leave the nest."

Carolyn snorted. "Still not funny."

Maybe not, Phyllis thought, but in a way Sam was right. All three of them had grown, married children. They'd had to watch as those children left home and established lives on their own, and while that was the way it should be, the happiness that parents felt was a bittersweet one, mixed with an undeniable sensation of loss that tightened the chest and made the eyes grow misty. You watched children grow up and raised them to be able to take care of themselves, but when the time came . . .

Of course, it wasn't the same with Eve. That was just a friend leaving, Phyllis told herself. But Eve had become part of her family, just as Carolyn and Sam had. And now, as the taillights of Roy's car turned the corner and disappeared, Phyllis knew nothing would ever be the same.

Sam must have sensed what she was feeling. He put his arm around her shoulders and said, "Come on, I'll help you clean up those dishes. And if I remember right, there was one more piece of pie left. If nobody else wants it . . ."

Phyllis laughed. "It's all yours," she said.

Chapter 8

It was amazing how quickly things settled back into a routine. A different one than before, to be sure, but still a routine. People needed that, Phyllis thought.

She spoke to Eve almost every day on the phone. A few days after the newlyweds returned from their honeymoon, Phyllis, Sam, and Carolyn went out to the bed-and-breakfast to see where they were living now. They brought along some of Eve's belongings from the house that she wanted with her, and Sam drove Eve's car, which had been parked at Phyllis's house since before the wedding.

The place was every bit as charming as Roy had made it sound. In January, the scenery wasn't as nice as it would be in the spring, summer, and fall, but it was still a picturesque landscape with wooded hills rolling away and then dropping into the valley of the Brazos River.

"It's lovely," Phyllis told Eve as they all stood on the house's front porch, looking down toward the river.

Sam rested his hands on the porch's railing, which was made from rustic cedar posts, and nodded. "Yeah, a fella could get used to this view," he said.

"And it really is peaceful here," Carolyn admitted.

"Yes, it's so beautiful and serene that we've had trouble working up the enthusiasm for getting out and looking for a place of our own," Eve said with a smile. "It's been easier just to sit back and enjoy this place."

"Well, that's all right . . . for a while," Phyllis said.

"Oh, I'm sure we'll find a house soon," Roy said. "It's just a matter of time."

A car turned off the farm-to-market road that ran between the hills and started up the long gravel drive toward the house. As it approached, the door went up on the much newer two-car garage that was attached to the old farmhouse.

"Those are the owners, Pete and Jan Delaney," Eve said. "Very nice people."

Instead of closing the garage door after the car had pulled in, the woman who got out walked around to the front of the house instead and gave them a friendly smile as she said, "Hi, folks. Eve, are these your friends?"

"That's right. Jan, this is Phyllis Newsom, Carolyn Wilbarger, and Sam Fletcher."

The woman came up the steps to the porch and shook hands with all of them. "Jan Delaney," she said. "I'm so glad to meet you. Eve has talked a lot about all of you."

Jan was in her mid-forties, Phyllis guessed, a very attractive woman with short chestnut hair. She wore jeans and an open flannel shirt over a sweatshirt. She had a down-to-earth air about her that probably came from living in the country.

Phyllis had seen that attitude in her own parents, both of whom had been raised on farms.

The man who followed Jan from the car was a little shorter and stockier, with graying dark hair and an open, friendly face. Jan held out a hand toward him and said, "This is my husband, Pete."

"Nice to meet you folks," Pete Delaney said with a nod. He didn't seem to be as outgoing as his wife, but he was certainly pleasant enough. Phyllis found herself liking both of them right away.

Pete went on, "I'll get those groceries taken in and put up, Jan."

"Let me give you a hand," Sam volunteered.

"I'd be glad to help, too," Roy added.

Pete shook his head. "Oh, no, I wouldn't want to bother you folks."

"No bother," Sam insisted. "Come on."

Pete smiled and said, "In that case . . ."

The three men went to the garage, leaving the women on the porch.

"You have a lovely home here," Phyllis said to Jan.

"Thank you. As soon as I saw the place, I knew I had to have it. There's something about it that affects nearly everybody the same way. They want to stay for a while." Jan laughed. "But Pete and I decided to stay forever. We'd had enough of moving around." She paused. "Pete was a colonel in the army before he retired. We lived all over the world. I guess that made me always want a place of my own, a place where I could just stay and stay and never have to pack up and move again."

"I can imagine," Carolyn said.

Pete Delaney hadn't really seemed like the military type to Phyllis, but she knew that appearances could be deceiving.

"It's nice of you to let Eve and Roy stay here like this," she said.

"Oh, we were happy to give them a good rate and have them move in for a while. At this time of year we don't do much business except on the weekends, and we're hardly ever full even then. It's no problem having full-time guests."

"I don't know how long we'll be here," Eve said. "You've made it so pleasant, I'm not sure we'll ever want to leave!"

Jan laughed. "Then we're doing our job, aren't we? I hope that even after you and Roy find a home of your own, you'll come back to see us every now and then."

"We certainly intend to," Eve said with an emphatic nod.

The rest of the visit passed pleasantly. Phyllis, Sam, and Carolyn headed home well before dark, and as Phyllis drove her Lincoln along the country roads toward Weatherford, Carolyn said, "Well, she does seem happy, I suppose."

In the backseat, Sam chuckled. "As happy as any newly-wed is, I'd say."

"You mean the glow hasn't worn off," Phyllis said with a smile.

"That's right," Sam agreed.

"Oh, it will," Carolyn said. "It always does sooner or later; we all know that."

Carolyn was in the passenger seat in front while Sam sat in the back, turned sideways a little to accommodate his long legs. Phyllis glanced in the rearview mirror and caught Sam's eyes for a second. Carolyn's comment had been edged with bitterness, and Phyllis understood why her friend felt that way.

But Phyllis knew that at least in some cases, Carolyn was wrong. The glow of the love she'd felt for Kenny had never gone out. It might have waned some over the years, and every now and then it even flickered a bit as the stresses of everyday life took their inevitable toll. But at other times it burned brightly, and it had never, ever gone out. Phyllis knew that Sam felt the same way about his late wife. Her long struggle with cancer had only made them grow closer, and her eventual death had been a loss from which he would never fully recover. Phyllis felt the same way about Kenny.

But then Sam had moved into the house because Dolly Williamson didn't think he ought to be living alone, and the friendship that had grown up between him and Phyllis had been very good for both of them. There were broken places in both of them that would never heal, but the pain of those breaks had faded because now they had each other to lean on. The glow that was between them was different, but it was warming and sustaining, and Phyllis had come to realize that it would never go out, either. Carolyn was wrong. It wasn't the same for everyone.

Phyllis knew that when she met Sam's eyes and knew as well that he felt the same way.

And that put a little smile on her face, all the way back home.

Several more days passed. The weather turned cold again as a front came through, but it didn't bring any snow or ice with it. The temperature was low enough to make Phyllis's bones ache a little, even though it was warm enough in the house.

She was sitting in the living room knitting when she glanced up through the picture window and saw a cruiser from the Parker County Sheriff's Department stop at the curb in front of the house. She enjoyed knitting, needlework, and other crafts like that, but she lacked the patience to stick with any of it for too long at a time, so she was glad to set the needles and yarn aside for a while. She stood up as she watched her son, Mike, get out of the car and come across the yard toward the porch.

Clouds of steam formed in front of Mike's face as his breath fogged up in the frigid air. He was carrying his hat instead of wearing it, and Phyllis's mothering instincts kicked in. She would have to tell him that in cold weather like this, he ought to wear his hat whenever he wasn't in the car, even if he just got out for a minute. A lot of body heat escaped through the top of the head, after all, and she didn't want him to get chilled. She thought she remembered reading somewhere that that wasn't really true, that the top of the head didn't lose warmth any faster than any other part of the body did, but that was what she'd been taught and what she'd believed for years, and she wasn't going to change now. Anyway, any scientist who didn't think that a child ought to wear a hat when it was cold was a quack, as far as she was concerned.

Phyllis opened the wooden door and watched Mike through the glass of the storm door. He didn't look particularly cold . . . but he did look worried and upset about something, she realized.

As soon as that thought went through Phyllis's head, fear for Bobby gripped her. She loved her grandson dearly. Hard on the heels of that came concern for Sarah. She was the best daughter-in-law any woman could ever want.

But if something was wrong with Sarah or Bobby, Mike would have looked even more upset, Phyllis decided. This was something else. Something bad, no doubt, but not the worst.

Phyllis opened the storm door as Mike came up the porch steps. "Come in here out of the cold," she told him.

He summoned up a slight smile. "Hi, Mom." He was a handsome, broad-shouldered man, especially impressive in his uniform. "Are Sam and Carolyn here?"

"Sam's out in the garage, and I believe Carolyn's upstairs," Phyllis said as she closed the door behind him. The fact that Mike had asked about them reinforced her feeling that something was wrong. "What is it?"

"I want to talk to all three of you," he said. "I'll go get Sam."

"I'll call Carolyn," Phyllis said. "But can't you tell me what's wrong?"

Mike shook his head. "It'll be better if I can sit down with all of you."

So it was nothing to do with the family, Phyllis thought, but her heart was hammering harder than usual anyway as she went part of the way up the stairs and called to Carolyn. Maybe she was wrong, she told herself. Maybe the bad news was personal and it was so bad Mike wanted to have Sam and Carolyn there so they could support her when he told her.

But nothing could be that bad as long as Mike and Sarah and Bobby were okay, she thought. It had to be about somebody else . . .

Eve.

Phyllis's breath seemed to freeze in her throat, just as surely as water would freeze outside on a frigid day like today. Something had happened to Eve.

They had been wrong all along to trust Roy.

That was a terrible thing to think, she scolded herself. She had no idea what was wrong, but it wasn't right to jump to such horrible conclusions.

Carolyn appeared at the top of the stairs and started down. "What is it?" she asked.

"Mike's here, and he wants to tell us something."

Carolyn frowned. "Mike? Is he here as a deputy or your son?"

"I don't know, but I don't think it's good either way."

By the time they reached the bottom of the stairs, Mike and Sam were starting up the hall from the kitchen. Mike had gone out that way to fetch Sam.

"What's going on here, Mike?" Carolyn demanded.

"Let's go in the living room and sit down," Mike said. "Then I'll tell you all I know, Mrs. Wilbarger."

"This is pretty bad, isn't it?" Sam asked.

"It's not good," Mike admitted.

"And it's something about Eve," Phyllis said. Her voice sounded strained to her ears.

"Let's just sit down," Mike said as he herded them into the living room.

Everyone sat, but no one relaxed. Phyllis said, "All right, you've frightened us enough, Mike. Tell us what's wrong."

"One of our cars answered a 911 call an hour or so ago," Mike said. "There was a call for an ambulance, too. Something had happened at a place out in the country, a little bed-and-breakfast—"

"I knew it," Carolyn said. She put a hand to her mouth. "Oh, my God. Eve—"

"Eve's fine, as far as we know," Mike said. He took a deep breath. "It's Roy. When the responding units got there, he was dead."

"Lord," Sam said. "Heart attack?"

Mike shook his head. "I'm afraid not. He'd been murdered."

Chapter 9

*P*hyllis sat back, stunned—although a part of her brain wondered why she would be surprised. Hadn't murder seemed to follow her around for the past several years? It was as if some cosmic switch had been flipped, and after leading a nice, normal existence for more than six decades, suddenly she was cursed to find herself dealing with violent, unexpected death on a regular basis.

That grim thought occupied her for only a fraction of a second. Then she asked the questions that were really uppermost in her mind.

"Where is Eve? Does she know?"

Mike took another deep breath, and Phyllis steeled herself for another answer she didn't think she was going to like.

"We don't know where Eve is," he said.

"Oh, my God," Carolyn said, her voice cracking from the strain she was under. "She's been kidnapped! The murderer kidnapped her!"

"There's no evidence of that," Mike said with a shake of his head. "In fact, right now . . . right now I guess you'd say she's considered a person of interest."

"A suspect, you mean," Sam said.

"That's crazy!" Phyllis burst out.

Mike lifted both hands and patted at the air. "No, that's not it, exactly. I wouldn't say that she's a suspect. She's just somebody that we want to talk to."

"Have you issued an arrest warrant for her?" Carolyn asked, and her words were jagged with anger now. "I know how quick you people are to arrest people who are innocent!"

That "you people" comment wasn't fair to Mike, Phyllis thought, but she could understand why Carolyn felt that way. Several years earlier, Carolyn herself had been suspected of murder, and she had never forgiven the authorities for that.

To get Carolyn off that track, Phyllis asked, "What about the people who own the bed-and-breakfast, Jan and Pete Delaney? Have they been questioned?"

Mike nodded. "Jan Delaney was the one who found the body."

A little shudder went through Phyllis at the way Mike said *the body* instead of using Roy's name. But that was his training, she supposed. Roy's death was a murder case now, and that's how he had to regard it. He had put aside any personal feelings he might have.

"I suppose Mrs. Delaney and her husband have both been questioned by now, and any other people who were in the house at the time," Mike went on. "I don't know that for sure. I haven't been on the scene. When I heard that a unit was going to be sent here, I asked for the job. I don't think Sheriff Haney much wanted to give it to me, but I guess he decided it would be all right."

"Wait a minute," Sam said. "You came here lookin' for Eve, didn't you?"

"I knew it!" Carolyn said. "You're going to arrest her!"

Phyllis could tell that Mike was getting annoyed. She said, "Eve's not here."

Mike nodded. "I know that. I could tell by the way you reacted, so I didn't figure there was any point in even asking. I'd already found out what I needed to know. But now I have to tell you . . . if you see her or hear from her, you need to tell her to come to the sheriff's department and ask to speak to the investigators in charge of the case."

"Turn herself in, you mean," Carolyn said.

"Look, Mrs. Wilbarger, this isn't any easier for me than it is for you."

Normally Phyllis might have said something to Mike about speaking to Carolyn in that tone of voice, but she understood why he was upset. Eve had been one of his English teachers in high school, and since she had moved in here, she'd become almost like a member of the family. To him this was like having one of his aunts suspected of murder.

"What else can you tell us?" she asked.

He looked even more uncomfortable as he said, "That's it. Just tell Mrs. Turner . . . I mean, Mrs. Porter . . . to come talk to us if you see her."

"You sounded mighty sure it was murder," Sam said. "How'd Roy die?"

Mike shook his head. "I can't go into any details."

"You can't go into them, or you don't know them?" Phyllis asked.

Mike made a face and said, "Look, Mom, the sheriff had a talk with me before he agreed to let me come over and see if Eve was here. The district attorney doesn't like the fact that the sheriff's department has shared information with you in the past. DA Sullivan doesn't *know* that information came from me, but it's pretty obvious, isn't it?"

"So Sheriff Haney's walkin' on eggshells when it comes to Phyllis, just like Chief of Police Whitmire does," Sam said as he frowned. "What Sullivan doesn't like is that Phyllis has solved those murders that the cops couldn't."

"The district attorney feels that everything should go through proper channels."

"The district attorney's got a big ol' stick up his—"

"Sam," Phyllis said. "Let's not make things any more difficult for Mike than they have to be."

"Thanks, Mom. I appreciate that."

"So, do you have an APB or a BOLO or whatever you call it out on Eve?" Carolyn asked.

"Descriptions of her and her car have been broadcast," Mike acknowledged.

"Is it possible that she's come to any harm?" Phyllis asked. "Could whoever killed Roy have kidnapped her?"

"Honestly, I haven't heard anything to make me believe that. I think we'd be handling things differently if that's what the evidence indicated."

Sam nodded and said, "Yeah, that makes sense. Sorry I snapped at you a minute ago, Mike."

"That's all right. I don't blame you for being upset, Sam. I don't blame any of you. Mrs. Porter . . . Eve . . . means a lot to all of us." Mike got to his feet and hesitated. "Look, I don't want her coming in by herself. If she shows up here, could you call me? I'll come get her and make sure she's treated properly."

"We'll do better than that," Phyllis said as she stood up, too. "We'll come with her, and you can meet us there."

Mike winced. He looked like he tried to control the reaction, but he couldn't quite manage that.

"I understand," Phyllis went on. "Me being there would look bad to the sheriff and the district attorney, wouldn't it?"

"How about if we get her a lawyer?" Sam suggested. "She's gonna need one, isn't she?"

Mike shrugged. "That wouldn't be a bad idea," he admitted, "but I can't recommend it officially."

"Of course not," Phyllis said. "It was all our idea."

"Okay." Mike put a hand on Phyllis's shoulder. "I'm sure sorry about all this, Mom. Eve seemed so happy at the wedding. I'm sorry her marriage only lasted a few weeks."

"Not half as sorry as the varmint who ruined it for her is gonna be," Sam said. "It's only a matter of time until you catch him."

Mike nodded and said, "I hope so. I'll be in touch."

"Put your hat on before you go outside," Phyllis told him as he started toward the front door.

When Mike was gone, Carolyn sat in one of the armchairs and shook her head. "I can't believe this," she said. "I just can't believe it. I knew something was going to go wrong."

That attitude wasn't going to help anything, Phyllis thought, but it wouldn't do any good to fuss at Carolyn, either.

Carolyn looked up at her and went on. "You're going to have to find out who killed Roy, you know."

"Absolutely not," Phyllis said. "You heard what Mike said. I think I'd be risking his career if I were to get mixed up in this investigation."

"But you know good and well they think Eve did it, and once they get an idea like that in their heads, they stop looking for anybody else! You saw what happened in those other cases. If you hadn't stepped in and uncovered the real killers, innocent people would have gone to jail . . . probably including me!"

"Those were isolated cases," Phyllis insisted. "Most of the time, the police and the sheriff's department are very good about finding out what really happened—"

"Are you prepared to risk Eve's life on that?" Carolyn broke in. "Because that's what you'll be doing if you turn your back on this, you know. Do you honestly believe she could survive being sent to prison? Do you want to have to go to Huntsville to visit her and see her wasting away to nothing in there behind those iron bars?"

"I think they send most of the female convicts to Gatesville instead of Huntsville," Sam said, then when Carolyn gave him an angry look hurried on, "Anyway, it doesn't matter, because Eve's not gonna be convicted of anything, and she's not gonna be convicted of anything because she's innocent. We all saw her with Roy the past couple of months. There's no way she would ever hurt him, let alone kill him."

Phyllis knew that was true. The conventional wisdom was that anybody was capable of anything under the right circumstances, but she didn't believe that. Maybe it was true in most cases, but some things were so far beyond the pale that they simply were impossible.

She turned toward the phone, and Carolyn asked, "What are you going to do?"

"I thought I'd call Juliette Yorke," Phyllis replied. "We said we'd get a lawyer for Eve, and Juliette's the best one I know."

Despite her relative youth, Juliette was a highly competent defense attorney, and she had been involved in several of the cases Phyllis had solved in the past. If Eve was going to turn herself in, she would be better off if Juliette was with her.

Phyllis had barely picked up the phone, though, when Sam, who was looking out the window, said, "Better wait a minute."

"Why?" Phyllis asked.

"Because Eve just pulled her car into the driveway."

Chapter 10

It was all Phyllis could do not to rush out the front door to meet Eve.

Carolyn was on her feet, too. She said, "We need to tell her to run!"

"No!" Phyllis cried. "That's the absolute worst thing she could do. That'll just convince the investigators more than ever that she's guilty!"

"Hang on, both of you," Sam said. "Look at her. You want proof? There it is."

The three of them stood in front of the picture window and watched as Eve got out of her car, walked around the front of it, and started along the walk toward the porch. She seemed perfectly calm, and as she looked up and saw the three of them there, she smiled brightly and waved.

"Good Lord," Sam breathed. "She doesn't know a thing about it yet."

The expressions on their faces must have told Eve that

something was wrong. Her step faltered a little, but then she came on. By the time she reached the porch, Phyllis had the door open, and Sam and Carolyn were standing right behind her.

"Oh, dear," Eve said as she stepped into the house. "Something's wrong, I can tell. What is it? What's happened?"

"Eve," Phyllis said miserably, not knowing how to begin, "there's something you need to know . . ."

She didn't get any further before Eve's eyes suddenly widened in horror and she cried out, "Roy!"

There was nothing suspicious about that, Phyllis told herself. At their age, naturally the prospect of bad news would make someone who was married think immediately of their spouse.

Phyllis moved to Eve's right side, Carolyn to the left. Phyllis linked her arm with Eve's and said gently, "Let's go into the living room—"

"No!" Eve cried. Tears were already running down her face. "Tell me! He's dead, isn't he? Roy's dead?"

Phyllis swallowed hard and nodded. "I'm sorry, Eve. I'm so sorry."

Eve would have collapsed then if Phyllis and Carolyn hadn't had ahold of her. She sagged in their grip and sobbed brokenly. Step by halting step, they managed to walk her into the living room and get her over to the sofa. They lowered her onto it and sat down on either side of her.

Phyllis looked up at Sam and asked, "Could you go make that phone call we were talking about?"

He nodded. "Sure, I'll handle it. Don't worry."

But it was too late for that bit of advice, Phyllis thought as

Sam hurried out of the room to make the call in the kitchen. Eve's world had already crumbled around her.

And it was about to get even worse.

A box of tissues sat on the coffee table in front of the sofa. Carolyn picked it up and pressed one of the tissues into Eve's hand. Instinctively, Eve wiped her flowing eyes.

"Wh-what happened?" she managed to ask between sobs. "Was it his heart? Did he have a stroke? He has high b-blood pressure, you know, but he's on m-medication for it . . ."

"It wasn't his heart or a stroke," Phyllis said. "Mike is the one who came here and told us about it. Jan Delaney found him at the bed-and-breakfast. He . . . he'd been murdered, Eve."

Eve stared wide-eyed at her for several seconds, as if she couldn't comprehend what Phyllis had just told her. Then she said, "You! This is all your fault!"

"Eve!" Carolyn exclaimed in horror as Phyllis recoiled from the accusation, just as she would have from a physical slap in the face. "How can you say something like that? Phyllis didn't have anything to do with this. None of us did!"

"She did! She's a jinx! She's cursed! Think about all the murders. Did you ever know anybody who had anything to do with murder until people started dropping dead around her?"

Carolyn took hold of Eve's shoulders and shook her a little. "Stop it! That's not fair! Phyllis wasn't to blame for any of those other deaths, and she didn't have anything to do with this one, either." Carolyn looked over at Phyllis. "Tell her, Phyllis. Tell her!"

But Phyllis could only sit there feeling stunned. Maybe Eve was right. Lord knew she had thought often enough that she was some sort of jinx. How else could she explain her involvement in several murders over the past few years? She was some sort of . . . of . . . murder magnet, she thought crazily.

Eve blotted at the streams of tears from her eyes and asked, "Do the police know who did it?"

"Not yet," Carolyn admitted.

Eve nodded as if that confirmed everything she had just said. "So she'll have to solve it. She'll have to find the killer."

"That's what I told her," Carolyn said. "Because—"

"B-because what?" Eve asked.

Carolyn didn't answer, and it didn't take long at all for the silence to become extremely uncomfortable.

"Oh, my God!" Eve said. "They think *I* did it! They think I killed Roy!"

That brought on a fresh round of wracking sobs. Phyllis shook off her own stunned feelings and leaned closer, trying to put an arm around Eve's shoulders to comfort her.

Eve pulled away, though, and huddled instead against Carolyn's formidable figure.

Phyllis told herself not to be offended by that or by anything Eve had said. Eve was in a terrible emotional state right now. Later, when some of the initial shock had worn off, she would be able to think straighter.

Sam came back into the living room, caught Phyllis's eye, and said, "I got hold of that, uh, person on the phone, and she said she'd be right over."

"Person?" Eve lifted her tear-streaked face. "What person?"

Sam hesitated, but when Phyllis nodded, he said, "Juliette Yorke."

Phyllis could tell by the look on Eve's face that her grief was mixed with confusion for a moment, but then the confusion cleared and was replaced by outrage.

"The lawyer? But that . . . that means they seriously think . . ."

"That's right, dear," Carolyn said. "The police think that you killed him."

Phyllis wished that Carolyn hadn't put it so bluntly, especially when Eve began to wail again. But it was hard to sugarcoat such news, and anyway, Eve had to know what the situation was sooner or later.

Sam went on, "Ms. Yorke said to tell all of you that if the cops show up again, not to say anything to them, especially you, Eve."

"They really think that I . . . that I could ever . . ." Eve turned to look at Phyllis again. "Mike came here to *arrest* me?"

"No, no, of course not," Phyllis said as she hastily shook her head. "They just want to talk to you; that's all."

"They want to interrogate you," Carolyn put in. "Mike said you were a person of interest. Why, that's the same thing as a suspect!"

Phyllis couldn't contain herself any longer. "Carolyn," she said, "you're just making things worse—"

"No!" Eve said. "I want to know how bad things really are, and she's telling me the truth! They think I did it! They think I killed my . . . my own husband . . ."

Her voice trailed away into sobs again as she leaned against Carolyn and shudder after shudder rolled through her body.

Phyllis stood up and rubbed her temples, where a dull headache had sprung up. She wasn't doing any good here. She motioned with her head for Sam to join her and went out to the kitchen.

"What did you tell Juliette?" she asked quietly when they were alone.

"Just that Roy's been murdered, the cops are lookin' for Eve and want to talk to her, and that she's here. Juliette said we did the right thing by callin' her. She'll go in to the sheriff's department with her."

Phyllis frowned. "I started to worry that it would look bad for Eve to bring a lawyer along when she turns herself in."

"Like she's guilty, you mean?"

"You know that's the first thing everybody will think. If she's not guilty, then why would she need a lawyer?"

"Anybody who'd think that doesn't know anything about dealin' with the cops," Sam said. He shrugged. "Anyway, I figure it's better to run that risk than take a chance on Eve sayin' something that would get her in even more trouble."

"But how is that even possible, if she didn't do anything wrong? And you and I both know, Sam Fletcher, that she didn't."

"Yep," Sam agreed. "We know that. The trick's gonna be convincin' the investigators of it."

Phyllis turned toward the counter. "Well, I'm going to fix some coffee. I need to be doing *something*."

When she had the coffee brewing, she and Sam went back up the hall to the living room. Eve wasn't wailing now, but she was still sobbing quietly as she leaned against Carolyn's shoulder. Phyllis didn't say anything as she sat down in one of the armchairs. She wanted to be there if she could do anything for her friend, but she wasn't going to force Eve to talk to her right now, not with the state of emotional turmoil Eve was in.

Phyllis had been sitting there only a few minutes when she saw an SUV pull up at the curb in front of the house. Juliette Yorke got out of the vehicle and came toward the house with long-legged strides.

Juliette was in her middle thirties, with fairly long brown hair that she usually kept pulled back in a ponytail, which was the case today. She must not have had to be in court, because she wore jeans and a quilted jacket over a dark red blouse. She had her briefcase with her, something no lawyer ever liked to be without.

Sam opened the door for her before she could ring the bell. Juliette gave him a brief smile as she stepped past him into the living room. She nodded to Phyllis as she took off her jacket.

"Let me get that for you," Sam said. He took the jacket and hung it up in the hall closet.

"Eve," Carolyn said, "Ms. Yorke's here."

Juliette sat down on Eve's other side, where Phyllis had been sitting earlier, and placed her briefcase on the coffee table. She put a hand on Eve's shoulder and said, "Mrs. Porter, I'm so sorry to hear about your loss. Please accept my condolences."

"Th-thank you, dear," Eve said. "Sam told you what h-happened?"

Juliette nodded. "As much as we know now. But we're going to find out a lot more, I promise you that. We're going to find out the truth, and we're going to see justice done. But to do that . . . and I know it's terribly hard right now . . . I'm going to have to ask you some questions."

"I . . . I know. I'll tell you anything I can."

Juliette reached over to the coffee table and opened her briefcase. She took out a small digital recorder and said, "It's all right if I record our conversation?"

Eve swallowed and nodded. "Of course."

Juliette switched on the recorder and said, "First interview with Mrs. Eve Porter." She gave the date and time, then went on, "Mrs. Porter, I need to know everywhere you've been today."

"Wait a minute," Carolyn said. "You're asking her for her *alibi*?"

"I'm trying to establish the facts of the case, Mrs. Wilbarger." A steely tone came into Juliette's voice. "It might be easier if I talked to Mrs. Porter in private."

"That's not necessary," Phyllis said. "We won't interfere, will we, Carolyn?"

"Of course not," Carolyn said, but the irritation was easy to hear in her voice. "We just want what's best for Eve."

"Fine." Juliette turned back to Eve. "Mrs. Porter, where have you been today?"

"Well, I . . . I've been out looking at houses," Eve said. "You know, Roy and I have been trying to find a place to buy."

"Do the two of you normally do this together?"

"Yes, but . . . Roy said he didn't feel very well today . . . That's why I thought it might have been his heart, or a stroke, when Phyllis told me . . . told me . . ."

Juliette took hold of Eve's hand. "It's all right," she said in a steady, calming tone. "I know what a terrible thing this is to deal with. Just take a deep breath, and then we'll go on."

Eve nodded, took that deep breath, and a moment later she nodded.

"Roy didn't feel well. I would have stayed to take care of him, but he said he didn't like people fussing over him when he was sick, so I told him I'd take a look at some of the places we were considering. We printed out a list from a real estate website . . . it's in the front seat of my car."

"That's good," Juliette said. "Did you stop and talk to anyone at any of these houses?"

"No. I . . . I just drove around and looked at them . . ."

"Did you stop anywhere and buy anything? Gas for your car, or something at the grocery store?"

Phyllis knew why Juliette was asking that. Receipts would have the time of purchase printed on them.

Eve shook her head. "No, I just . . . drove around, like I said."

Phyllis saw Juliette's lips tighten slightly. If what Eve was saying was true, then she had no alibi, no way to prove that she hadn't been at the house murdering Roy in some as-yet-unknown fashion. Of course, they didn't know the time of death yet, Phyllis reminded herself. But from the sound of it, Eve had been out by herself for quite a while.

Juliette followed up on that same thought, asking, "When did you leave the bed-and-breakfast?"

"It was right after lunch. Twelve thirty, I suppose. Somewhere around there."

"Did anyone see you leave? The people who own the place, maybe?"

Eve shook her head and said, "Goodness, I don't know. I don't believe Jan was there, and I don't know where Pete was.

There are a few other people staying there, but I don't know any of them except to nod to. I didn't talk to anyone when I left, and I didn't see anyone watching me."

"Don't worry. I'll talk to everyone who might have seen you. We won't leave anything to chance. This list you printed out of houses you were considering buying . . . did you check them off or cross them out or anything like that as you drove around?"

"No. There weren't any of them I could actually eliminate without Roy looking at them. I wanted his opinion . . ."

Her voice broke, and tears started to well from her eyes again.

Juliette leaned closer and said, "I'm sorry, Mrs. Porter, but I have to know . . . had you and your husband been getting along all right? Had you had any disagreements recently?"

"No!" Eve said. "We'd only been married a few weeks! This was still like . . . like an extended honeymoon for us . . ."

She couldn't go on. She collapsed against Carolyn again.

Juliette stood up and came over to Phyllis and Sam. "Have you noticed any signs of friction between Mrs. Porter and her husband?" she asked.

"Absolutely not," Phyllis answered without hesitation. "They were as happy a couple as I've ever seen."

Sam nodded and said, "Yep, I feel the same way. There's no chance in the world Eve would've ever hurt that fella."

"You've known Mrs. Porter for a long time, haven't you?"

"Ten years," Phyllis said.

"It hasn't been that long for me," Sam said, "but long enough to know she didn't do anything wrong."

Juliette smiled faintly. "Well, it never hurts to have good character witnesses. A good solid alibi is better, but . . ." She stopped and shook her head. "What about Roy Porter? How long have you known him?"

Phyllis glanced up at Sam, who stood beside her chair. "We met him when Eve brought him here for Thanksgiving."

"This past Thanksgiving? Not even two months ago?"

"Well . . . yes."

"So you barely knew him," Juliette said.

"We knew him well enough to know that he loved Eve," Phyllis said. "That's all that mattered to us."

"Yes, of course." Juliette looked at Sam. "You said that investigators from the sheriff's department want to talk to Mrs. Porter?"

"Yeah. Phyllis's son, Mike, came by here lookin' for her. He said that if we saw her, we should call him and he'd come get her."

Juliette shook her head. "Absolutely not. Mrs. Porter is going to talk to the authorities of her own volition, and if I don't like the line of questioning, we'll be leaving."

"If you try to do that, won't they just arrest her?" Phyllis asked.

"Not if they don't have a case. And if they do have a case . . . then we'll deal with that. Right now, though . . ." Juliette turned back toward the sofa. "Mrs. Porter, it's time to go talk to the investigators."

Eve managed to nod. "If . . . if I have to."

"I'm afraid it's necessary. The sooner we convince them that you had nothing to do with your husband's death, the sooner they'll be able to find out who's really responsible."

"Of course. Is it all right if I . . . if I go upstairs and wash my face?"

"I think that would be all right. Mrs. Wilbarger, would you go with her?"

"Why?" Carolyn demanded. "Do you think she's going to climb out a window and go on the lam or something?"

"I just think it's a good idea that Mrs. Porter not be alone right now," Juliette said. "Please."

"Oh, all right." Carolyn stood up. "Come on, Eve."

They left the living room and went upstairs. Juliette picked up her recorder and switched it off. As she was putting it in her briefcase again, Phyllis asked her, "Things don't look very good, do they?"

"I can't really discuss the case at this point, Mrs. Newsom, but I will say it would have looked better if certain things had been different."

"Like an alibi," Sam said.

Juliette shrugged. "I'll do everything I possibly can," she promised. "If Mrs. Porter isn't taken into custody, will it be all right to bring her back here for the night? I'm assuming that she won't want to stay at the bed-and-breakfast."

"Of course," Phyllis said. "Some of Eve's things are still here, in fact, so it won't be any problem for her to stay in her old room for as long as necessary."

"That's good. And it's good that she has loyal friends in a situation like this." Juliette paused. "She's going to need them."

Chapter 11

$\mathcal{E}$ ve and Carolyn came down the stairs a few minutes later. Eve had washed her face and looked a little better now, although her eyes were red rimmed and she looked like she might start crying again at any minute.

Juliette met them at the bottom of the stairs. "Are you ready to go?" she asked Eve.

"Yes, but first there's something I have to say." Eve turned to Phyllis. "I'm so sorry for what I said earlier, Phyllis. I didn't mean it—you know that. I don't blame you for Roy's death, I really don't. I was just so . . . so shocked."

Juliette frowned at Phyllis and asked, "Why would Mrs. Porter blame you for what happened to her husband?"

"It's nothing—," Phyllis began.

"I said that she was cursed," Eve interrupted. "I said that she was a jinx because murders happen all the time around her. But that's crazy. There haven't really been all *that* many murders."

"There have been a few, though," Juliette said in a musing tone that seemed to say she was considering Eve's theory. Then she gave an abrupt shake of her head and went on, "But you're right. That's crazy." She put a hand on Eve's arm. "Let's go."

As they headed toward the front door, Eve looked back and said, "I'm sorry, Phyllis. I really am."

"It's all right," Phyllis assured her. "I know you didn't mean it."

But even as she spoke, she wasn't a hundred percent convinced that Eve was wrong. She wasn't convinced of that at all.

With Eve and Juliette gone to the sheriff's department, it was impossible to concentrate on anything else. Time dragged by as Phyllis, Sam, and Carolyn sat in the living room and drank coffee. Now and then one of them would speak up and make some comment about how Eve would be back soon and everything would be fine, and the others would agree, but the undercurrent of doubt in their voices was unmistakable. They weren't convinced that everything was going to be all right. Not at all.

It was starting to get dark when headlights stopped at the curb in front of the house. Sam stood up quickly and went to the window. "Looks like Ms. Yorke's SUV," he said as he looked out through the gap in the curtains.

The three of them crowded into the foyer. Phyllis opened the wooden door and turned on the porch light. She expected to see Eve and Juliette walking toward the house, but her heart sank as she realized that the lawyer was by herself. Juliette didn't even have her briefcase with her this time.

She didn't waste any time, either, as Phyllis opened the storm door. As she was coming up the steps to the porch, Juliette said, "Mrs. Porter has been taken into custody."

"They've arrested her!" Carolyn said. "Oh, my Lord!"

"Let's get down there and bail her out," Sam said.

Juliette shook her head as she came inside. "There won't be a bail hearing until tomorrow morning. She'll have to spend the night."

"In jail!" Carolyn said. "She'll have to spend the night in jail! Locked up in the tank with God knows what sort of degenerates! I've seen *Caged Heat*, you know."

Juliette managed to smile faintly. "Take it easy, Mrs. Wilbarger," she advised. "The sheriff's department isn't a bunch of ogres. Eve has her own cell. I wouldn't go so far as to say that it's comfortable, but she'll be all right there. No one's going to bother her."

"Let's go in the living room and sit down," Phyllis suggested. "I'll bring you some coffee."

Juliette nodded. "Thanks. I can use it."

A few minutes later, they were all settled down in the living room, Phyllis and Sam on the sofa, Juliette and Carolyn in armchairs. Phyllis let Juliette take a couple of sips of the hot coffee before she asked, "How is Eve taking it?"

"As well as can be expected, I suppose. She seems to be a strong woman. I get the feeling, though, that her strength doesn't run all that deep. I wouldn't want to leave her locked up for very long. But I think she can stand it until we get her out of there tomorrow morning."

"First thing tomorrow morning," Carolyn put in.

"I'll do what I can," Juliette said, "but a lot of the timing is up to the judge."

"Whatever you need, we'll come up with it," Phyllis said.

"The bail could be pretty high," Juliette warned. "I'll try to get Eve released on her own recognizance, since she doesn't exactly come across as a flight risk, but this is a murder case, after all. It's hard to predict."

"If you need to put up this house as security with a bail bondsman, I'll sign whatever papers are necessary," Phyllis said without hesitation.

"And I can put my hands on some cash," Sam added.

"We all can," Carolyn said. "Do whatever you have to. We're good for it."

Juliette smiled again. "Mrs. Porter certainly has some devoted friends. That's good."

"Did they actually charge her with murder?" Phyllis asked.

"I'm afraid so. They brought out a letter opener while they were questioning her and wanted to know if she recognized it. I stopped her from answering, but it didn't really matter. Her fingerprints were the only ones on it."

"A letter opener," Phyllis repeated. "That was the murder weapon?"

"They didn't say so, but from the way it was bagged and tagged, yeah, I'm sure it was."

"What did it look like?"

Juliette held up her hands about ten inches apart. "That long, with a narrow blade and a handle with a little cat's head at the end of it."

Phyllis and Carolyn looked at each other.

"You recognize the description, don't you?" Juliette asked. "It's all right. I was able to talk to Eve in private later, and she admitted that it was her letter opener."

"I've seen her use it a thousand times," Carolyn said. "One

of her students gave it to her the last year she taught." A frown creased Carolyn's forehead. "But I haven't seen it lately, come to think of it. Have you, Phyllis?"

Phyllis shook her head. "No, I don't believe I have."

"Eve said that it should have been in her room here at the house," Juliette continued. "She claims she didn't take it with her when she moved some of her things to the bed-and-breakfast. But she couldn't recall the last time she actually saw it."

"Didn't she tell this to the investigators?" Phyllis asked.

"The conversation didn't get that far," Juliette said. "When they brought it out, I stopped Eve from answering and told them the questioning was over, that we were leaving." She shrugged. "That's when they took her into custody."

"You keep calling it that," Carolyn said. "They *arrested* her."

"Yes, they did," Juliette admitted. "It doesn't really matter what you call it."

"Maybe not, but I don't think we need to lose sight of just how serious this is."

"There's no chance of that," Phyllis said. "Were you able to find out anything else when you talked to Eve in private?"

"All of this really should be privileged, you know," Juliette said. "But I can make an exception since Mrs. Porter gave me permission to tell you, and you're all so close to her, and since you have, well, a history of figuring things out, Mrs. Newsom."

"Solving murders, you mean," Carolyn said.

Juliette ignored that and went on, looking at Phyllis, "I'm not your lawyer, so I can't give you any legal advice . . . but just as an acquaintance, I'd say that the sheriff's department really seems like they don't want anybody interfering in this investigation."

"You mean that's what the district attorney wants," Sam said.

"Timothy Sullivan will be running for reelection in less than a year," Juliette said. "That tends to make a person very sensitive to appearances."

"So he doesn't want Phyllis showing up the legal system again," Carolyn said.

"I've never tried to show up anybody," Phyllis said.

Juliette held up her hands and said, "We're getting off the track here. Mrs. Porter told me again that she didn't kill her husband, and I believe her. Now, don't take this the wrong way, but what have the three of you been doing all day?"

Carolyn's eyes widened. "Oh . . . my . . . God. Now you're asking *us* for our alibis?"

"You can't be serious," Phyllis said to Juliette.

"I'm just trying to nail down all the facts I possibly can," Juliette explained. "I'll be asking the same questions of everyone who has any connection to the case."

"Well . . ." Phyllis shrugged. "I guess that sounds reasonable."

Carolyn's "Hmmph!" made it clear that she wasn't going to go that far.

"I've been right here in the house all day," Sam said. "Well, either in the house or out in the garage. And I'm pretty doggone sure that Phyllis and Carolyn have been, too."

"That's right," Carolyn said. "We haven't gone anywhere. We're each other's alibis."

Juliette looked at Phyllis. "Mrs. Newsom? Is that true?"

Phyllis nodded and said, "It certainly is. I don't suppose any of us can actually prove that we've been here without relying on the testimony of the other two, but that's what happened."

"That's good enough for me," Juliette said, "and I think it would be for any reasonable person, too. We can move on."

"What should we do about the bail hearin'?" Sam asked.

"I'll call you in the morning as soon as I find out when it will be. I'd be ready to come down to the courthouse right away, if I were you."

"We will be," Phyllis promised.

"That's all any of us can do tonight," Juliette went on as she stood up. "But if you think of anything that might be helpful, anything you've seen or heard that might indicate someone else had a reason to want Roy Porter dead, please call me. You've got my cell phone number."

"Isn't it obvious that someone else wanted Roy dead?" Carolyn asked. "Someone killed him, and we know Eve didn't."

"But you don't have a defense except for creating reasonable doubt, do you?" Phyllis said to Juliette. "You have to point the finger of suspicion at someone else."

Juliette's voice and expression were grim as she said, "Without an alibi and with Eve's fingerprints on the murder weapon, a weapon that a number of people can identify as belonging to her, we're not going to prevail on the merits of the evidence. I'm sorry, but there's no getting around that."

Sam said, "What you mean is, you need to find the real killer."

"Well, that would be nice, but I'd settle for some big, fat reasonable doubt in the minds of some of the jurors." Juliette looked at Phyllis. "So I'm definitely not saying that you need to conduct your own investigation, Mrs. Newsom."

"I understand that," Phyllis said.

She also understood that there was no way she was going to allow Eve to be convicted for a murder she didn't commit.

No way in the world.

Chapter 12

*P*hyllis didn't sleep well, and according to Carolyn and Sam the next morning, neither did they. So they were all up early, dressed and ready to go as soon as Juliette Yorke called with the information about Eve's bail hearing.

Sam was the only one who had much of an appetite. He fixed his own breakfast, heating up a bowl of oatmeal with bananas cut up in it while Phyllis and Carolyn just drank coffee and nibbled on toast.

They all jumped a little when the phone rang at eight forty-five. Phyllis was the closest, so she answered it.

"The bail hearing is at nine o'clock," Juliette said. "I know this isn't much notice, but I just got off the phone with the court clerk myself."

"Don't worry," Phyllis said. "We'll be there."

By the time she hung up, Sam and Carolyn were both on their feet, ready to go.

Juliette had said that the hearing would be in one of the

courtrooms on the second floor of the main courthouse on the square. That was only a few blocks away, so the three of them were able to get there, park, and walk inside with a few minutes to spare. As they went along the hall toward the open double doors that led into the courtroom, Phyllis spotted Juliette standing near the doors, talking on her phone.

Juliette was dressed for court today in a sober gray suit. She was wearing her glasses instead of the contacts she'd had in the day before. She broke the connection on the phone and then turned it off before she slipped it into a jacket pocket.

' "I was just talking to a bail bondsman," she said. "I don't think we'll have any problem arranging things once bail has been set."

"Have you had any indication what the judge will do?" Phyllis asked.

"None whatsoever. We won't know until we're in there." Juliette hesitated. "Are you prepared to testify if I call you, Mrs. Newsom?"

"Testify? Me? Why would I need to testify?"

"Mrs. Porter will be staying at your house. The judge may want to hear from you. I could ask you how you feel about that."

"And I could say that I don't have any objection to Eve staying with us because I know she's not capable of committing murder." Phyllis smiled. "Like you said, a character witness."

"It can't hurt," Juliette said. She lowered her voice. "Here comes the district attorney."

Phyllis glanced around and saw a slender man of medium height, with carefully styled brown hair, walking along the hall toward the courtroom. He was talking to a couple of other men in suits who weren't as photogenic as he was. As they passed Phyllis and the others, District Attorney Timothy Sullivan nodded to Juliette and said, "Good morning, Counselor."

Sullivan didn't speak to Phyllis, but she saw his eyes flick toward her for a second and knew that he knew who she was. She hadn't set out to make an enemy of this man . . . but there wasn't an iota of friendliness in his gaze.

Sullivan and his associates went on into the courtroom. Juliette nodded toward the doors and said, "Let's go."

Phyllis, Sam, and Carolyn slipped onto one of the half dozen benches set up for spectators while Juliette went through a gate in a wooden railing and set her briefcase on the defense table at the front of the room. She sat down, opened the case, and began taking papers out of it.

"I don't care much for bein' in court," Sam said quietly. "I never would've made a good lawyer."

"Neither would I," Carolyn said. "I'm too outspoken. I tell the truth as I see it, not the way some judge wants to hear it."

Sam smiled and said, "I was thinkin' more of the fact that I don't like wearin' a tie."

By now it was five minutes after nine o'clock, but the judge hadn't come into the courtroom yet. That wasn't unusual, Phyllis thought. Like any other bureaucracy, the legal system worked on its own schedule, and everyone else had to accommodate that. She would have liked to see all the judges and attorneys in the world try to function in a school environment, where you had to be in your seat and ready to get down to work as soon as the bell rang. She was willing to bet that things would be a lot more efficient that way.

A few more maddeningly slow minutes went by, and then a uniformed bailiff came into the courtroom through a side door, followed by the court clerk. The bailiff called, "All rise."

Phyllis didn't know the judge who came in and went behind the bench. He was a stocky, mostly bald man in his fifties or sixties, with thick glasses and a fringe of gray hair. When he sat down, he told the others in the room, "You may be seated," in a rather high-pitched voice.

The bailiff announced that court was in session, the Honorable Phillip J. Hemmerson presiding. The court clerk read a docket number and said that this was a hearing to determine bail, and then a uniformed female deputy brought Eve into the courtroom through a different door. Phyllis was glad to see that Eve was wearing her own clothes, even though those clothes were getting wrinkled by now. She was sure Eve wouldn't have liked wearing one of those orange jumpsuits prisoners usually had to wear.

Eve saw the three of them sitting there and managed to smile, but she was pale and haggard, as if she hadn't slept a bit the night before. Phyllis wouldn't be surprised if that was true. Eve sat down at the defense table next to Juliette, who leaned over and spoke quietly to her.

The judge was looking through some papers on the bench in front of him. Phyllis had no doubt that he already knew the particulars of the case, but judges always did that anyway. Then he looked up and asked, "Do you have a recommendation for bail in this case, Mr. Sullivan?"

The district attorney stood up and said, "Yes, Your Honor, we do. The state recommends that bail be set in the amount of five hundred thousand dollars."

Phyllis drew in a deep breath. Half a million dollars sounded like a tremendous amount, but she remembered that a bail bondsman usually only asked that the client put up ten percent of the bail amount. Her house was worth more than three times what that ten percent would be even in the current market, and she was more than willing to let Eve use it as surety for the bond.

Juliette wasn't going to let Sullivan's demand go unchallenged, though. When Judge Hemmerson turned to her and said, "Ms. Yorke?" she stood up and said, "Your Honor, half a million dollars is the sort of bail you set on a professional criminal who represents a flight risk. My client is a retired schoolteacher who has led a quiet, decent life and never been in trouble with the law. We ask that you release her on her own recognizance."

Well, this was normal so far, Phyllis thought. Both sides had established their starting positions, and now they could negotiate toward something in the middle.

"Your Honor," Sullivan responded instantly, "Ms. Yorke clearly doesn't know everything there is to know about her client; otherwise, she wouldn't describe Eve Porter as simply a retired schoolteacher."

Phyllis stiffened. She didn't like the smug tone of Sullivan's voice or the self-satisfied smile on his face. Neither did Juliette, who turned sharply toward the district attorney and demanded, "What are you talking about?"

Instead of answering her directly, Sullivan addressed the judge again as he said, "Your Honor, Mrs. Porter has been questioned by the police regarding more than one suspicious death in the past."

It would have been hard to say who looked more shocked: Phyllis, Sam, and Carolyn in the spectators' section, Juliette at the defense table, or Judge Hemmerson on the bench, who peered at Sullivan over the glasses that had slipped down on his nose and said in a tone of disbelief, "Her?"

The only one who didn't seem surprised was Eve, who sat there looking straight ahead with her shoulders slumped in an air of resignation. Phyllis would have expected her friend to display indignation at such an outrageous accusation.

Unless, of course, what Sullivan had just said was true . . .

Still looking smug, the district attorney said, "Yes, Your Honor, Mrs. Porter was questioned by the police in Wichita Falls and Abilene about the deaths of two previous *husbands*."

The emphasis Sullivan put on the word made the implication clear. He had practically accused Eve of murdering not only Roy, but also two of the men to whom she had been married previously.

Phyllis's head was spinning. She knew that Eve had been married several times, of course. Eve had made no secret of that fact. But Phyllis had always assumed that those marriages had ended in divorce. Eve had never done anything to correct that assumption.

Juliette was quick on her feet. She said, "Was my client ever charged with any crime?"

"No," Sullivan replied with a shrug, as if that was just a formality.

"Were the deaths of those men ruled to be homicides?"

Now Sullivan didn't look quite so satisfied with himself. "There wasn't enough evidence for an official finding of homicide," he admitted. "But that doesn't mean—"

"Your Honor, I move for a dismissal of the charges against my client," Juliette cut in. "The district attorney has irreparably and irretrievably prejudiced any future proceedings involving Mrs. Porter with these outrageous, unsubstantiated, and irrelevant claims."

Hemmerson shook his head. "Nice try, Counselor, but this is a bail hearing, not a trial. Save it for the grand jury." He turned his attention to the district attorney. "And Mr. Sullivan, I don't appreciate theatrics so early in the morning, especially if you don't have anything concrete to back them up."

"My apologies, Your Honor," Sullivan said. "I was just trying to demonstrate a pattern of behavior on the part of the defendant that would indicate the need for the bail we've requested."

"Well, you didn't. On the other hand, I'm not inclined to release someone who's been charged with murder on her own recognizance, either." The judge picked up his gavel. "Bail is set in the amount of two hundred thousand dollars."

Eve slumped even more in her chair as Hemmerson rapped his gavel on the bench, but Phyllis thought it was with relief this time. Eve had to know they could manage that amount and that she would be out of jail soon.

Timothy Sullivan didn't look happy as he gathered up his papers and spoke to his associates. Had he really wanted to keep Eve in jail, Phyllis wondered? Surely that wouldn't look good to the voters, forcing an elderly retired schoolteacher to remain behind bars.

Unless Sullivan truly believed that Eve was guilty of several murders and that the public would see that eventually. That high level of confidence in the district attorney didn't bode well for Eve's chances.

Juliette sat down beside Eve and spoke to her in a low

voice. Eve nodded several times. The uniformed officer who had brought her into the courtroom came over and motioned for her to stand up. Eve did so, turning to look at Phyllis, Sam, and Carolyn. She smiled at them, but Phyllis could tell that the expression was forced. This bail hearing could have gone a lot worse, Phyllis knew, but its outcome didn't change the fact that Eve was still in deep, deep trouble.

After Eve had been taken out of the room, Juliette closed her briefcase and stood up. She came through the gate in the railing and told them, "Eve has enough cash in the bank to cover her share of the bond. I'll call the bondsman and start making arrangements."

"How long before she'll be out?" Carolyn asked.

"An hour, hour and a half, maybe," Juliette said. "Assuming everything goes smoothly, and there's no reason to think that it won't."

"Then what?" Phyllis said.

"Then she'll be arraigned, probably next week, and the case will go to the grand jury next month. They'll determine whether there's enough evidence to warrant an indictment."

"Maybe it won't get that far. Maybe before then, they'll find out who really killed Roy, and the charge against Eve will be dropped."

"They never should have arrested her in the first place," Carolyn added.

"Given the evidence, they didn't have much choice," Juliette said.

Carolyn frowned. "You're supposed to be on her side."

"I am. But we have to be practical about this." Juliette sighed. "And Eve's got to start telling me the truth—all of the truth—if she's going to have any chance at all."

Chapter 13

*J*uliette told the three of them to go home. There was nothing more they could do at the courthouse. As soon as Eve was released, she would bring her to Phyllis's house, Juliette promised.

They didn't say much during the short ride back to the house, but as soon as they were inside hanging up their coats, Carolyn burst out, "I swear, I wanted to wring that district attorney's scrawny little neck!"

"Then they would have locked you up, too," Phyllis pointed out. "I think Juliette already has her hands full with just one of us for a client."

"Maybe so," Sam said, "but I know how Carolyn feels. A fella actin' so snide like that always puts my teeth on edge. I was about ready to go to fist city with him when he started goin' on with all that junk about Eve."

"How do we know it was junk?" Phyllis asked.

The other two stared at her for several seconds before

Carolyn demanded, "What are you talking about? You can't possibly believe all that crazy stuff he was spouting about her!"

"I don't like Mr. Sullivan, either," Phyllis said, "but he doesn't strike me as an idiot. I don't think he would have brought up Eve's past unless he knew what he was talking about."

Sam shook his head. "I don't believe she ever killed anybody, let alone Roy and two husbands before him."

"Neither do I. I don't believe it for a second. But *something* happened, something Eve's never told us about."

"That's her right," Carolyn said. "There are things about my life I've never shared with any of you. I'm sure we could all say the same thing. Everyone has . . . well, not secrets, exactly, but things we like to keep to ourselves."

That was true, Phyllis thought, and she certainly believed that Eve had the right to be as discreet as she wanted to be about her past. Unfortunately, when murder was involved, discretion often flew right out the window.

Phyllis didn't want to waste time arguing with Carolyn, though, especially when they really wanted the same thing, which was for Eve to be able to put this horrible business behind her. The legal mess threatened to overshadow the fact that Eve was now a widow. The man she had married only weeks earlier was dead, and she ought to be able to mourn.

"I'm going to get some fresh coffee brewing," Phyllis said. "I'm sure Eve will need some when she and Juliette get here."

Carolyn started for the stairs, saying, "I'll go up and make sure her room is ready for her."

From the front window in the living room, Sam said, "Better hold on a minute, both of you. Looks like we've got company."

"Eve and Juliette are here already?" Phyllis asked.

Sam shook his head. "Nope. But a sheriff's department car just pulled up out front. And it's not Mike gettin' out."

Phyllis went to the window and stood beside him to look out. Two men wearing Western-cut suits and gray felt Stetsons were coming toward the house. They had badges on their belts. Phyllis didn't recognize either of them.

She didn't wait for them to ring the bell. Instead she met them at the door, figuring that whatever this was about, it would be better to get it over with before Eve and Juliette got there.

"Mrs. Newsom?" one of the men asked.

"That's right."

"I'm Deputy Ward Burton. This is Deputy Richard Conley. We're the lead investigators on the Roy Porter case."

"What can I do for you?" Phyllis asked.

Burton took a paper from his pocket. "We're here to execute a search warrant for the room occupied by Mrs. Eve Porter."

"You're going to paw through Eve's things?" Carolyn asked from behind Phyllis. "Hasn't she suffered enough indignities already?"

"We're just doing our jobs, ma'am," Burton said.

Phyllis knew it wouldn't do any good to argue. She stepped aside to let the deputies into the house. "Will there be a forensics team, too?" she asked.

"No, ma'am. Well, probably not. Depends on what we find, I guess."

Both deputies were middle-aged, rawboned men who looked like cowboys. They probably took part in the annual Sheriff's Posse Rodeo. But despite their appearance, Phyllis had no doubt that they were experienced, competent investigators. Ross Haney was a good sheriff who hired skilled people for his department.

"I'll show you where Eve's room is," she said as she took the search warrant from Burton.

Carolyn frowned. "You're just going to cooperate with them?"

"Wouldn't be any point in doin' otherwise," Sam said. "And it wouldn't do Eve any good for the three of us to get locked up, would it?"

"I suppose not," Carolyn said, but she didn't hide her disapproval as Phyllis led the two deputies to the stairs.

When she had opened the door of Eve's room, Burton said, "We'd like for you to stay, Mrs. Newsom. This is your house, after all."

"Yes, of course." Phyllis didn't honestly think the deputies would try to plant any evidence or do anything else underhanded . . . but if they found anything unusual, she wanted to know about it.

The deputies' experience showed in the swift, efficient, and completely thorough way they searched Eve's room. They checked all her clothes, everything in the desk, and every drawer. Watching them, Phyllis felt bad for Eve and was glad that she wasn't here to witness this invasion of her privacy.

Because that's what it amounted to, no matter how polite and professional Burton and Conley were about it. They were poking around in Eve's life, and it made Phyllis both embarrassed and uncomfortable to be part of it. She looked at the search warrant. Everything on it seemed to be in proper legal order, but maybe it would have been better to wait until Juliette was here to look it over, she thought.

But that would have meant exposing Eve to even more stress, and Phyllis didn't think that was a good idea, either.

After half an hour, the deputies were finished. Ward Burton held up two photo albums, each of which had been slipped into a clear plastic evidence bag of its own.

"We'll be taking these with us," he told Phyllis. "That's all."

"Why do you need Eve's photo albums?" she asked.

Burton smiled and said, "I'm afraid we can't discuss that, ma'am."

She could make a pretty good guess anyway, she thought. Those albums probably had pictures in them of Eve's former husbands. The ones who had died. The ones Timothy Sullivan had all but accused her of murdering. Phyllis could picture the district attorney in her mind's eye, standing in a courtroom in front of a jury, pointing to huge, blown-up photographs of those men and shouting about how Eve was some sort of black widow serial killer . . .

"Will she get them back?" Phyllis asked.

"I couldn't really say, ma'am," Burton replied. He held out a hand toward the stairs. "After you."

She led the way back downstairs. Sam was sitting in the living room. Phyllis didn't see Carolyn, but she smelled coffee brewing and figured that Carolyn was in the kitchen. Probably didn't trust herself to be around the deputies without saying or doing something that might get her in trouble.

After the lawmen were gone, Sam stepped out into the

hall and said, "Carolyn went to put on that coffee. I told her I thought it might be a good idea."

"And I'm sure it was," Phyllis agreed.

"I saw they had somethin' with 'em. What'd they find?"

"Photo albums," Phyllis said.

"Ah. The ex-husbands."

"Late husbands, to hear the district attorney tell it."

"Did you know they died?" Sam asked.

Phyllis shook her head. "No, today is the first I've heard about that. Eve always talked more like she was divorced from them."

"But she didn't come right out and say that?"

Phyllis thought back on the conversations she'd had with Eve over the years. She couldn't possibly remember all of them, of course, but as far as she could recall . . .

"No, I don't believe she ever did."

"Then she didn't exactly lie to you. She just let you think what you wanted to think."

"I suppose you could say that."

Phyllis knew that Sam was right, but she couldn't help but feel a little hurt anyway that Eve hadn't trusted her and Carolyn. Of course, Eve's past was none of their business. She had to keep things in perspective here.

Carolyn came up the hall from the kitchen. "Are they gone?" she asked.

"Yes," Phyllis said.

"You shouldn't have let them in here."

"I didn't have any choice. They had a search warrant."

"You could have demanded that they wait until Juliette was here to look at the warrant."

"And they could have refused," Phyllis said. "Plus that would have meant that Eve was here, too, and it would have just been harder on her to know they were rooting around in her things."

"She'll find out about it anyway."

"Yes," Phyllis admitted, "I suppose she will."

Sam said, "And speakin' of Eve . . . they're here."

Phyllis hurried to the door. Sam and Carolyn were right behind her. When Phyllis opened the door, they saw Eve and Juliette coming toward the porch. Juliette had hold of Eve's arm, supporting her.

"She looks like she's aged ten years since yesterday," Carolyn whispered.

Phyllis agreed, but she wasn't going to say anything about that to Eve and hoped that Carolyn wouldn't, either.

"Well, I'm back," Eve said as she came into the house. She summoned up a smile, but Phyllis could tell that it cost her an effort.

"And we're glad to see you," Carolyn said with a false note of hearty cheer.

Eve stopped short. The smile disappeared from her face.

"You may not be," she said. "You may not want anything more to do with me once you know the truth . . . but it's high time you did."

Chapter 14

"Don't say that," Carolyn said as she put an arm around Eve's shoulders. "There's nothing you could tell us that would make us feel any differently about you, dear."

Eve's smile came back, but it was rueful this time. "Don't be so sure about that," she said.

"Let's go in the living room," Phyllis suggested. "I'll get coffee for everyone."

"Thank you," Eve said. "That sounds wonderful right now."

"I'll give you a hand," Sam told Phyllis. The two of them went into the kitchen while Carolyn led Eve into the living room and Juliette Yorke followed.

Quietly, Sam said, "I've only known Eve for a few years, but I don't reckon I've ever seen her as down as she is now. She's usually a ball of fire."

"I know," Phyllis agreed. "This experience has taken a lot out of her, and I'm afraid it's only going to get worse before it gets better." She paused. "She's going to have to deal with Roy's funeral, you know."

"Bound to be hard. Maybe we can give her a hand with all that."

Phyllis nodded. "That's a good idea. Of course, the sheriff's department probably hasn't released the body yet. They may not have even done . . . the autopsy . . . yet."

But Phyllis was sure an autopsy would be done because it was standard procedure in all suspicious deaths. She just didn't want to think about it.

She poured coffee and placed the cups on a silver tray along with creamer and sweetener. Sam carried the tray into the living room and set it on the coffee table. Carolyn and Eve were sitting on the sofa. Juliette was in one of the armchairs.

When everyone had their coffee, Phyllis and Sam sat down as well, and a few moments of silence went by. It didn't take long for that silence to become uncomfortable, though, and Eve broke it by saying, "Well."

"Well, well," Carolyn said.

"I appreciate the effort, dear," Eve told her, "but you don't have to try to be cheery. There's nothing cheery about any of this. Roy's dead, and the police think I killed him."

"They're insane," Carolyn said. "You'd never hurt anyone."

"That's not what the district attorney believes. According to him, I not only murdered Roy; I also killed two more of my husbands and got away with it scot-free." Eve took a sip of her coffee. "And he doesn't even know yet what happened in Sweetwater."

The implications of that statement left them all silent again. Then Phyllis said, "Why don't you just start at the first, Eve, if there's something you want to tell us?"

Juliette said, "I think that's a good idea. Certainly a better idea than not leveling with your lawyer."

"You two stop fussing at her," Carolyn snapped. "You know the kind of strain she's under—"

"That's right," Eve said, "and part of that strain is keeping everything bottled up inside. It's all right, Carolyn, really. I want to talk about this." She took a deep breath. "You know I'm from West Texas."

Phyllis nodded. "You told me once you were born in Midland."

"That's right. And my first teaching job was in Sweetwater. That's also where I married my first husband, Doyle McGinnis. He was a truck driver." Eve smiled sadly. "We weren't happy. Doyle was gone a lot, and I was lonely. It was . . . difficult. I had opportunities to turn to other men, but I resisted. I'm not sure Doyle was as good at resisting temptation as I was. He was on the road so much . . . But then he was hauling cattle one day and the brakes on his truck went out and he wound up going into an embankment. It was a terrible, terrible accident."

"How awful," Carolyn said.

"As far as the authorities could determine, it was simple mechanical failure due to improper maintainance," Eve went on. "Doyle never did take good care of his things. But I'm sure if Timothy Sullivan wanted to, he could make it sound like I tampered with those brakes because Doyle was cheating on me, even though there was absolutely no proof of that."

"That was just a tragic accident," Phyllis said. "It doesn't have anything to do with what's happened now."

Juliette nodded and said, "I agree, but Eve's right. Sullivan might use it to try to sway a jury . . . if there's something else to go with it."

"Oh, there's more," Eve said. "After that I didn't want to live in Sweetwater anymore, so the next school year I got a job teaching in Abilene. I met a man there. Thom Lewis. Thom with an *h*. He was in real estate, and very successful at it. He'd made a fortune when they built the interstate highway through there. We were married for almost ten years. I kept teaching, even though we didn't need the money, of course, because I loved it, and Thom didn't mind. He was always occupied with his business. But it was a good marriage, much better than the one with Doyle. Until Thom got sick and died after a short illness."

"What was wrong with him?" Juliette asked.

Eve shook her head. "The doctors were never able to make a final determination."

"And since you inherited his money, the police questioned you, thinking that you might have poisoned him," Juliette said.

"That's exactly what they thought, my dear," Eve agreed. "But they could never prove anything, because there was nothing to prove. I loved Thom. I wouldn't have hurt him."

"Of course not," Carolyn said.

"And they never determined the cause of death?" Juliette asked.

Eve shook her head. "Eventually they ruled it natural causes because there was nothing to indicate otherwise. But medical science wasn't as advanced in those days. I know they thought I'd given him some sort of exotic poison."

"Ludicrous," Carolyn muttered.

"So you *did* inherit your husband's money?" Juliette asked. "I just want to be sure."

"Yes, I did. It was . . . several million dollars."

Phyllis and Carolyn stared at her in disbelief, while Sam said, "And a million bucks was real money back in those days."

Eve smiled and said, "Yes, it was, dear. It certainly was."

"I never had any idea," Phyllis said. "You kept teaching . . ."

"What else was I going to do? That was what I was trained for, and I liked it. I liked the kids and wanted to make a difference in their lives. Oh, it didn't happen often, of course, you know that, a lot of them are just putting in the time, but every now and then . . . every now and then you really reach one of them . . ." Eve took a deep breath. "Anyway, I moved to Wichita Falls and got a job there and told myself that I was never going to marry again. That resolve lasted a few years, but then it wore off."

"You started dating again," Carolyn said.

"Oh, I never stopped dating, once a suitable amount of time had passed after Thom's death. I've never been a woman who can function without masculine attention. But I never took it seriously. After what happened with Doyle and Thom, I didn't want another husband. Then I met Alex."

"Your third husband," Phyllis guessed.

Eve winced slightly. "Fourth, actually. I was married once between Thom and Alex, but it lasted less than a year and we parted on friendly terms." She lifted a finger. "He didn't die. In fact, he's still alive, as far as I know. It's just that, well, he was gay. But he didn't want to be, and he figured that if *anyone* could possibly cause him to . . . steer in the other direction, shall we say . . . it would be me. Times were different then, you know."

"Did you know about this?" Carolyn asked in a slightly strangled voice.

"Not at first. But it didn't take long to figure out." Eve sighed. "The poor dear. I did my best, but it just didn't take. So we went our separate ways with no hard feelings."

Juliette took off her glasses, rubbed her temples, and put the glasses back on. "What about Wichita Falls?" she said. "You were telling us about Alex."

"Oh, yes, Alex Martinez. God, what a gorgeous man! He looked just like Ricardo Montalban. And he even sounded like him. Rich Corinthian leather, oh, my word!"

Juliette frowned in confusion. "What?"

"Before your time," Phyllis told her. "Go on, Eve."

"Alex was in the oil business. Quite the globe-trotter. He was always jetting off to South America or the Middle East to set up some multimillion-dollar deal. He simply swept me off my feet with the same sort of panache. We were married for five years. Five very happy years."

"Until he died suddenly," Juliette said.

Eve sighed and nodded. "Yes, that's right. And I suppose the police looked into my background and found out what happened with Thom, and since the doctors had a hard time determining what killed Alex, I was brought in for questioning."

"I reckon this fella Alex was rich, too?" Sam said.

"Oh, my, yes. But he didn't leave his entire estate to me. Some went to his other relatives, and he made a number of endowments to various charities. I only inherited about five million dollars."

"Good Lord!" Carolyn burst out. "We've been living with Miss Moneybags and didn't know it!"

"Oh, dear," Eve said, looking hurt.

"I'm sorry, Eve," Carolyn said quickly. "I didn't mean that. Well, not the way it sounded, anyway. But you're rich! Why did you move in here and live such a simple life? You could've bought a mansion!"

"But I didn't want a mansion," Eve said. "I wanted a simple life, like you said. I wanted friends. And before that, I wanted to teach. You see, I already thought I had everything I needed. All that money in the bank, well . . . that was just money in the bank. It didn't really *mean* anything to me, not like all of you do."

Phyllis was so touched that she felt tears forming in her eyes. But she swallowed hard and brought her emotions under control, saying, "What happened about Alex's death?"

"Nothing, really," Eve said. "I was under suspicion for a while, but there was no evidence against me, again, because I hadn't done anything. Finally the doctors said they thought he had contracted some sort of bizarre virus during a recent trip to the jungles of South America. That's what I think happened, too."

Juliette said, "So you lost two rich husbands to mysterious illnesses. I can see why Sullivan jumped to conclusions . . . or at least why he would want a jury to jump to that conclusion."

"But none of those deaths were Eve's fault," Carolyn said. "It's not fair that she should be blamed for them."

"Contrary to what some people believe, the legal system isn't about fairness," Juliette said. "It's about what you can prove. Or rather, it's about what you can get a jury to believe you've proved, whether you really have or not."

"This is going to make the case against Eve stronger, isn't it?" Phyllis asked.

"I'm afraid so. But we've got time to work on our defense. For everything that Sullivan digs up to make Eve look bad, we'll find something to counter it."

"For one thing," Carolyn said, "even if she had been knocking off her husbands for their money, that doesn't apply here. Roy wasn't rich!"

"I'm right here, dear," Eve said.

Carolyn put a hand on her arm. "Oh, I didn't mean to imply that you did! I was just saying—"

"Carolyn's got a point," Phyllis broke in. "Eve has absolutely no motive. Which brings us to the most important question of all."

"Who *did* have a reason to want him dead?" Eve said. "I wish I could tell you, dear, I really do. But I have no idea."

Chapter 15

*E*ve was exhausted, naturally enough. She hadn't gotten much sleep in jail the night before, she said, and she wanted to go upstairs and lie down for a while, even though it wasn't noon yet.

"You can't imagine how good it will feel to stretch out in my own bed again," she said.

"Is there anything else you haven't told me about your past?" Juliette asked.

"Well, I'm sure there's a great many things, dear, but they don't have any bearing on this case."

"Nothing else that Sullivan can use against you?"

"I can't think of what it might be," Eve said.

Juliette nodded. "All right, then. Get some rest. As soon as I find out when the arraignment will be, I'll let you know. It's just a formality where the charge against you will be entered officially into the court records."

"All right." Eve clasped both of Juliette's hands. "Thank you so much for everything you've done."

"I'm not finished yet," Juliette said. "We're just getting started."

Eve smiled and went to the stairs. She looked back at Phyllis, Sam, and Carolyn and said, "Thank you all. I'd never make it through this without . . . without my friends."

"We'll be here for you," Sam said with an emphatic nod.

"You can count on that," Phyllis added.

Once Eve had gone upstairs and Phyllis heard the door to her room close, she turned to Juliette and asked, "How do things really look? The district attorney's going to use Eve's past against her and try to make the jury think she got away with murder before, isn't he?"

"I'm sure he will," Juliette said. "I'll do my best to keep him from bringing it in at the trial. It's really immaterial and irrelevant to this case, and once I get the witness list and know for sure that's what he's planning, I'll go to the judge and try to get him to rule against that testimony before the jury ever hears it. Sullivan's pretty slick, though. He's good at getting what he wants."

"You're assuming that there's going to be a trial," Carolyn said.

"Oh, there'll be a trial," Juliette said. "The murder weapon and Eve's lack of an alibi is more than enough to get an indictment, I think. I can't imagine the grand jury deciding otherwise."

"But she doesn't have any motive," Phyllis objected. "Like Carolyn said, Roy wasn't rich. At least, not that I know of."

"And evidently Eve *is* rich," Carolyn said. "Why would she need to keep on bumping off husbands for the inheritance?"

Juliette said, "I'll look into Roy's finances—that's for sure.

If we can demonstrate that Eve didn't have any hope of financial gain, and if we can prove that there's no evidence of any trouble between them, that's a start on reasonable doubt, anyway."

"We can all testify that they were very much in love," Carolyn said. "We'll make that jury believe us."

Juliette smiled. "Like I said, that's a good start." She nodded to them. "I'll be in touch."

"I can't believe all this," Carolyn said when Juliette was gone. "It's like the whole world has been turned upside down. Eve's no murderer."

"Of course not," Phyllis said. She started gathering up the empty coffee cups to take them into the kitchen.

"I'll give you a hand," Sam offered.

When they had all the cups in the kitchen and Phyllis was rinsing them in the sink before putting them in the dishwasher, Sam went on, "I've been thinkin' about that letter opener."

"So have I," Phyllis said. "I assume it was used to stab Roy, and despite the fact that it belonged to Eve, I think the fact that the killer used it argues for her innocence. It doesn't fit the pattern. In those other cases, she was accused of poisoning her husbands."

"Which she didn't do," Sam pointed out. "So that means there isn't really a pattern."

"You're right, of course. But if Sullivan does take that tack, I think Juliette can turn it against him. What were you thinking, Sam?"

"Well, once you mentioned it, I sort of remember seein' that letter opener around here, too. I may have even borrowed it from Eve a time or two myself. It's not very sharp. Seems to me it'd take more strength than a lady like Eve has to stick it in a fella's chest. *If* that's what happened."

"So it would be more likely a man who did the killing," Phyllis said as she frowned in thought. "That's good, Sam. We'll have to mention that to Juliette."

"She may have thought about it already. She seems to be pretty smart. I hope so, anyway."

"So do I," Phyllis murmured. "So do I."

Mike came to the house that afternoon with news from the sheriff's department.

"Roy's body has been released so that funeral arrangements can be made," he told Phyllis. Eve hadn't eaten any lunch, claiming that she wasn't hungry, and was still upstairs. "Whatever funeral home Eve wants to use can pick it up anytime."

"Thank you, Mike. I'll talk to her about it."

Mike nodded and started to leave, then hesitated. "How's she doing?" he asked.

"Not very well, I'm afraid. She's trying to put up a good front, but I know she's had just about all she can take."

"I'm sorry. I heard about that stunt the DA pulled at the bail hearing this morning." Mike shook his head. "I hate that she's having to go through this. When Eve got back here, did she say anything about those allegations Sullivan made?"

Phyllis opened her mouth to reply, but she stopped herself before she said anything. Mike worked for the sheriff's department, she reminded herself, and it was the sheriff's department that was handling the investigation into Roy's death. They were a vital link in the chain of the prosecution.

"Not much," Phyllis said in response to Mike's question. "I suppose that since Roy's body has been released, they've finished the autopsy and determined the time and cause of death."

"Yeah, I guess," Mike said, and the awkwardness he felt was obvious. In the past, he and Phyllis had always talked freely, sharing information about cases, but it appeared that circumstances—and a touchy district attorney—had placed them on opposite sides this time. Phyllis didn't care for that feeling at all.

Mike went on, "I guess I, uh, better be going. See you later."

"Of course. Give Bobby a big hug and kiss for me."

He smiled and lifted a hand in farewell as he said, "Will do."

Once he was gone, Phyllis sighed. She would be glad when this terrible affair was over, so things could go back to the way they had been before.

Right now she faced another unpleasant task: talking to Eve about Roy's funeral.

She went to Carolyn's room first. She wasn't going to do this by herself.

"Mike was just here and said that the sheriff's department has released Roy's body," Phyllis told Carolyn. "We need to find out what Eve wants to do."

"Oh, Lord," Carolyn muttered. "I'm not looking forward to this. But I suppose it has to be done."

When Phyllis knocked on Eve's door a moment later, Eve

said, "Come in." When they entered the room, they saw her sitting in a rocking chair, facing the window.

"Eve, there's some news," Phyllis said. "We can make arrangements for Roy's funeral now."

"Will you be taking him back to Houston?" Carolyn asked. She looked over at Phyllis and whispered, "Can she do that while she's out on bail?"

The rocker creaked a little as Eve sat forward and stood up. Moving slowly, as if weighed down by infinite weariness, she turned and said, "It doesn't really matter, Carolyn, because I'm not taking him back to Houston. He'll be buried here in Weatherford. We talked about that. Not in any specific terms, you know, just in general, because at our age it's smart to do so. His first wife is buried there, with her family, but they didn't have any children, and since Roy doesn't have any close relatives, he said that when his time came he'd rather be up here with . . . with me." Eve took a deep breath as she struggled to bring her emotions under control. "We just never dreamed that his time would come . . . so soon."

Tears started to roll down her cheeks again.

Phyllis and Carolyn hurried over to her and embraced her. As she lightly patted Eve's back, Carolyn said, "If that stupid district attorney could see you now, he'd know that you would never hurt Roy!"

After a few minutes, Eve was able to stop crying. Phyllis turned the rocking chair away from the window and helped her sit down again. Phyllis sat on the bed, and Carolyn took the room's other chair. When Eve said, "I suppose I should call the funeral home . . . ," Phyllis told her, "I can take care of that for you. Do you have a . . . a plot picked out?"

Eve smiled faintly. "As a matter of fact, I do. Right next to mine. I bought two, you see, because I always knew there was a good chance I'd be married again. I always considered myself . . . between marriages."

"I know," Phyllis said with a solemn smile of her own. "I think we all knew you'd find yourself another man."

"That does seem to be one of the things I'm good at." Eve grew more serious. "But never again. I can see now, after everything that's happened to all of them, that it's just not meant to be."

"Oh, goodness, I wouldn't go that far," Carolyn said.

"Why not, dear? You barely believe in the concept of marriage anymore."

"Well . . . maybe not. Not for me, anyway. But that doesn't mean you have to feel the same way."

Eve shook her head. "No, it's time to recognize the obvious. Being divorced once and widowed four times is enough for anybody!"

Phyllis couldn't argue with that. Losing Kenny had been devastating enough that she didn't want to ever go through something like that again. When he passed away, she had sworn to herself that she would never remarry. It had taken years—and knowing Sam Fletcher—for her to get to the point where she might even start to reconsider that vow, and even now she seriously doubted that it would ever come about.

She leaned over and patted Eve on the arm. "You don't need to concern yourself with that right now. I'll go call the funeral home. Do you want the service at the church or at their chapel?"

"The chapel, I think. There probably won't be very many people there."

"That's fine. I'm sure you'll have to go down there and talk to them, probably tomorrow, but we'll deal with that when the time comes."

Eve nodded. "Yes. I'll be stronger by then."

Phyllis hoped that was true. The next few days were going to be awfully hard on Eve. There was no way of getting around that. But she and Carolyn and Sam would be there to help her in any way they could. They would all just have to get through it somehow.

And then, once Roy Porter had been laid to rest, they could start trying to figure out who had killed him.

Because no matter what District Attorney Sullivan or Sheriff Haney or her own son thought, Phyllis told herself, there was no way she was going to let Eve be convicted for a murder she didn't commit. If she had anything to say about it, there wouldn't even be a trial, because by then the real killer would be behind bars.

Chapter 16

*S*he had been to too many funerals in her life, Phyllis thought two days later as she sat in the cemetery, trying not to shiver as a chilly wind blew across the rolling green hills around them.

She wondered, if she tried, could she count them all up, going as far back over the years as she remembered? Or were there too many for that?

It hadn't been long, only a few weeks, since she'd attended another graveside service in this very cemetery. The person who'd been murdered on her own front porch had been laid to rest that day, which had also been cold and windy. Phyllis looked across the cemetery, but although she could pin down the area, she couldn't see the actual grave.

Not that it really mattered. Life had moved on without the person who was resting there, just as it would one day move on without her. Funerals, graveside services, memorials . . . it was often said that these things actually were for the living, not the dead, and that was true.

They were meant to remind everyone who attended them that someday the end would come for them, too.

Phyllis closed her eyes and tried to banish those grim thoughts. The minister was droning on, the wind was cold, and even the day was gloomy, with thick clouds clogging the sky and the potential for snow in the forecast for that night. Suitable weather for what had brought them here. Phyllis was ready for it to be over.

Eve sat beside her, with Carolyn on Eve's other side. As Eve began sobbing quietly, Phyllis and Carolyn took hold of her hands and squeezed to give her strength. They all wore gloves and hats and sober dark suits. Sam stood to the side with the other pallbearers, the wind ruffling his thick salt-and-pepper hair and plucking at his tie.

Mike and Sarah sat in the second row of folding chairs under the canopy that had been set up over the grave and the casket. They had left Bobby with a sitter this afternoon. Mike wasn't in uniform, thank goodness. He was off duty today. In fact, no one from the sheriff's department was here officially, although a Weatherford police car had led the procession from the funeral home to the cemetery. The officer hadn't stayed for the service, though.

Juliette Yorke was here, too, also in the second row, next to Sarah. And Dolly Williamson and a number of other retired teachers and administrators had shown up for the funeral and also come out here to the cemetery. There were more mourners than Eve had expected. She was well liked, even loved, in the educational community. In fact, many of the same people who had been at the bridal shower on Christmas Eve and the wedding on New Year's Eve had come today to bid farewell to

Roy, even though they hadn't known him well. They knew Eve, and that was enough, Phyllis had thought as she looked at all the solemn, familiar faces.

She had spotted Loretta Harbor and Velma Nickson and remembered the spat the two women had had at the bridal shower. That seemed so far in the past now, and so unimportant, too. Phyllis hoped their feud wouldn't lead them to say or do anything to disrupt the service. It didn't seem likely, since they were sitting as far away from each other as possible.

There were other familiar faces besides the retired teachers. Jan and Pete Delaney were there, looking solemn. They had to be upset about the fact that a murder had been committed in their bed-and-breakfast, and Jan had been the one who had found Roy's body, Phyllis recalled. That must have been a terrible thing for her. She wouldn't have blamed them if they had stayed away, but like everyone else, they were here for Eve.

Finally, the minister seemed to be wrapping up his remarks. When he said, "Let us pray," Phyllis bowed her head not only in reverence but also in relief.

After the prayer, Sam and the other pallbearers, all of them retired teachers Phyllis had recruited, took off the carnations that had been pinned to their lapels by the funeral director and placed them on the casket with the other flowers. Then they moved along the front row of chairs to shake hands with Eve and offer their condolences. The rest of the mourners followed suit. Jan Delaney bent down to hug Eve, as did several of the other women.

Now that the service was over, most of the people headed for their cars, obviously eager to get out of the cold wind, and who could blame them, Phyllis thought. Others remained behind briefly to talk to old friends. The Delaneys were among them, and when Jan caught Phyllis's eye, she knew that the woman wanted to talk to her.

"I'll be right back," she told Eve, who only sighed and nodded. Phyllis stood up and walked back among the other grave markers to join the Delaneys.

"We're so sorry about all this," Jan began. "And I really hate to bother you with it, but we need to know what to do about the things that are still at the house. You know, the things that belong to Eve and . . . well, that belonged to her and Roy."

Phyllis nodded and said, "That's all right. I understand. I assume the police have already conducted all their searches and the room isn't taped off as a crime scene anymore?"

"That's right," Jan said, which confirmed Phyllis's guess that Roy's body had been found in the room he'd shared with Eve at the bed-and-breakfast. Until now she hadn't known that for certain.

"Did the investigators take some of their belongings?"

Jan started to answer, but before she could, Pete said, "The officers told you not to talk about that or anything else about the case, Jan, remember?"

"Oh, yes, of course. I'm sorry, Mrs. Newsom."

"Oh, no, I didn't mean to pry," Phyllis said quickly.

Which wasn't exactly the truth. She *had* meant to pry. She was a prying, meddling, self-righteous old snoop. More than likely that was what some people thought of her, anyway. She didn't care. All that mattered to her was finding out the truth, clearing Eve's name, and bringing Roy's killer to justice.

"I guess I can't talk about anything the investigators did," Jan went on, "but I can tell you that quite a few things are still at the house. I'd be glad to box them up so that someone can get them and take them back to your place. Eve's going to be staying there, isn't she?"

Phyllis nodded and said, "Yes." She started to add, *for the time being,* but then she realized that sounded like she expected Eve to be going somewhere else—prison, maybe—and she wasn't going to entertain that notion even for a second.

She went on, "Sam and I can come out and pick them up in a few days, whenever you're ready. Will that be all right?"

"That'll be fine," Jan said with a smile. "Thank you for being so understanding about this."

"Well, you don't need the room just sitting there empty when you can rent it again."

Pete said, "Yeah, we'll be lucky if we're able to do that. I don't know if anybody will ever want to stay in a room where a murder took place, but I worked hard getting the blood-stain out of the rug . . . Blast it, now I'm saying things I shouldn't."

"It's all right," Phyllis told him. "I know how hard it is not to talk about something when it's all you can think about."

"Yeah, you've been mixed up in cases like this before, haven't you? I remember reading about you in the newspaper."

Phyllis shrugged and didn't say anything.

Jan clasped her hands and said, "I'll give you a call."

"That'll be fine," Phyllis said. She waved good-bye as the Delaneys headed for their car.

Turning, Phyllis went back to the canopy. Eve was on her feet now, standing with Carolyn and Sam, talking with Dolly

Williamson. The former superintendent was still a formidable figure despite her age. Phyllis didn't know exactly how old Dolly was, but she had to be in her eighties.

Dolly hugged Eve and said in her booming voice, "Anything you need, you just let me know, you hear?"

"Of course, Dolly," Eve said.

Dolly hugged the other three of them in turn before going to her car. Carolyn shook her head as she watched her go.

"I miss the days when if you had a problem, you could tell Dolly about it and she would make it go away."

"I'm not sure if it was ever really like that, or if she just made it seem that way," Phyllis said.

"Either way, life seemed a lot simpler then. I thought once you retired, everything was supposed to be simpler. That's what I planned on."

"Well, you know the old sayin'," Sam said. "Life is what happens when you're makin' other plans."

Phyllis glanced at the flower-bedecked casket sitting on the mechanism that the funeral directors would use to lower it into the grave vault once everyone was gone. It was vivid evidence of the futility of making too many plans.

She linked her arm with Eve's and said, "Let's go home."

"That's a good idea," Carolyn said. "People have brought so much food, we're going to be doing nothing but eating for a week just to keep up with it."

Eve shook her head. "I don't think I can eat."

"Now, don't start that," Carolyn said as the four of them walked toward Phyllis's Lincoln. "The past few days you haven't eaten enough to keep a bird alive, and it's time you got your appetite back."

"Life goes on, you mean?" Eve said. "I appreciate the sentiment, dear, but—"

"But, nothing," Carolyn said, her voice even blunter than usual. "Nobody's saying that you have to stop mourning Roy. You'll do that when the time is right, and not before. But you do have to keep living, and part of that is eating. You know good and well that's what Roy would want you to do. He always had a healthy appetite, didn't he?"

"Oh, yes. He loved to eat." Eve smiled. "He would have loved all the potato salad and the casseroles and the pies . . ."

"You see what I mean? He would expect you to eat and enjoy all that good food."

"You know, I think you're right," Eve said. "Thank you, Carolyn. Maybe I can eat a little when we get back to the house."

That reaction was encouraging, Phyllis thought. Sometimes, what a person needed more than anything else was some straight talk. And nobody could be counted on for straighter talk than Carolyn Wilbarger.

Almost everyone had left now. The hearse and the funeral director's car were still here, of course, and in the distance there was a pickup that probably belonged to the man who would use a tractor to cover the grave later on, but Phyllis didn't want to think about that.

There was also one car parked not too far from her Lincoln, but Phyllis didn't recognize it or the woman who was sitting in it. When the woman saw them coming, she got out of the car.

She wore a long dark brown coat, the tails of which swayed a little in the wind. Even though the coat mostly concealed her shape, Phyllis could tell that she was tall and slender. Sunglasses covered her eyes despite the overcast sky. She had blond hair that fell in wings around her face.

For a second Phyllis thought that this was one of the teachers she didn't know, one of Eve's coworkers from her last years at the high school. But then Phyllis realized she had never seen this woman before. Clearly, though, the woman wanted to speak to them.

"Mrs. Porter?" she said as she stepped away from her car.

Eve and the others all stopped. "Yes?" Eve said. "Do I know you, dear?"

The woman took her sunglasses off, revealing blue eyes. She smiled, which relieved the rather stern lines of her face. "No, we've never met," she said.

"Did . . . did you know my late husband?"

"I'm afraid I never met Roy Porter, either, although I wouldn't have known him under that name. But I've been looking for him for quite a while."

Eve shook her head in confusion and said, "I'm afraid I don't know what you're talking about. Why were you looking for Roy, and what do you mean about his name?"

Phyllis was confused, too, and a bad feeling had cropped up suddenly inside of her. She had a hunch that Eve wasn't going to like whatever this woman was about to say.

"My name is Tess Coburn, Mrs. Porter, and I'm a private investigator. I've been looking for your husband because he was a con artist and a thief."

Chapter 17

In the shocked silence that followed Tess Coburn's statement, Sam was the first one to react. He moved quickly, putting himself between his three friends and the stranger and saying, "I think you'd better get on outta here now, miss."

Carolyn spoke up next, bristling with fury as she said to Tess Coburn, "How dare you—"

The woman ignored both of them and went on, "I'm sorry to have to break it to you like this, but you have a right to know the truth."

Sam crowded closer to her. "Look, lady, I'm tryin' to be a gentleman because that's the way I was raised, but I'm tellin' you, you better leave."

She gave him a cold stare and said, "Back off, Mr. Fletcher. I don't bully easily."

"Everyone settle down," Phyllis said as she took hold of Sam's arm and got a firm grip on it. She glared at Tess and went on, "Have you no sense of decency, Ms. Coburn? We just buried my friend's husband."

Tess stuck her hands in the pockets of her coat and said, "Actually, I do have a sense of decency, Mrs. Newsom. That's why I don't want your friend there to waste one more minute mourning the death of that man when he doesn't deserve it."

"Stop it!" Eve cried in a ragged voice. "Please, stop saying things like that!"

"I don't blame you for not believing me. He was good, very good, at what he did. But just let me show you one thing."

Tess took her hand out of her pocket, and for one crazy second, Phyllis thought she was going to pull a gun. Instead, it was a photograph Tess took from her pocket. A police mug shot, in fact, and when she held it up where they could see it, another shock jolted Phyllis as she recognized Roy. He was considerably younger in the photo, but there was no doubt that it was him. Eve exclaimed in pained recognition.

"His name then was Jack DeWalt," Tess said. "At least that's what he was calling himself. This photo was taken twelve years ago in Sarasota, Florida, when he was arrested for fraud. He had married a woman named Doris Tilley and cleaned out her bank accounts. She realized what he'd done in time to alert the police, and they arrested him at the airport just as he was about to fly out of town. Unfortunately, he was released on bail and promptly disappeared. He changed his identity, and Mrs. Tilley never got her money back. The police were never able to find out where DeWalt stashed it."

Phyllis and the others listened to this recital in stunned disbelief. Tess wasn't finished, though. She took a notebook from her pocket and opened it.

"The next place he cropped up was Louisville, Kentucky, using the name Harry Evans. He got married there, too, to a woman named Patrice Wilson. She owned a very successful horse farm. Evans talked her into giving him power of attorney; then he sold the place out from under her, pocketed the proceeds of the sale, and vanished, leaving her up to her neck in litigation and broke, to boot."

"Wait just a minute," Carolyn broke in. "How do we know this man Evans was the same person?"

Tess took a newspaper clipping from the notebook and held it out. The clipping was from a society section, and the photo in it showed Roy dressed in a tuxedo at some fancy affair. Standing next to him was an attractive older woman in a stunning gown. Both of them held drinks as they smiled at the camera. Phyllis leaned forward to read the caption under the photo, which identified the couple as Harry and Patrice Evans of Oakdale Farms.

"I don't know if it was his next stop after Louisville or not, but the next place I was able to identify him was Tulsa," Tess started to go on, but Eve cried out and stopped her.

"No more," Eve moaned. "Please, no more."

"I hope you're proud of yourself," Carolyn snapped at Tess. "You've destroyed this poor woman."

"Not at all," Tess said briskly as she closed her notebook. "I've saved her from spending the rest of her life mourning that man. And I've probably helped her defense as well. Now her lawyer can point out that she had a good reason to kill him, once she found out that he'd been lying to her and planned to steal all her money and abandon her. She ought to be able to plea-bargain the charge down to manslaughter without much trouble."

Eve burst out in a miserable wail.

"She didn't kill him," Phyllis said, "and I don't care what Roy did in the past; he never hurt her. You're terrible for doing this, Ms. Coburn, just terrible."

Tess shrugged. "Think whatever you want. I can't stop you. But I still think Mrs. Porter has a right to know the truth."

"A right, maybe, but not an obligation."

Even as Phyllis spoke, she wasn't sure she was correct about that. Of course, Eve could have gone the rest of her life without knowing what appeared to be the dreadful truth about the man she had married. She might have been happier that way. But that happiness would have been based on a lie.

And Phyllis had already realized something else. All along they had been asking themselves why anyone would have had a reason to want Roy Porter dead.

If what Tess Coburn had told them was true, then she might have just given them that reason.

"Carolyn, take Eve to the car," Phyllis went on. "I need to talk to Ms. Coburn."

"I want to give her a piece of my mind, too—," Carolyn began.

"Please," Phyllis said, and a steely edge had come into her voice despite its polite tone.

"All right," Carolyn said. "Come on, Eve." She tightened her arm around Eve's shoulders and led her toward Phyllis's Lincoln as Eve continued to sob. Sam stayed behind with Phyllis and Tess Coburn.

"Look, I'm sorry—," Tess said.

"I don't think you really are," Phyllis said. "But I'll grant that you probably believed you were doing the right thing."

She took a deep breath. "I'd like to talk to you some more about Roy's past."

Tess nodded. "We can do that. It would be a good thing if you could help Mrs. Porter to understand that this wasn't her fault. Whatever his real name was, that man had been taking advantage of women like her for years and years. He was very talented at it."

"Is that the only reason you came here today? To tell Eve about him?"

A thin smile appeared on Tess's face. "Not completely. I've been on his trail for a while. I guess I just wanted to see for myself that he was really dead, that it wasn't another of his tricks to get away. Now I know. He won't be swindling any other women."

"No," Phyllis said. "He won't." She paused. "Since you obviously know who we all are, I assume you've been stalking us for a while."

Tess frowned and said, "Hey, hold on there. I haven't stalked anybody. I just got to Weatherford yesterday. It didn't take me long to find out what's been going on, though. All of you turn up in the online newspaper archives. You're sort of like Texas's version of Miss Marple, aren't you, Mrs. Newsom?"

"Not at all," Phyllis said. "Your investigation must have told you where we live."

"Sure," Tess said with a nod.

"Can you come by there in an hour or so? I'd really like to talk to you some more about this."

Tess hesitated as she glanced at the car where Eve and Carolyn sat in the backseat. Eve was resting her head on Carolyn's shoulder, and her back was shaking a little as she continued to cry.

"Look, maybe I got carried away a little—," Tess began.

"Maybe?" Sam said. "You reckon?"

"I'm sorry, okay? It might be better if I just left you folks alone from here on out. The guy's dead, which means that my part of the case is over."

Phyllis shook her head. "I'm sure Eve will go up to her room when we get home. We'll be discreet and try not to let her know that you're even there. But I'd really like to hear whatever you know about Roy."

"I wouldn't mind hearin' about that myself," Sam put in with a shrug.

"So you're a detective, too?" Tess said.

Sam shook his head. "Not me. Phyllis is the one who always figures out everything."

"Well, I don't mind talking to both of you, I suppose. If you're sure it won't upset Mrs. Porter even more."

"It's a little late to be worrying about that," Phyllis said. "But please come by anyway."

"All right," Tess said. "If it's that important to you, I'll be there in an hour or so."

"Thank you."

Tess put her sunglasses back on and got into her car. As she drove away, Sam said, "That gal's got a lot of nerve, showin' up at the cemetery this way and sayin' all those rotten things to Eve."

"You saw the pictures she had," Phyllis said. "From the looks of them, she wasn't lying about Roy."

"Maybe not, but her timing still stinks. She was at the funeral home, wasn't she?"

Phyllis nodded. "Yes, I remember seeing her there. I just thought she was one of the women who taught at the high school the last year or two that Eve was there. I don't know most of them."

"Me, neither. But I figure I know why you want to talk to her . . . You're thinkin' that if Roy really was a con man like she claimed, that's a good reason for somebody from his past wantin' him dead."

"You know what Juliette said about trying to establish reasonable doubt."

"Yeah, and Roy havin' a bunch of enemies is one way to get it." Sam nodded. "I guess it's a good idea findin' out all we can . . . but that doesn't mean we have to like that Coburn woman."

"No," Phyllis said, "it doesn't mean that at all."

Chapter 18

It was a painful ride home with Eve sobbing in the backseat and Carolyn trying to comfort her. Clearly, today's events had pushed Eve to the end of her emotional rope. She had collapsed now in the grief that overwhelmed her, grief not only because of Roy's death but also over the way Tess Coburn had destroyed everything she'd believed about him.

If she ever found herself in such a situation, Phyllis thought, she would be just as distraught as Eve was. She wanted so badly to do something to help her friend.

But no matter what she wanted, she couldn't change the past. Roy was what he was, and based on what Phyllis had seen so far, that wasn't very good. But at least maybe she could prove that Eve hadn't had anything to do with his murder.

When they got back to the house, Carolyn took Eve upstairs. Phyllis and Sam followed. Phyllis was anxious to get out of her funeral dress, and Sam had already taken off his tie and unbuttoned his shirt collar. Blue jeans and comfortable shirts were in the near future for both of them.

When Phyllis got back downstairs, she took some of the food that had been dropped off from the refrigerator and set it out on the counter, uncovering the bowls and casserole dishes. Sam came into the kitchen, and Phyllis nodded toward the spread and said, "Help yourself."

"I don't have as much of an appetite as I did, but I guess I can still eat," he said as he got a plate from the cabinet. He started filling it.

Carolyn came in a few minutes later, still wearing the dress she had worn to the funeral. "I got her to lie down," she said. "She dozed off quicker than I thought she would. The poor dear is just exhausted."

"Bein' so upset will do that to you," Sam said from the kitchen table, where he and Phyllis were sitting.

"Would you like a plate?" Phyllis asked.

"Maybe in a few minutes," Carolyn said. "As soon as I go get this blasted girdle off." She blushed, clearly embarrassed that she'd been so upset she had said something that intimate in front of Sam. Phyllis could tell that he was pretending not to have noticed any of it.

The food helped. Later, they would try to get Eve to eat something, Phyllis thought. Right now, though, a nap would probably be as good for her as anything.

After Carolyn had come back downstairs, Phyllis told her, "Tess Coburn is coming by here in a little while."

"That horrible woman? Why? Hasn't she done enough damage already?"

"I want her to tell me everything she knows about Roy," Phyllis said.

Carolyn shook her head. "I'm not sure why. It'll all be a pack of lies anyway."

"You saw that mug shot and that newspaper clipping," Phyllis pointed out.

"So she found someone who looks a little like Roy—"

"That *was* Roy. As much as we might like to believe otherwise, we saw the pictures with our own eyes. That was Roy, Carolyn."

For a moment, Carolyn glared across the table defiantly, as if she planned to keep denying what they all knew. But then she sighed and her shoulders slumped in resignation.

"I guess it was," she said. She brightened suddenly. "Unless he has a twin somewhere. An evil twin."

"A doppelganger," Sam said. "We didn't consider that."

"No, because this isn't a soap opera," Phyllis said.

"Hey, some of 'em aren't *that* far-fetched."

"It was Roy," Phyllis forged ahead, "and I want to know as much about his past as I can. That has to be where the key to his murder is."

"You're right about that," Carolyn said. "Since he's been here in Weatherford, nothing has happened that would cause someone to want him dead."

Phyllis tended to agree with that, yet she didn't know it for sure, she reminded herself. Roy had spent most of his time with Eve since coming to Weatherford, and Eve hadn't mentioned any incidents that might have led to murder. But they hadn't been together twenty-four hours a day, and Phyllis had no idea what Roy might have been doing when he wasn't with Eve. That might be something else to look into.

First things first, though, and that meant the private investigator Tess Coburn. Would Tess be willing to reveal who had hired her to track down Roy, or would that be considered a breach of ethics? Phyllis didn't know, not having had many dealings with private investigators.

Sam stood up and said, "I'm gonna go wait for Ms. Coburn in the livin' room. I can keep an eye out through the front window. We don't want her ringin' the bell. That might wake up Eve."

"Yes, whatever we do, we don't want Eve to know that woman has been here," Carolyn said. Her expression made it clear that she still thought inviting Tess to the house was a bad idea.

After Sam had left the kitchen, Carolyn picked up her plate, which was still half-full of food, and said, "I think I'll go upstairs to finish this, if that's all right with you."

"Of course it is," Phyllis said. She understood why Carolyn was angry. But she was confident that once Carolyn thought it over, she would realize how important it was to learn as much as they could about Roy's background.

Phyllis put the rest of the food away. The refrigerator was full. They would be able to make meals from what was left for several more days. She wasn't sure how it was in other parts of the country, but in Texas, food went hand in hand with funerals, especially where Baptists were concerned.

Because hunger reminded people they were still alive, she mused, and so did satisfying that hunger.

She had just closed the refrigerator door when Sam called quietly from the hallway, "She's here."

Phyllis hurried into the hall and said, "Can you get the door?"

"You bet," Sam said. He went to it and opened it before Tess could ring the bell.

"Thank you," she said as she came in.

"I'll take your coat," he offered.

She nodded, said, "Thanks," again, and took off the long brown coat, revealing that she wore brown slacks and a tan blouse underneath it. She handed the coat to Sam.

"Eve's upstairs asleep, so we won't disturb her. You can put your purse on that table," Phyllis said, nodding toward the small table in the foyer.

"Thanks, I'll keep it with me," Tess said.

"Fine," Phyllis said. She wondered if Tess had a gun in her bag. She was a private eye, after all. "Can I get you something to drink? Coffee, iced tea?"

Whether she liked Tess Coburn or not, she wasn't going to be inhospitable.

"We've got soft drinks, too," Sam added.

"A Diet Coke would be good, thanks," Tess said.

"Be right back with it," Sam said.

"Have you eaten lunch already?" Phyllis asked. "We have plenty of food. People have been dropping off covered dishes ever since . . . well . . ."

Tess smiled and nodded. "I know what you mean. And yes, I've eaten, but thanks anyway. What I'd really like to do is get down to business. You want to know about the man you knew as Roy Porter."

"Can't we go ahead and call him by that name?" Phyllis asked as she ushered Tess into the living room. "That's the only name we ever knew him by."

"Sure, I don't see why not. It'll certainly simplify matters, since he's had at least a dozen names over the years. And those are just the ones I know about. There's no telling how many more aliases he used."

Sam came in with a can of Diet Coke. "You want a glass and some ice . . . ?"

"No, that's fine," Tess said as she took it from him.

Phyllis waved to the armchair directly across from the sofa and said, "Have a seat." She and Sam settled on the sofa facing the visitor.

Tess took a sip from the can and then set it on a coaster on the small table next to her chair. "So, Roy Porter," she said. "If you don't mind me asking a question first, what did he tell you about his background?"

"Well, he said he was from Houston," Phyllis replied, "and that he was semiretired from a company that does consulting work for the oil and gas industry. He claimed he was able to handle all his jobs on the computer, so it didn't matter where he lived."

"He said he was a widower, too," Sam added. "He was married to a woman named Julie who sold real estate down there. But she died a while back."

Tess nodded. "If you were to look up any of that online, I'd be willing to bet that the company he mentioned really does exist. Also, I know that there was a real estate agent in Houston named Julie Porter who was married to a man named Roy until she died. But Roy's dead, too, and I'm not talking about the one who was buried today. The real one died sixteen months ago, which probably wasn't very long before your friend Eve met the fake Roy online. That *is* the way they met, isn't it?"

Phyllis nodded. "On the Facebook," she said, quoting what Eve had told them.

"The Internet has certainly made life easier for the con men and swindlers, and I'm not just talking about the Nigerian princes," Tess said. "Before that, men like Roy had to find their victims through correspondence or actually go out and meet them through singles' clubs and things like that."

"Roy was good on the computer," Sam said. "A real whiz compared to fellas like me."

"I don't doubt it. He would have had to be good to create all the false identities he did. It never seemed to take him long to find a dead man who would have been about the same age and general description that he was. My theory is that he was able to hack into various databases and create new Social Security cards, driver's licenses, and things like that to match whatever new identity he was adopting. I'll give him credit: You don't find too many people his age—no offense—who are so proficient with computers."

"Yeah, he had good Google-fu," Sam agreed. "How did you get onto him?"

Tess smiled. "I have pretty good Google-fu myself. I wrote a program to cross-reference the Social Security death index with new applications for those documents I was talking about. Most of the hits were simple, innocent cases of similar or even identical names, but there were enough matching parameters in some of them to prompt a deeper search. I put together a list of possibles and then did on-site investigations. That allowed me to come up with a fairly complete history of Roy Porter, as we're calling him."

Phyllis frowned and said, "I thought private detectives shadowed people."

"That's what I was doing," Tess said, "only I was doing it with technology. By the time I had boots on the ground anywhere, Roy was already long gone, of course, but I was able to talk to some of the people who had crossed paths with him, usually to their great regret. He left a trail of broken hearts and empty bank accounts behind him."

Phyllis leaned back against the sofa cushions and shook her head. It was so hard to believe that the Roy they had known was this manipulative criminal genius Tess was describing. And yet, to do the things she claimed he had done, he would have had to be a master of getting people to like him and trust him.

"You have actual evidence of all these previous identities you say he had?"

Tess nodded. "Photos, copies of marriage licenses and bank records, newspaper clippings like the one I showed you . . . Most of the women were fairly involved with the society scene where they lived, since they were all well-to-do. I can document seventeen different cases of fraud and embezzlement over the past twenty years, stretching from Florida to Maine to Colorado."

"You happen to know what the fella's real name was?" Sam asked.

Tess shook her head. "I was never able to uncover that. He seems to have surfaced for the first time in Virginia. But he was in his forties at the time, so either he had a long career as a swindler before that and managed to cover his tracks completely, or else he took up the game rather late in life. Now that he's dead, I don't suppose we'll ever know the answer."

"That's a shame. I'd like to know what would prompt a fella to do things like that."

"So would I, Mr. Fletcher." Tess shrugged. "But in my

business, sometimes you have to settle for knowing what happened and try not to worry about the why."

"Speaking of your business," Phyllis said, "could you tell us who hired you? I'm assuming it was one of the women who Roy bilked out of their money. Not all their money, of course, or else they wouldn't have been able to hire someone as competent as you seem to be."

Tess smiled and said, "Thanks. That's a good deduction on your part, Mrs. Newsom. Unfortunately, the identity of my client is confidential, but I can say that in general terms, you're right. As a matter of fact, I've been working for more than one of Roy's victims. As you can imagine, there's a long line of people who'd like to see him brought to justice."

"Who'd like to get even with him, you mean," Sam said.

"You could call it that," Tess admitted. "Now, of course, they're out of luck. Although they may take some satisfaction out of knowing that he's dead."

"I would think some of them might take a great deal of satisfaction out of that," Phyllis said.

Tess took another drink of her Diet Coke and asked, "Is there anything else I can tell you?"

"What are you going to do now?"

"I'll prepare reports for all my clients. In fact, I'll probably send e-mails even to the ones who didn't hire me, just so they'll know what happened. I think they have a right to know, too, don't you?"

"Yes, of course," Phyllis said. "Just like you told Eve she had a right to know."

Tess shifted uncomfortably in her chair and shook her head. She said, "Look, I've been thinking about what happened, and I admit I was a little too zealous. I could have waited for a better time to talk to Mrs. Porter, and I'm sorry about the way things turned out. Please tell her I apologize for the extra pain I caused her."

"I can do that," Phyllis said, nodding and thinking that she liked Tess Coburn a little better now that the woman had exhibited some contrition.

"It's just that I've been on his trail for quite a while," Tess went on, "and I've seen with my own eyes how much pain and trouble he caused for all those women . . . and I guess I was kind of satisfied myself to know that he wouldn't be doing it any more. So I got carried away. Again, I'm sorry."

"Well, it's gracious of you to admit that you were wrong. What are you going to do about the police?"

"About the investigation into his death, you mean?" Tess looked uncomfortable again. "I'll have to turn over the information I have to the sheriff's department. The victim's background is evidence in a murder case. If I didn't give it to them and it came out later, I could be in trouble myself. At the very least I might lose my license."

"I understand, but it's liable to make the authorities even more convinced that Eve's guilty."

Tess nodded and said, "I know. They'll think that she found out somehow what he was planning and killed him to stop it. But like I said before, that makes her actions more reasonable. Look, it would certainly be easy to argue that she confronted him with it, he attacked her, and she was only defending herself when she killed him. She's looking at a possible manslaughter plea, and she might even get off with a claim of self-defense."

Phyllis was about to respond to that when a clear voice rang out from the door into the hall. "The only thing wrong with that idea," Eve said, "is that I didn't kill my husband!"

Chapter 19

*P*hyllis was on her feet instantly, turning toward the door and saying, "Eve, you really shouldn't be down here—"

"So I wouldn't know that you brought this woman into our home?" Eve snapped. "To spread her lies about Roy and about me?"

Eve's eyes were still red rimmed from crying, but no tears welled from them now. Instead, they sparked with anger.

Despite the terrible situation, for the first time in days Eve actually looked a little like herself again, Phyllis thought.

Tess had stood up, too, and now she extended a hand toward Eve. "Mrs. Porter, I'm sorry—"

"Save your breath," Eve snapped. "I don't accept your apology, and I don't accept anything you have to say about Roy. You didn't know him."

"It's true I never met him," Tess said, "but I have proof of everything I've said. Solid proof that would stand up in court. If he were still alive, he'd be behind bars now, because I would have turned over everything to the cops and had him arrested. It was just a matter of locating him." She shrugged. "I was a little late on that score."

"Get out," Eve said in a low, dangerous voice.

Tess looked at Phyllis. "Mrs. Newsom . . . ?"

"I think it would be best if you left," Phyllis said. She believed what Tess had said about Roy. It was hard to argue with the proof she had assembled. But right now the important thing was to get her out of here and get Eve calmed down, Phyllis thought.

Tess shrugged and said, "Sure. I really am sorry if I've made things worse for you folks."

Phyllis went to Eve's side, took hold of her arm, and gently urged her toward the kitchen as Eve continued to glare at Tess. "Sam, if you could get Ms. Coburn's coat . . ."

"Sure," Sam said. Phyllis maneuvered Eve into the kitchen so she couldn't see what was going on anymore, but she heard Sam open the hall closet. He and Tess spoke briefly in low voices; then the front door opened and closed. Sam came down the hall to the kitchen and said, "She's gone."

Eve sank into one of the chairs at the table. The momentary strength that anger had given her appeared to be fading fast. "Why did you let her come here, Phyllis?" she asked.

"I'm the one who asked her to come," Phyllis replied. "It wasn't her idea."

Eve stared up at her. "Why would you do that?"

"Because I wanted to know as much as I could about Roy. You're still in trouble with the law, Eve, and as much as we might hate to think about it, the only sure way to clear your name is to figure out who really did kill Roy."

"But the things that woman said . . . they were all lies . . ."

Phyllis shook her head. "I don't think so. She has a lot of evidence—"

"Did you see it? Did she show you anything?"

"Well . . . not really. Just that mug shot and the newspaper clipping she had at the cemetery. But I don't think she'd lie about the other things if she couldn't produce them."

"You don't know that!" Eve insisted. "It could have been faked, all of it."

"Eve's got a point," Sam said. "With all the things folks can do with computers these days, it probably wouldn't be too hard to come up with a mug shot and a newspaper clippin' that looked real."

Phyllis hadn't considered that, but as she thought about the possibility, she knew Eve and Sam were right. Tess Coburn *could* have fabricated the evidence she claimed to possess. But to what purpose? Phyllis didn't have an answer for that.

"If she's lying, the truth will come out eventually," she said. "But if she's not, we need to know the facts."

"The only facts that matter to me are that I loved Roy and he's gone." Eve started to cry again. "Gone."

Carolyn came along the hallway from the stairs. "What's going on here?" she demanded. "Eve, I thought you were taking a nap."

"I . . . I woke up," Eve said. "I came downstairs to see where everyone was . . . and I found that woman in the living room! The one spreading all those lies about Roy!"

Carolyn glared at Phyllis. "I thought we were going to try to protect Eve from all that."

"You knew about it?" Eve asked.

"It was Phyllis's idea."

What was it they said on those horrible reality TV shows about people being thrown under buses? Phyllis knew what that felt like now. But she still thought she had done the right thing by trying to find out what Tess knew about Roy.

Despite that, she said, "I'm sorry, Eve. I hope you'll forgive me."

"Well, of course, dear." Eve had taken a handkerchief from her pocket. She dabbed her eyes. "I know you were just doing what you thought was best."

That's right, Phyllis thought. She was going to find Roy's killer and clear Eve's name, no matter what anybody thought about her.

And as always, coming to that decision was a great weight off her mind. From here on out, she could take action, knowing that she was doing the right thing.

Eve refused to eat any lunch, but that evening Carolyn took a plate of food up to her room and persuaded her to eat a little. As time passed, her appetite would come back and her strength would return, Phyllis thought.

She hoped that was true, anyway.

In the meantime, Phyllis got on the computer and did some searching of her own. Her "Google-fu," whatever that was, was no match for Tess Coburn's, but she was able to confirm several things. The company that Roy had claimed he worked for in Houston did exist, but in all the newspaper business section stories Phyllis could find about it, there was no mention of him.

She found an obituary notice for a Houston Realtor named Julie Porter who was survived by her husband, Roy. But that Roy Porter had survived his wife by less than a year. Phyllis found an obituary notice for him, too. Roy—Eve's Roy—must have figured that while someone might check up on his claims about his late "wife," no one would think to see if there was an obituary for *him*, too. Why would they, when they would all be convinced the real Roy Porter was still hale and hearty and standing right in front of them?

Phyllis looked up the other cases Tess had mentioned and found more information about both of them, including photos that were unmistakably of the man they had known as Roy. She wanted to stop calling him by that name, since it obviously didn't belong to him, but she didn't know how else to think of him.

She was at the computer in the living room when she heard a car door outside. Eve, Carolyn, and Sam were all upstairs. She stood up, moved the curtain aside at the front window, and looked out to see a sheriff's cruiser parked at the curb. Mike was walking toward the house.

Phyllis met him at the door. "Come in out of the cold," she told him. She smiled. "You're wearing your hat this time."

He took it off as she closed the door behind him. "I can't stay but a minute," he said. "And I really shouldn't be here at all. But I wanted to tell you . . . a woman named Coburn came to see Burton and Conley."

Those were the investigators in charge of the case, Phyllis recalled.

"You don't look surprised," Mike commented with a slight frown.

"I'm not. I know who she is, Mike. She confronted Eve at

the cemetery after the graveside service. You and Sarah had already left."

"She came there?" Mike shook his head. "Man, that takes a lot of . . . brass. What did she want?"

"To tell Eve the same thing she told Burton and Conley, I imagine. The truth about the man we all knew as Roy Porter."

"Then you already know." Mike looked relieved and troubled at the same time. "I worried about coming here and talking to you about it. If the sheriff found out . . ."

"I don't want you getting in trouble," Phyllis said. "I certainly don't want you risking your job." She hesitated. "But what did the investigators think about the evidence Ms. Coburn turned over to them?"

"They'll check it all out, of course, and confirm it. But from what I heard, it all looked pretty convincing. I think Burton and Conley are convinced."

Phyllis nodded. "I was afraid they would be."

"And it doesn't exactly help Eve's case, either."

"I know. It just gives her a motive, where she didn't really have one before."

"Yeah. Mom, are you going to—" Mike stopped short, held up his free hand, and shook his head. "No, forget what I was about to ask you. Forget I said anything."

Phyllis smiled and said, "Consider it forgotten." He didn't want to know if she was going to investigate the case and try to find Roy's killer. And since she had already talked to Tess Coburn and learned about Roy's criminal background, he hadn't revealed that information to her, either. He was still in the clear as far as doing anything that could cause the sheriff or the district attorney to be angry with him.

"You'd better go," she told him. "There's nothing wrong with stopping by to say hello to your mother, but that's all you did. Right?"

"Right," Mike said. "Although Sullivan might not believe that."

"He can't prove otherwise. And for that matter, I don't care what Mr. Sullivan believes, because he's obviously wrong about a great many things."

"Yeah," Mike said with a grin. He leaned over to kiss her on the cheek, then put his hat back on. "Good night, Mom."

As she closed the door, Sam asked from the bottom of the stairs, "Was that Mike?"

She turned to him and nodded. "That's right. He told me that Tess Coburn went to see the investigators in charge of the case."

"Well, we expected that," Sam said with a shrug. "She told us she was goin' to."

"I know. But it just makes things look worse for Eve." Phyllis nodded toward the computer in the corner of the living room. "I've been trying to look things up. She was right about Roy, Sam. Everything she told us checks out."

"Yeah, we figured it would. But that didn't stop me from doin' some searchin' of my own. I reckon I probably found the same things you did."

"The question is, what do we do now?"

Sam smiled. "If Roy went around stealin' from folks for twenty years, you know what that tells me?"

"No, what?"

"That you got twenty years' worth of suspects to sift through, so you better get a good night's sleep. You're liable to need the energy to find this killer."

Chapter 20

Before Phyllis could figure out where to begin the next morning, the telephone rang and took care of that decision for her.

"This is Jan Delaney, Mrs. Newsom," the voice on the other end said. "We have everything Eve and Roy left here packed, anytime you'd like to pick it up."

"Already?" Phyllis asked. "I thought it might take a few days."

"Well, there really wasn't that much," Jan said. "Clothes, mostly."

"In that case, thank you. I'll come out this morning, if that's all right."

Even though there had been a chance of snow in the forecast overnight, none had fallen. The sky was still overcast, but the temperature was above freezing, so even if there were a few flurries, they wouldn't stick.

"This morning is fine," Jan said. "I'll see you later."

Phyllis went out to the garage. Sam had headed for the workbench as soon as he finished breakfast. He was sanding some boards to make more bookshelves. He had built a couple of sets for his room already and planned to add a couple more at least. It wouldn't take him long to fill them up with the paperback Westerns, thrillers, and science fiction novels he read voraciously.

"Jan Delaney just called and said that she had Eve's things packed up," she told him. "I could tell that she wanted us to go ahead and come get them, so I said that I'd come on out there this morning."

"And you want me to come along and give you a hand?" Sam asked.

"Do you mind?"

"Nope, not at all." He smiled. "That's one good thing about bein' retired. Whatever I do now, it's on my own schedule."

Phyllis understood that. She didn't miss having to live her life according to which bell had just rung. That structured environment had never really bothered her, but she was just fine without it, too.

They took Phyllis's car. She knew they would be able to carry everything in the backseat and the roomy trunk. Eve and Roy hadn't had all that much with them, after all, since they'd come back from their honeymoon and moved right into the country bed-and-breakfast.

There were several cars in the graveled parking area when Phyllis and Sam arrived. It appeared that Jan and Pete still had customers. Maybe what had happened to Roy wouldn't cost them too much business.

Jan must have been watching for them. She came out onto

the front porch and smiled and waved. Phyllis wondered whether Pete was here. He was the one who had stepped in at the cemetery to remind Jan that they weren't supposed to discuss the case, by order of the sheriff's department investigators.

Maybe if Pete wasn't around, Jan might be more willing to talk.

Phyllis felt a little bad about thinking that, but not too much. Now that she had made up her mind that she was going to find out who killed Roy, she was willing to do whatever it took. Eve's freedom was at stake, after all, not to mention her reputation. It wouldn't be enough just to create reasonable doubt, as Juliette Yorke had talked about. That might keep Eve from being convicted, but it wouldn't stop some people from being convinced that she was guilty anyway. The only way to make sure everyone knew she was innocent was to positively identify the actual murderer.

"Hello, you two," Jan said as Phyllis and Sam approached the porch. "My, it's still gloomy, isn't it?"

"Looks like those gray clouds have settled in for a while," Sam said.

"Well, it is winter, after all." Jan waved them onto the porch. "Come on in. Would you like some coffee? I have plenty of doughnuts, too."

Sam grinned. "I have a long-standin' rule about not turnin' down doughnuts."

"Good! Maybe we can visit for a few minutes before you load up Eve's things." As they went in the house, Jan motioned for them to follow her. "Let's go back to the kitchen."

She led them into a large, rustic, farmhouse-style kitchen.

The maple cabinets gave the kitchen an inherent glow and warmth. The cabinets matched the kitchen table, which had four chairs with cushions. There was also a counter area with stools that had cushions matching the ones in the chairs. It was a room that encouraged people to visit with the cook. There were plenty of homey decorating touches as well, with lacy curtains, plants on the windowsill, and vintage knick-knacks, including a glass bowl full of fruit. She took the cover off a plate of doughnuts sitting on the counter. "Help yourself," she told Sam with a smile as she rested a hand on his arm for a couple of seconds.

"Thanks," he said. "Don't mind if I do."

Jan poured coffee for all of them, herself included. They sat on the stools around the big counter, and Jan asked, "How's Eve doing?"

"As well as can be expected," Phyllis said. She didn't mention Tess Coburn's arrival in Weatherford or the startling revelations about Roy that the private investigator had brought with her. "She was able to eat a little last night, and Carolyn took a tray up to her this morning and said her appetite seemed even better."

"Oh, I'm so glad to hear that! Eve's just the sweetest thing in the world." Jan took a sip of her coffee, then added, "Of course, I thought Roy was, too."

Phyllis wondered what she meant by that, but she decided to pass it over for the time being. Instead she said, "I believe I'll have one of those doughnuts, too."

"Sure, help yourself. I like those chocolate ones with the little sprinkles. How about you, Sam?"

"Ummm," Sam said. That was all he could manage since his mouth was full at the moment.

Phyllis picked out a doughnut with a caramel glaze on it, since she knew the sprinkles on the chocolate ones were full of artificial food coloring and sometimes that bothered her. As she sat down again, she asked, "Is Pete here this morning?"

"No, he's gone into town to run errands. He had to go to the bank. I've told him we can do nearly everything online now, but Pete's an old-fashioned guy in a lot of ways." Jan flashed another smile. "Not that I mind. That just makes him more romantic."

Phyllis heard people moving around on the second floor of the old farmhouse and glanced toward the ceiling. "You have people staying here," she commented.

"Yes, only a couple of guests canceled their reservations when they heard about what happened. I didn't blame them, of course. But I'm glad the others decided not to cut their visits short. We have two couples and a single lady staying with us right now."

Sam said, "Kind of unusual for somebody to stay at a bed-and-breakfast by themselves, isn't it?"

"Well, it's certainly not as common as couples, but it's not unheard of," Jan replied. "Alice is widowed and likes to travel around antiquing. When she's checked out all the stores in Weatherford, she plans to move on to Ranger, Eastland, and Cisco. That's Alice Jessup, by the way. She's from Louisiana."

"How long has she been staying here?" Phyllis asked.

"Oh, goodness, about a week now, I guess. She's leaving tomorrow."

"Then she was here when . . ." Phyllis let her voice trail off.

Jan grew solemn and nodded. "Yes, she was here while Eve and Roy were. They were friendly but not particularly close. Alice was gone a lot, hitting the antique stores."

"What about the others?" Phyllis asked in apparently idle curiosity. She knew that Jan liked to talk, and the woman was also the sort who was everybody's friend as soon as she met them, calling them by their first name and touching their arm or shoulder. Phyllis had wished sometimes that she was that outgoing, but it just wasn't her personality.

"We have Frank and Ingrid Pitt and Henry and Rhonda Mitchum, all of them newlyweds." Jan smiled. "Although Frank and Ingrid are like Eve and Roy were. This isn't the first marriage for either of them. They're in their sixties, I'd say. For that matter, Henry and Rhonda are a little older than a lot of newlywed couples, too, although they're just in their thirties. A lot of people wait longer to get married these days, don't they? They like to be settled in their careers first, I guess. I can't say that I blame them for that."

Phyllis ate the last bite of her doughnut, washed it down with a sip of coffee, and then asked, "How long have they been here?"

"Henry and Rhonda just got here last night. Frank and Ingrid came in several days ago."

"Well, I'm glad you have enough guests to keep you busy," Phyllis said.

"So am I," Jan said. She shook her head. "If I was here by myself, I'm not sure I could stop myself from thinking about . . . about . . ."

Phyllis did some touching then, resting her hand on top of

Jan's where it lay on the table. "That must have been so awful, finding him like that."

"Oh, you just can't imagine!" A look of horror came into Jan's eyes. "When I heard that big thump upstairs, I just thought somebody must have dropped something, so I didn't go up right away. But then I got to worrying that one of the guests had fallen down and might be hurt, so I thought I should go check. Roy didn't answer when I knocked on the door, and honestly, I try not to be nosy, but I couldn't stand the thought that he might be in there unconscious or dying of a heart attack or something, and the door wasn't locked . . ."

Jan had to stop to gather herself, and Phyllis's nerves stretched taut as she worried that the woman might realize she was talking more than the sheriff's department—and her husband—wanted her to.

But then Jan went on in a hushed voice, "When I saw all that blood, though, I knew it wasn't a heart attack, and then I stepped into the room and saw Roy lying there on the rug beside the bed with that letter opener sticking in his throat . . . I'll bet they heard me screaming all the way over in Dallas."

"It must have been terrible," Phyllis said.

"Think I'll get another one of those doughnuts," Sam said, a comment that seemed inappropriate at first, but Phyllis realized what he was doing. He was keeping Jan off balance, distracting her so she wouldn't start thinking about how much information she was revealing.

Either that or he just really wanted another doughnut.

"Who was here at the time?" Phyllis asked.

"Pete was out back working on the well. Frank and Ingrid were in their room. They were the first ones to get to me. I didn't know where Eve and Alice were." Jan frowned a little. "Although come to think of it, I heard a car leaving just a minute or two after that big thump upstairs. You can hear it pretty easily when somebody pulls out on that gravel."

That thump Jan had heard had been Roy falling to the floor to bleed to death, Phyllis thought. If she had gone upstairs as soon as she'd heard it, instead of waiting for a few minutes, would she have been able to save his life?

Probably not, Phyllis decided. From the way Jan had described the scene, the blood and the fact that Roy had been stabbed in the throat, it was likely the letter opener had severed an artery. It was unlikely that Jan would have been able to slow down the bleeding enough to keep him from dying.

"You didn't see anyone coming or going?" Phyllis asked. "You just heard a car pull out?"

"That's right. I was busy back here in the kitchen."

"And Pete wouldn't have seen anything if he was out back in the well house."

"No, but he heard me carrying on and came running," Jan said. "He wanted to know why I was screaming bloody mur—" She stopped and put a hand to her lips as her eyes widened.

"You really were screamin' bloody murder," Sam said. "No need to be ashamed of that. Anybody would have, if they'd walked in on what you did."

"I suppose so. All I could think about was Eve."

"You didn't think about Roy?" Phyllis asked.

Jan's lips tightened. "Of course I did, but I was more worried about Eve."

This was the time to bring up that earlier matter, Phyllis

thought. "You said that at first you thought Roy was sweet, too. What changed your mind?"

"Nothing, really. I'm not going to speak ill of the dead." Jan waved a hand. "Anyway, it's not that unusual for an older man to sometimes say or do things around a younger woman that aren't really that appropriate—"

"Roy made a *pass* at you?" Sam burst out as he turned away from the plate of doughnuts with a jelly-filled one in his hand.

For a second Phyllis wished he hadn't been quite so blunt about it, but then Jan said, "Oh, Sam, I didn't mean any offense to you when I said that about older men! I'm sure you're an absolute gentleman."

"But Roy wasn't?" Phyllis asked.

"He was a little free with his hands," Jan admitted with a shrug. "And he said some things that were a little . . . questionable. Always whenever Eve wasn't around, you know. I just ignored it as much as possible and didn't really think anything about it." She paused. "He was hardly the first guest to hit on me, you know. Goodness, plenty of the female guests flirt with Pete, too. Even some of the, uh, male guests have been known to do that. I just tell Pete not to let it bother him."

"Maybe so, but I'm really surprised to hear that about Roy," Phyllis said. "I thought he was so much in love with Eve."

Phyllis wasn't actually surprised. A man who would marry a woman just to swindle her out of her money wouldn't draw the line at some racy talk or a little fanny patting with another woman. But Jan didn't know anything about Roy's background, so she didn't have any idea what his real plans had been.

"Just because he flirted a little doesn't mean he wasn't in love with Eve," Sam said. "Some fellas are just that way."

"I suppose," Phyllis said.

Jan glanced at the clock on the wall and said, "Goodness, you've let me blather on for nearly half an hour, when all you came out here to do was pick up those things." She had a worried look on her face now, as if she had realized at last that she was talking too much. "Once I get wound up, it's hard to stop me."

"Don't worry about it," Phyllis said. "I always enjoy visiting with people."

"Yes, but I, uh, wasn't supposed to talk about what happened."

Phyllis held up both hands. "Don't worry, Sam and I are both very discreet."

"Good, because Pete wouldn't be happy with me if he found out."

"We don't have any reason to tell Pete anything," Sam said.

Jan looked relieved. "You go ahead and finish that doughnut, Sam," she said, "and then we'll load up those boxes."

It didn't take long to put the handful of boxes in the Lincoln's trunk and lay Eve's clothes across the backseat. All of Roy's clothes were in the boxes, Jan explained.

"But I left Eve's on the hangers to keep them nicer," she added.

"That was very considerate of you," Phyllis said. "I'm sure Eve's not going to want to deal with any of this for a while, but I've got plenty of storage space in my house, so we'll just leave everything in the boxes."

"You'll give Eve my best?"

Phyllis smiled. "Of course."

"And tell her that if there's anything I can do . . ."

"I'm sure she knows that."

Jan hesitated, then hugged both Phyllis and Sam. "She's really lucky to have friends like you two and Carolyn. I feel like I've known all of you for years."

They said their good-byes, then got into the Lincoln; Phyllis pulled out, hearing the crunch of gravel under the car's tires and remembering what Jan had said about hearing someone leaving just before she found Roy's body. Phyllis wondered if she had told the sheriff's men the same thing. She probably had.

Sam cleared his throat and said, "Friendly woman."

"And you enjoyed that hug she gave you, didn't you?"

"I'd be lyin' if I said I didn't."

"Well, you don't have to grin quite so big about it. But I've been thinking," Phyllis went on. "What if things went a little further with Roy than Jan was willing to admit?"

Sam's grin disappeared. "Are you sayin' that maybe the two of 'em . . . well, you know? That doesn't seem likely to me. Gals like Jan sometimes get a mite touchy-feely themselves, but that doesn't mean they're lookin' to play around."

"No, but what if Roy got more aggressive than she told us? What if she was trying to fend him off and things got out of hand and . . ."

"And she grabbed that letter opener and stuck it in his neck?" Sam thought about it and nodded slowly. "Could've happened that way. All we've got is her word for it that she heard somethin' fall upstairs."

"And that she heard a car pulling away," Phyllis said. "She could have said that just to throw suspicion on someone else, most likely Eve."

Sam rubbed his chin. "Here's another one for you. Maybe ol' Pete knew what Roy was tryin' to pull. From the way Jan was talkin', he can be a little hot tempered. She said he was old-fashioned in some ways, too. An old-fashioned sort of fella might confront a lounge lizard like Roy and tell him to stay the heck away from his wife. Then Roy says somethin' that makes Pete even madder, and like you said, things get outta hand . . ."

"Did you just call Roy a lounge lizard?"

Sam laughed. "Yeah, I guess I did."

"You're not old enough to be using terms like that."

"Oh, but I am," he said. "Heard fellas called that many a time when I was growin' up."

"Anyway," Phyllis said, "there's two more possible suspects right there."

"Reasonable doubt," Sam said.

Phyllis shook her head. "No, I don't want reasonable doubt," she said, putting into words the thought that had gone through her head earlier. "I want Roy's killer . . . signed, sealed, and delivered."

Chapter 21

When they got back to the house, it was almost time for lunch. Sam volunteered to take the boxes in while Phyllis fixed something to eat.

"Put as many of the boxes as you can into that back hall closet," she told him. "The others can go in the cabinets in the utility room. I think between those two places, there's plenty of room for everything."

"What about Eve's clothes?" Sam asked.

Phyllis frowned in thought for a moment before she said, "Lay them on the bed in my room. I didn't tell her we were going out to the bed-and-breakfast, so she doesn't know we were bringing those things back. I don't want to spring them on her without preparing her first. I'll talk to her, and then I can hang the clothes in her closet later."

Sam nodded. "Sounds good to me."

Phyllis made grilled ham and pepper sandwiches for lunch. One of the neighbors had brought them a ham, so she used big slices to make the sandwiches. That was the quickest and easiest thing to do, and it didn't take much thought. Her brain was already busy going over everything Jan Delaney had told her and Sam that morning, as well as the things Jan had done to reveal her personality.

Both theories she and Sam had come up with—that either Jan or Pete Delaney could have killed Roy because of his advances toward Jan—seemed reasonable. There was no proof to indicate that either of those things had happened, but the Delaneys had had both motive and opportunity, and if the letter opener was in Eve and Roy's room, either of them could have picked it up and used it just as easily as Eve could have. Only the facts that spouses were always suspects in homicides, Eve had no alibi, and only her prints were on the weapon made the authorities believe she was guilty.

But Eve had said that she didn't have the letter opener at the bed-and-breakfast, Phyllis recalled, which opened up even more questions. How else could it have gotten there and been used to commit murder? She supposed Roy could have taken it along. The sheriff's department investigators just assumed that Eve was lying about it, of course. To them, her denial might just make her seem even more guilty.

It was a dizzying situation, Phyllis thought, made even more so by the fact that one of her friends was accused of the crime.

Carolyn came into the kitchen as Phyllis was browning the sandwiches in a large frying pan. "I was just going to see about some lunch," she said. "I knew you and Sam were back, but I thought you might be helping him carry things in from the car."

"There really wasn't that much," Phyllis said. "How's Eve?"

"Slowly getting better. I got her working on some needle-work. I think it takes her mind off of everything that's hap-pened."

It was also unlike Eve, Phyllis thought. Eve had never had the patience for crafts. She liked to be out doing things, rather than sitting quietly.

"I can tell she still has her dark moments," Carolyn went on, "but that's to be expected, I suppose."

"Yes, certainly," Phyllis agreed.

"Did those people from the bed-and-breakfast have any-thing to say?"

For a moment Phyllis considered sharing the ideas she and Sam had come up with. She decided not to, however. It was too early in the investigation, and Carolyn might say some-thing to Eve about it, getting her hopes up prematurely. At this point, Phyllis had no reason to think that either Jan or Pete had killed Roy . . . only that they *might* have.

Phyllis settled for saying, "Mr. Delaney wasn't there. And Jan just said to give her best to Eve." She held out one of the plates to Carolyn. "Do you think you could get her to eat some of this sandwich?"

"I can certainly try," Carolyn declared. She marched out of the kitchen like a woman on a mission.

Phyllis was on a mission, too, but it didn't involve food. Its only goal was to find a killer and clear Eve's name.

After lunch, Phyllis went into the living room and sat down at the computer in the corner. She didn't turn the monitor on immediately, though. Instead she took a legal pad and a pen from one of the drawers in the desk and wrote down five names.

Alice Jessup
Frank Pitt
Ingrid Pitt
Henry Mitchum
Rhonda Mitchum

She paused for a moment, frowning in thought, and then wrote down two more names, those of Jan and Pete Delaney. She didn't consider the five people who were staying at the bed-and-breakfast to be possible suspects in Roy's death, as she did with Jan and Pete—the Mitchums couldn't be, because they hadn't even arrived at the place until after the murder—but she wanted to know more about them anyway. It was a matter of being thorough. After another brief hesitation, she added Julie Porter's name to the list and then finally wrote down one final name.

Roy Porter

The real Roy Porter, not the one they had believed they knew, Phyllis thought. Was it a mere coincidence of similar age and appearance that had led "Roy" to adopt the other man's identity? Or was it possible there was some other connection between the two men, something that would provide a reason for the fake Roy's death?

Phyllis considered that unlikely, but again, it was something she wanted to look into.

She was about to turn on the monitor when she heard a car door close outside. A glance through the front window showed her Juliette Yorke's SUV parked at the curb and the lawyer herself coming toward the house. Juliette's breath fogged in the cold air in front of her face. Phyllis got up and went to meet her at the door.

Juliette didn't look particularly upset, Phyllis thought, but she certainly wasn't jubilant, either, so it was probably too much to hope for that the investigators had found Roy's killer and the charges against Eve had been dropped.

"Hello," Phyllis said. "Come in. How are you today?"

"I'm fine, I guess," Juliette said. "I have some news for Eve."

"Good news, I hope?" Phyllis didn't really believe that was what was coming, but it didn't hurt to hope.

With a solemn little smile on her lips, Juliette shook her head. "No, not good news," she said, "but not bad news, either. At least, not as bad as she's been getting. More like expected news."

"Well, come on in. Eve's upstairs."

Phyllis took Juliette's coat as Juliette went on, "I suppose I could have just called her, but I wanted to see her, too. To find out how she's holding up."

"I haven't seen much of her myself," Phyllis said. "She's been holed up in her room. But Carolyn's spending quite a bit of time with her."

"Good," Juliette said with a nod. "Maybe that keeps her from brooding too much."

Before all this happened, Phyllis would have said that Eve wasn't the type to waste even a minute brooding about anything. Eve had never suffered quite the same level of shocks as she had recently, though. Even when those earlier husbands of hers died and she came under suspicion in their deaths, she had never been arrested and charged with their murders. She had been considerably younger then, too.

"I'll tell her you're here," Phyllis said. "Unless you'd rather go up to her room and speak to her in private."

Juliette shook her head. "Oh, no, that's all right. We can talk down here. This is nothing that you and the others can't hear."

"All right. I'll be right back."

She climbed the stairs and went to the door of Eve's room. When she knocked, Eve called, "Come in."

Phyllis opened the door to find Eve sitting in the rocking chair while Carolyn sat in the other chair. Both of them were doing needlework. Carolyn was saying, "Now, if you'll just tighten up those stitches a little—"

"What is it, dear?" Eve asked Phyllis.

"Juliette is downstairs and wants to talk to you."

"Oh. All right." Eve put the needlework aside with what seemed to Phyllis like eagerness and stood up. "Should I go downstairs, or should she come up here?"

"She said there was nothing private about it."

"Fine. I haven't been downstairs today. I suppose I should make the effort."

Eve was starting to look and sound more like herself, Phyllis thought. True, it was just flashes so far, but that was better than nothing.

"I suppose we can come back to this later," Carolyn said as she set her own needlework on the dresser.

By the time the three of them got downstairs, Sam was in the living room talking to Juliette. "I'd be glad to," he was saying.

Juliette said, "Fine. I'll let you know the dimensions. Thank you, Mr. Fletcher."

"Call me Sam. And it's my pleasure."

Juliette turned to Eve and asked, "How are you feeling today?"

Eve smiled faintly. "Well, I suppose that'll depend to a certain extent on what you've come to tell me, dear."

"It's nothing we weren't expecting. The arraignment will be Monday morning at nine o'clock."

Eve nodded. "Do I need to be there?"

"It's not absolutely necessary. As your attorney I can enter a plea for you, but it would be better if you were there. For appearance's sake."

"Then I'll be there," Eve said.

"We all will," Carolyn said.

"Actually, that's not a bad idea," Juliette said. "A show of support for the media. I'm not trying to influence the jury pool . . . Oh, who am I trying to kid? Of course I am. So is the district attorney. That's why Sullivan—"

Juliette stopped short. When she didn't go on, Phyllis said, "That's why Sullivan did what?"

Juliette looked uncomfortable, but she shrugged and said, "He had a news conference this morning to announce the arraignment. Actually, I'm surprised you hadn't heard about it already."

"We've all been busy," Phyllis said.

"Yes, Carolyn and I have been doing needlework samplers," Eve said.

"Sullivan's just trying to make it look like he's right on top of everything and handling the whole case himself. Like a tough district attorney."

Carolyn said, "Yes, as if prosecuting a harmless old woman makes him tough on crime."

Eve winced a little at that description of herself, but she didn't say anything for a moment. Then she said, "I don't want people feeling sorry for me."

Carolyn turned to her. "But you've been wronged—"

"I said I don't want people feeling sorry for me. I made my own choices, just like I always do, and if Roy fooled me, it's my own fault for being so gullible. I'm not some dotty old lady who can't think for herself."

"No one has claimed that you are," Carolyn said.

Eve looked at Juliette and went on, "I don't care what you do as long as you don't make me look feeble and defenseless."

"We have to be careful about what image we present—," Juliette began.

"I don't present an image," Eve said. "I am who I am."

Phyllis tried not to smile. Eve was sounding more like herself by the minute.

"I didn't kill Roy," Eve went on, "but if I had found out the truth about what he was trying to do, I might have."

It was Juliette's turn to wince. She shook her head and said, "You definitely don't need to be saying things like that, especially in public. Here among your friends it's one thing, but—"

Eve interrupted her again. "If it comes to a trial, I don't want a jury voting to acquit me because they feel sorry for me. I won't play the poor-little-old-lady card, Juliette, and if you try to, I swear I . . . I'll stand up in court and fire you right there on the spot!"

Juliette met Eve's intense gaze for a moment before nodding. "I believe you would, too," she said. "All right, Eve. You're the client, which means you're the boss."

"Darned right I am."

"As long as it doesn't go against my best legal judgment," Juliette went on. "If that happens, then maybe we will have to come to a parting of the ways. But I hope it doesn't come to that."

Eve smiled. "It won't, dear. I like you."

"Anyway, we'll meet at the courthouse at eight thirty Monday morning, okay?"

"We'll all be there," Phyllis promised. "Have you heard any more about the investigation?"

A bleak look came over Juliette's face. "At this point, the investigation is closed. The sheriff's department has turned over everything to Sullivan's office. They believe they have the killer, so that's how they're going forward."

"They're not questioning anyone else, looking for evidence to corroborate their theory?"

Juliette shook her head. "No, and that tells me they think they've got plenty already. Sullivan is confident of a conviction."

Eve said, "Well, then, we'll just have to prove him wrong, won't we?"

"That's right," Juliette said, summoning up a smile. "And

now that I've talked to you, Eve, and seen how you've gotten some fight back in you, I'm sure that's exactly what we're going to do."

"That's the spirit," Sam said.

Yes, that was the spirit, all right, Phyllis thought, but spirit wasn't going to save Eve by itself. They needed evidence, too.

And judging by what Juliette had said about the sheriff's department closing its investigation, the responsibility for finding that evidence fell to her, Phyllis told herself.

She just hoped she was up to the task.

Chapter 22

This was Friday afternoon. The arraignment was Monday morning. That gave her two days to start looking into the case. It wasn't much time. Phyllis wanted to spare Eve the ordeal of going through another court appearance if she could, but that might not be possible.

Before she started, she was curious about something else. As soon as Juliette was gone and Eve and Carolyn had gone back upstairs, Phyllis said to Sam, "When we came in you were talking to Juliette about something. She said she'd call you with the dimensions?"

He smiled. "Yeah, she asked me if I could make a book-shelf for her office. I guess the word's gettin' around about what a good carpenter I am."

"You *are* a good carpenter," Phyllis said. "Is she hiring you?"

"She offered to pay me," Sam said with a shrug, "but I told her that if she'd just cover the cost of the materials, that'd be fine. It's not like my time's worth a whole lot."

"You ought to get paid for your trouble."

He shook his head. "No, woodwork's just a hobby with me, and somethin' I can do as a favor for friends. If I start takin' money for it, it becomes just another job . . . and I'm retired."

Phyllis nodded and said, "I can understand that, I suppose."

"Anyway, Juliette's not makin' all that much money, even if she is a lawyer, and she's got a daughter to raise. Seems like there are as many single parents these days as there are married ones, but it still can't be easy."

"I didn't know Juliette had a daughter," Phyllis said. "I'm not sure I even knew that she was single, although I'd noticed that she doesn't wear a wedding ring."

Sam shrugged again. "Guess I'm easy to talk to. Folks just naturally open up to me."

"I know. That's one reason I like to take you along when I'm looking into things."

"And here I thought it was so I could subdue all the suspects."

"That, too," Phyllis said.

The banter concealed an actual worry of hers. More than once, her investigations had put both her and Sam in danger. If she kept looking for Roy's killer, it was possible that could happen again. Anyone who would drive a letter opener into a man's throat like that was capable of, well, just about anything, Phyllis thought.

Unfortunately, she had no choice. She had faith in Juliette's skill as a defense attorney, but she wasn't going to let Eve's fate fall into the hands of a jury if there was anything she could do about it.

Sam went back out to the garage, and Phyllis sat down in front of the computer. She turned on the monitor, checked her e-mail, then did a search for the first name on her list. A lot of Alice Jessups turned up, too many for her to go through all of them in a reasonable amount of time. Jan had said that the Alice Jessup staying at the bed-and-breakfast was from Louisiana. Phyllis added that to the search to narrow down the number of hits.

There were still quite a few, and a quick scan of the list didn't make any of them jump out at her. She would come back to Alice later, Phyllis decided. She moved on to Frank and Ingrid Pitt. Again there was a multitude of results, and she didn't even know where they were from. The same was true of Henry and Rhonda Mitchum.

Phyllis was starting to feel like she was wasting her time. She didn't consider it likely that there was anything important to the case in the background of Jan or Pete Delaney—their involvement was more immediate than that, and if either of them was involved in Roy's death it was because of something that had happened at the bed-and-breakfast, not before—so she moved on to Julie Porter and the real Roy Porter.

"Roy" had done a good job of identity theft. Phyllis called up the real Roy's obituary again, which included a photograph. There was a slight resemblance between the two men. No one would have ever mistaken one of them for the other, but it wasn't as if they were totally unlike each other. The real Roy had worked at the same company the fake Roy claimed to. The fake had done his homework and had moved right in to take over the real Roy's life. Was it possible the fake had known the real Roy?

Phyllis wasn't sure how to go about discovering that, so she switched her attention to the late Julie Porter, searching out older mentions of her. She was quite a successful saleswoman when it came to real estate. Even in these lean economic times, she had managed to sell more than a million dollars' worth of property several times in past years. Phyllis called up a newspaper story about Julie receiving some sort of award. There was an accompanying photograph that showed a number of other agents from her company applauding as a smiling man handed her the award.

Phyllis's eyes narrowed, and she leaned closer to the monitor. That didn't really do any good, she realized, so she saved the image instead and then opened a photo-editing program to enlarge it. There was only so much she could increase the resolution—it was an Internet image of a newspaper photo, after all—but as she stared at the group of clapping real estate agents, the face of one man in the picture seemed awfully familiar to her.

She couldn't be sure, but she thought she was looking at the fake Roy Porter.

That made sense, Phyllis thought as her pulse beat a little faster. Working as a real estate agent would be a good way for a con artist to meet wealthy women. That way "Roy" would have been acquainted with Julie Porter and probably with her husband, as well, so when Julie had passed away and then the real Roy had followed her, the fake Roy was presented with a ready-made opportunity to assume a new identity. Maybe the real estate scam wasn't working out. Maybe he was just restless and ready to move on. He'd found a new target in Eve, established himself with her as "Roy," and come to Weatherford to marry her and get his hands on as much of her money as he could manage. It was a reasonable theory.

It didn't put Phyllis any closer to finding a previously unknown motive for the fake Roy's murder, though.

With a sigh, she backtracked to the searches she had done earlier and started going through the results again. As she did, an idea occurred to her. The Pitts and the Mitchums were newlyweds, Jan had said, so Phyllis ran a search for *Frank Pitt, Ingrid*, and the word *bride*.

A link to their wedding announcement popped right up.

Not everyone ran wedding announcements in the newspaper these days, of course. That was one more sign of the general decline in the newspaper business. But Frank and Ingrid were an older couple, so Phyllis thought they might be old-fashioned enough to have done so, and sure enough, there they were, an attractive older couple, Ingrid with quite a bit of her Scandanavian beauty intact, and Frank looking distinguished. More important, Ingrid's name was given as Ingrid Olsen Callahan, and that gave Phyllis something else to search for.

A few moments later, Phyllis leaned back in her chair, staring wide-eyed at the monitor.

She had a ten-year-old newspaper story from Minneapolis on the screen. It told how the police were looking for a man named Monte Callahan so they could question him about a sizable amount of money missing from the accounts of his wife, local businesswoman Ingrid Olsen Callahan. There were no photographs accompanying the story, but Phyllis didn't need them to know what she was looking at.

She had found another of the fake Roy's victims.

And that victim had been staying at the same bed-and-breakfast where Roy was killed.

How was that possible? Had Ingrid tracked him down after all these years and taken her revenge on him? It was an appealing theory, but that's all it was. Even though the possibility of a coincidence seemed too far-fetched for Phyllis to believe, she knew she couldn't eliminate that idea entirely. They were called coincidences for a reason, after all, and some of them were pretty wild.

She suppressed the urge to go out to the garage and drag Sam into the living room to look at her findings. Now that she'd had the wedding idea, she wanted to delve deeper. She tried the same search technique with Henry and Rhonda Mitchum, even though she didn't expect to find anything, since the Mitchums hadn't even shown up at the bed-and-breakfast until after "Roy" was dead.

A few minutes of searching uncovered Rhonda's maiden name—Gilbert—but she had never been married before and Phyllis couldn't find even a glimmer of anything that would connect either her or Henry to the fake Roy.

She moved on to Jan and Pete Delaney and found their wedding announcement from seventeen years earlier in the Fort Worth paper. Jan had been Janice Cresston then. More searching turned up a Janice Baker who had married a David Cresston a few years before Janice Cresston had married Peter Delaney. So Pete was her second husband, more than likely. Phyllis didn't find an obituary for David Cresston, so in all probability he and Janice had divorced.

And so what? Phyllis asked herself. This trail, like the one involving the Mitchums, was a dead end. If Jan or Pete had killed Roy, it was because he'd made a pass at Jan, not because of anything in the past. So it was still feasible . . . but the really exciting possibility was that vengeance had caught up to Roy at last in the person of Ingrid Pitt.

She didn't have to go out to the garage to get Sam. He came into the room behind her, paused, and said, "From the way you're starin' at that computer, you either found somethin' interestin' or you've been taken over by some evil artificial intelligence that's come out from the screen."

Phyllis turned to him and said, "Come take a look at this."

"I don't know if I want to. It's liable to turn me into some sort of zombie robot."

She didn't know whether to laugh or be exasperated with him. So she said, "There are no zombie robots in this computer . . . but there just might be a murderer."

Chapter 23

$\mathcal{S}$am stopped joking and pulled up a chair so he could look at the computer alongside Phyllis. She clicked through the various screens, pointing out the things she had discovered. When she was finished, Sam sat there silently for several seconds before he pointed out, "We don't know that this Monte Callahan fella who fleeced Ingrid Olsen is the same person as the Roy Porter who married Eve."

"Oh, come on," Phyllis said. "Who else could it be?"

Sam shrugged. "Lots of grifters and con men in the world. You didn't find a picture of Callahan, did you?"

Phyllis shook her head and said, "No, but it's got to be him."

"That was years ago, and clear across the country from here. How in the world would she know that Roy Porter in Weatherford, Texas, was the same fella who conned her in Minneapolis? For that matter, how do we know that Ingrid Pitt is even the same lady?"

"She has to be! The name is exactly the same."

"A few years ago the cops arrested Samuel J. Fletcher of Poolville for havin' a meth lab in his house. You know what my middle name is?"

"Of course I do. It's John. But you never had a meth lab."

"No, but Samuel James Fletcher who lived four miles from me did. I never heard of the fella, never knew there was another Sam Fletcher in Poolville until I came to work one day and noticed that folks were givin' me funny looks. I didn't know what was goin' on. The principal called me into his office and asked me if I'd started cookin' crystal meth because teachers were underpaid. He showed me the newspaper story. I'd missed it completely." Sam shook his head. "Took me a long time to convince everybody I wasn't some sort of drug kingpin."

"Well, that's just crazy," Phyllis said. "Everyone should have known right away that it was just a misunderstanding."

"My point is, there could be two Ingrid Olsen Callahans. Where did the one who tied the knot with Frank Pitt live?"

"They got married in Dallas," Phyllis admitted. "But she could have moved down here from Minneapolis. A lot of people have moved to Texas in the past forty years."

"That they have," Sam agreed. "And you sure might be right about this one. I just don't think you ought to go jumpin' the gun."

Phyllis sighed. "You're right. I was about to call Mike and ask him to come over so I could show all of this to him, but that would be a mistake, wouldn't it? I'd need more proof first."

"And you'd sort of put him between a rock and a hard place, too," Sam pointed out. "You're not supposed to be investigatin' this case. The DA told the sheriff, and the sheriff told Mike—"

"To tell me to keep my hands off. I know. But if you think I'm going to just sit back and let Eve go to prison for something she didn't do—"

"I never said I expected you to do that," Sam broke in. "I know you're gonna find the killer. We just got to be smart about it, though."

"You're right. I need to do some more digging before I go to the authorities. I've got to be absolutely sure." She turned back to the computer. "Here's something else."

A couple of mouse clicks brought up the photograph of Julie Porter accepting her award with her fellow agents applauding in the background. Without pointing out anything, so she wouldn't influence his reaction, she told Sam, "Take a look at this picture and tell me if you see anything interesting in it."

Sam squinted at the screen, then muttered, "Hold on." He took a pair of glasses from his shirt pocket and slipped them on. He studied the photograph for a few more seconds, then said, "Holy cow! Is that—"

His finger pointed at the same man Phyllis had spotted in the photograph earlier.

"I think it is," she said. "I think that's the man we knew as Roy Porter."

"He knew the two of 'em in Houston. Shoot, from the looks of this, he even worked with Julie Porter! When both of 'em died, that was a whole ready-made life he could just step into, especially if he was plannin' on leavin' town and just needed the background."

"That's what I think, too. It's interesting, but it doesn't really tell us anything else about who might have killed him, only about how he worked out his scheme to bilk Eve."

"I hate to say it, but I'm almost glad somebody stuck that letter opener in him. That fella was smart, and it doesn't look like he had any conscience at all. He would have stolen from Eve, and he would've just gone on stealin' from ladies and breakin' their hearts if somebody hadn't stopped him."

"Yes, he's no great loss," Phyllis agreed. "Other than the fact that Eve's being blamed for what happened to him."

Sam smiled. "Yeah, but you'll take care of that."

"I don't know," Phyllis said.

"You've already found out quite a bit already. It's just a matter of time."

Something had occurred to Phyllis. She called up another search and entered *Alice, Jessup, Louisiana*, and *marriage*.

"I looked up the Pitts and the Mitchums earlier," she explained to Sam, "but I didn't think to try the same thing with Alice Jessup."

Sam nodded. "Good idea."

A few minutes of searching turned up an Alice Nichols who had married Benjamin Jessup in Monroe, Louisiana, in 1982.

"That could be her," Phyllis said. She continued searching. "No obituary for Benjamin Jessup, though." She checked the Social Security death index. "Several Benjamin Jessups in the right time frame, but none in Louisiana."

"Maybe they got divorced," Sam suggested.

"Jan said that the Alice Jessup staying there was a widow." Phyllis frowned in thought. "But I'll bet that's what the woman told her. We can't assume that's the truth."

"If this Ben Jessup is the same as our Roy Porter, then this scam goes back earlier than any Tess Coburn talked about," Sam said. "Maybe it was his first."

"And all these years later, not one of his current victims but *two* of them happen to show up at the same bed-and-breakfast where he's staying with his current victim?" Phyllis shook her head. "I can't buy that, Sam. I just can't."

"Well, we're just brainstormin' here. We may be way off about all of it."

"Maybe," Phyllis said, "but I have an idea who might be able to tell us."

"Who's that?"

"Tess Coburn. She was working for some of Roy's previous victims."

"And she's not gonna tell you who they are, either," Sam said. "You've already been through that with her."

"She might look at things differently if she knew I'd already found out about Ingrid Pitt. She might confirm things she wasn't willing to reveal outright."

"Maybe," Sam said.

"The problem is that I don't know how to get in touch with her," Phyllis said. She swung around toward the computer. "Maybe she has a website . . ."

"Or you could just call her," Sam suggested.

"No, I can't. I don't have her number."

Sam grinned and took out his wallet. "The other night when she was leavin' and I was helpin' her with her coat, she gave me her card. Said if we had any more questions or if we ever needed a private investigator, we should call her."

He slipped a business card out of his wallet and held it out toward Phyllis.

She smiled and shook her head before she took the card from him. "The fact that women all seem to like you does come in handy sometimes," she said.

"I can't help it that I'm charmin'."

"Her office is in New Orleans," Phyllis said. "She's probably gone back there already. Louisiana . . . That's another connection with Alice Jessup."

"Lots of people live in Louisiana," Sam said. "I'll bet some of 'em don't even know each other."

Phyllis sighed. "I know. I'm reaching for straws here, aren't I? She'll probably refuse to talk to me, and all of these half-baked theories are probably wrong, anyway."

"Only one way to find out. Give her a call."

"I'm going to." Phyllis picked up the phone and punched in Tess Coburn's cell phone number, which was printed on the card.

She was expecting the call to go to voice mail, but to her surprise, a woman's voice answered. "Coburn Investigations."

"Ms. Coburn?" Phyllis said.

"That's right."

"This is Phyllis Newsom."

There was a second of silence on the line, as if Tess were trying to place the name. Then she said, "Mrs. Newsom, how are you? How's Mrs. Porter?"

"I'm fine, and Eve is holding up as well as can be expected." People always said that, Phyllis thought, and it was almost meaningless. She went on, "I was wondering if I could ask you a few questions about the case."

"Are you sleuthing?" Tess asked. Phyllis could almost see the smile on her face.

She swallowed the annoyance she felt at that and said, "I'm just curious about something."

"Well, I doubt if I can help you, but go ahead."

Phyllis took a breath and said, "I was just wondering how it is that two women who were swindled by Roy Porter in the past wound up staying at the same bed-and-breakfast where he and Eve were staying."

Once again there was silence on the other end of the line, but it lasted longer this time. Phyllis was starting to wonder if the connection had gotten broken somehow when Tess finally said, "What are you talking about?"

"Alice Jessup and Ingrid Pitt. They were victims of Roy's schemes, and they were there at the house."

"I don't know . . . That doesn't make any sense. I don't know what you're talking about."

Phyllis had heard the surprise in Tess's voice, though. She knew her shot in the dark had found its target.

"It's true, isn't it?" she pressed.

From the corner of her eye, she saw Sam start shaking his head. She wondered what had occurred to him, but she couldn't ask him right now.

Tess said, "Look, Mrs. Newsom, I think we need to talk."

"That's what we're doing."

"No, I mean face-to-face."

"You're coming back here from New Orleans?"

"I'm not in New Orleans," Tess said. "I'm still here in Weatherford. I can come to your house—"

"No," Phyllis said. She didn't want Eve walking in on another conversation with the woman who had destroyed all her illusions about the man she had married. "I'll meet you somewhere."

"There's a restaurant right up the street from my hotel. We could have dinner."

"All right." Phyllis glanced at Sam. "My friend Sam Fletcher will be coming with me."

"Mr. Fletcher? That's fine. I'll be glad to see him again. Make it seven o'clock." Tess named the restaurant.

"That's fine."

"I'll see you then." Tess paused but didn't hang up. "I think we have a lot to talk about."

"So do I," Phyllis said.

Chapter 24

"You were shaking your head like something was bothering you," Phyllis said to Sam after she'd broken the connection with Tess Coburn. "What is it?"

"If Roy swindled Ingrid Pitt and Alice Jessup in the past, how come he didn't recognize 'em there at the bed-and-breakfast?"

Phyllis frowned. That was a good point, and she hadn't even thought of it.

"I don't know," she admitted. "It was ten years ago that Monte Callahan stole that money from Ingrid Olsen, and even longer ago that Benjamin Jessup married Alice Nichols. It's possible the women could have changed enough that he wouldn't know them anymore."

"Yeah, but Alice Jessup is still goin' by that name," Sam said. "Don't you think Roy would have remembered his own aliases?"

"Maybe, maybe not. I mean, there's no telling how many

times he changed his identity over the years. He could have gone by so many different names that he doesn't remember them all, or the names of the women he married."

Even as she spoke, that sounded unlikely to Phyllis. And yet she couldn't rule it out. They couldn't ask Roy about it, either, since he was dead.

She went on, "Maybe Ms. Coburn can shed some light on all this, if she will. I hope it's all right that I said you were coming with me to meet her."

"Sure. I'm not gonna turn down a chance to eat out."

"It's Friday evening. The restaurant is liable to be busy, and I know you don't care much for crowds. I don't, either."

Sam shrugged. "When you're a detective, you've got to go where the answers are."

"But we're not professional detectives," Phyllis pointed out.

"Wouldn't want to be. It's a hobby, like woodworkin'. Only with more murders."

Phyllis laughed, despite the seriousness of the situation. "I suppose that's one way to look at it," she said.

Since she and Sam weren't going to be home for supper, she wanted to let Carolyn and Eve know. She went upstairs and knocked lightly on Carolyn's door.

"Come in," Carolyn called.

Phyllis opened the door and stepped into the room. Carolyn had brought her needlework back from Eve's room and was working on it as she sat by the window.

"I didn't know if you'd be here or still with Eve," Phyllis said.

"She wanted to be alone for a while after that meeting with Juliette," Carolyn explained. "I think it upset her more than she was letting on. Still, it's nice to see her showing some spunk again."

Phyllis nodded. "Yes, it certainly is. I came to tell you that Sam and I are going out for dinner this evening."

"With all of this trouble going on?" Carolyn asked with a frown.

Phyllis smiled and shrugged. If Carolyn wanted to think this was a date she was talking about, that was fine. That way Phyllis didn't have to explain the multitude of theories going through her head or admit that they were going to talk to Tess Coburn about the case.

"I'm sorry if it's a problem," she said.

Carolyn shook her head and waved a hand dismissively. "Oh, it's not, of course. I can throw some supper together for Eve and me. I don't mind at all. I was just a little surprised; that's all."

"We won't be out late."

"It doesn't matter. We'll be fine."

Phyllis nodded. "All right. I just wanted to let you know."

"Go ahead. Have fun." Carolyn's statement managed to sound a little disapproving, despite the words she spoke.

Phyllis left things at that. Carolyn might feel differently later, especially if Phyllis's efforts paid off and she discovered the identity of the person who really had killed Roy.

She spent the rest of the afternoon poking around on the computer, but she didn't find anything else related to the case. Around six o'clock she went upstairs to change. At this time of year, full night had fallen by then. With the stubborn overcast hanging on, it got dark even earlier than it might have otherwise.

The restaurant where they were going was one of the

chains, known for its informality, so Phyllis didn't see the need to wear anything fancy. She settled for a nice dress and jacket. As she came out of her room, Sam was leaving his, wearing jeans, a denim shirt, and a corduroy jacket. He looked very handsome in a rustic way, she thought.

"Too bad we're not really goin' out for a night on the town," he said with a smile. "We clean up pretty good, even if I do say so myself."

"Well, there's no reason why we can't enjoy ourselves at the same time," Phyllis said.

Sam linked his arm with hers as they went downstairs. He asked, "Did you let Eve and Carolyn know we were goin' out?"

"I told Carolyn. She said she'd fix some supper for her and Eve."

"We could bring somethin' back for them," he suggested.

"No, Carolyn has things under control. That's one thing you can say for her. It takes a lot to shake her out of her routine. Unfortunately, in recent years, we've had a lot going on."

"Retirement hasn't played out exactly like you thought it would, has it?"

"No, it certainly hasn't," Phyllis answered honestly. "But I think we've done some real good, too."

"So do I," Sam agreed.

They took his pickup, since Phyllis didn't particularly like to drive at night. The bright headlights bothered her. And there were plenty of headlights, since the area on the southern edge of town along the interstate was extremely busy at the best of times, let alone on a Friday evening. To Phyllis, it seemed like only a few years had passed since nearly all the land on both sides of the highway was pasture, but in reality, the area had developed at a tremendous pace over the past two decades. Now there were businesses and people and cars everywhere, and she seldom came down here unless she had to.

The restaurant was on the outer edge of the parking lot for a huge shopping center packed with big-box stores and specialty retailers. Sam found a parking place for the pickup, although it wasn't easy. As they walked in and saw the crowd of people waiting for tables, Phyllis hoped that Tess had thought to make a reservation.

Phyllis looked past the hostess into the restaurant and saw a familiar blond-haired figure sitting in a corner booth. She lifted a hand and caught Tess's eye. Tess returned the wave.

"How many?" the hostess asked. "And I'll need your name."

"There are two of us," Sam said, "but we're meetin' that lady over yonder in the corner."

When Sam pointed her out, Tess waved again and nodded to the hostess, who said, "All right, follow me, then."

She led them over to the booth, where Phyllis slid in first, opposite Tess, and Sam followed. "It's good to see you both again," Tess said. "Even though I didn't really expect to when I left your house the other day."

The restaurant was crowded and noisy, and a football game was playing on the big-screen TV that dominated the horseshoe-shaped bar area. Phyllis had no trouble understanding what Tess said, though.

A server came up to the table and got their drink orders— water for Phyllis, decaf coffee for Sam—and then Phyllis said, "I certainly didn't expect that you'd still be here in Weatherford. If you don't mind my asking, why haven't you gone back to New Orleans? Of course, it's none of my business—"

"No, no, that's all right," Tess said with a smile. "I don't have any pressing cases at the moment, and so much of my work is done on the computer, it doesn't really matter where I am most of the time, as long as I've got a fast Internet connection. I don't mind admitting, I'm curious to see how all this is going to play out, so I thought I'd hang around for a while."

"By all this, you mean Eve being charged with Roy's murder?" Phyllis asked.

"I don't mean to be insensitive about it. It's just that I was on his trail for so long. And then when I finally do find him, he's dead. I thought going to the funeral would give me a sense of—I don't know—closure, but it really didn't."

Sam said, "Maybe that's because you're a detective, and you've got your doubts about whether or not Eve really killed him. I'd think that'd bother somebody whose job is gettin' to the truth."

"You may be onto something there, Mr. Fletcher," Tess admitted. "But why would I have any doubts about whether your friend killed him? The district attorney certainly doesn't seem to have any."

"Timothy Sullivan is a horse's patoot. You can't go by what he thinks."

"What about the evidence, then?" Tess said.

Phyllis said, "It's circumstantial. The murder weapon belongs to Eve, and she doesn't have an alibi. No one has come forward to offer testimony that would put her on the scene at the time of Roy's murder, and until you showed up, no one had any reason to think that she might have a motive."

"But they do now," Tess said.

"If Eve has a motive, so do those other women."

Tess leaned back against the upholstered bench seat on her side of the booth. "And that's why we're here, isn't it? To talk about those other women you claim were victims of the man you knew as Roy Porter?"

"They had as much reason to want him dead as Eve did," Phyllis said. "More, really, because they knew what he had done to them. Eve didn't know what he was planning to do to her."

"You have only her word for that."

"That's enough for me," Phyllis said.

"And me," Sam added.

"That's all well and good but—"

Tess stopped as the server brought the drinks and then asked if they were ready to order. Phyllis hadn't even glanced at her menu, but she had eaten here before and knew what she liked. She ordered and so did Sam. Tess had looked at her menu before Phyllis and Sam arrived and knew what she wanted, too.

When the server was gone, Tess went on. "You know that ethically I still can't tell you anything about my clients, don't you?"

"Not even to confirm that Alice Jessup and Ingrid Pitt are two of the women you were working for?"

"I've never heard of Alice Jessup before in my life," Tess said.

"What about Ingrid Pitt?"

Tess's lips thinned. She didn't say anything.

"So I was only half right," Phyllis said. "Well, Alice Jessup was a long shot, anyway. But all three of us know that Ingrid Pitt used to be Ingrid Olsen Callahan, and that she was married to a man calling himself Monte Callahan who stole a considerable amount of money from her, ten years ago in Minneapolis, and then disappeared."

Tess sighed and said, "All right, I guess it doesn't make any sense to deny it. I didn't know anything about her being here in Weatherford, though. I was shocked when you told me."

"You didn't tell her this is where Roy was?"

"I sent reports to all my clients after the funeral, like I told you I was going to."

Phyllis shook her head. "That's not answering the question. Ingrid and her new husband were here *before* Roy was murdered. Why?"

Tess was starting to look angry now. She said, "I don't think we're going to be able to talk about this."

"I think that when you believed you had located Roy, you let something slip before you were able to confirm that he was the man you were looking for," Phyllis pressed. "You told Ingrid the name you believed he was using and that you thought he was here. The sheriff's department can find out from the Delaneys exactly when Frank and Ingrid Pitt made their reservations and arrived at the bed-and-breakfast."

Tess glared across the table for a couple of seconds, then, surprisingly, let out a laugh. "I have to say, Mrs. Newsom, you're as sharp as all those newspaper articles I read made you out to be. I'm not surprised you've been able to solve murders in the past. You wouldn't be interested in doing some consulting work as a PI, would you?"

As always, being praised didn't sit that well with Phyllis, especially being praised for her detective skills. She said, "All I'm interested in is finding out who really killed Roy Porter, because I know good and well Eve didn't."

"Maybe you're right," Tess admitted with a shrug. "And I hate to think about it, but maybe it's my fault."

"What do you mean by that?"

Tess sighed and shook her head. "Ingrid Pitt isn't the only one I told."

Chapter 25

A couple of servers arrived then with their food, so they stopped discussing the case until after the man and woman had placed their plates in front of them, asked if they needed anything else, and then went away.

When they had some measure of privacy again, Phyllis leaned forward and asked, "What do you mean, Ingrid isn't the only one you told?"

A look of dismay had appeared on Tess's face. "Look, I know it was unprofessional," she said, "but I was so excited about finally having a lead to the man I was after that I shared what I'd found with several of the clients I'd grown close to. If you'd heard these women's stories and seen the damage that man did to some of them—" She stopped and shook her head. "But that still doesn't excuse what I did. These things have to go through proper channels. I should have turned over the evidence I had to the authorities, let them arrest the man, and then reported to my clients . . . *all* my clients . . . instead of getting ahead of myself with some of them."

Excitement gripped Phyllis. "How many clients are we talking about?"

Now that Tess had revealed as much as she had, she must have thought there was no longer any point in being reluctant to answer. "Four," she said. "Counting Ingrid."

"Then that means there are four people who knew where Roy was and had a reason to want him dead."

"Maybe more than that," Sam put in. "This lady Ingrid was married. Some of the others may have been, too. I know if I found myself face-to-face with somebody who'd hurt my wife that bad, I'd be liable to do somethin' I'd regret. Or if I was mad enough, I might not regret it at all."

Phyllis nodded. "That's right. There could be half a dozen or more likely suspects that the authorities don't know anything about. You *have* to tell them, Ms. Coburn."

"And risk losing my PI license for ethical misconduct?" Tess said.

"The threat that's hanging over Eve's head is a lot worse than that," Phyllis said.

She and Tess looked intently at each other over the table. After a moment, Sam said, "There's been a whole lot to think about spilled out here in the last few minutes. We don't want our food to get cold, so why don't we eat while we mull it all over for a little while?"

Phyllis wasn't particularly hungry anymore. She didn't want Eve having to live with that cloud of suspicion over her head for even one minute longer than was necessary.

And yet she didn't know anything that would point the

finger of guilt at anyone else, she realized. Yes, the women Tess had unwisely told where they could find Roy had to be considered suspects, but that was all they were. It would be better in the long run if Phyllis knew exactly which one of them—or which of their husbands—had shoved that letter opener in Roy's throat. She would stand a better chance of doing that if she didn't make an enemy out of Tess Coburn.

So she took a deep breath and said, "I agree with Sam. We're getting carried away here. We need to stop and settle down, and then we can hash all this out."

The tension on Tess's face eased, too. "You're right." She managed to smile. "Hey, the food here's not great, but even so, we don't want to waste it, do we?"

For the next few minutes they ate in near silence, speaking up only to say inconsequential things about the meal or the weather. Finally Phyllis said, "You know, I was thinking. There's really no reason why we can't—"

"Work together," Tess finished for her. "Does this mean you're accepting my offer?"

"I was about to say there's no reason we can't work together, as you guessed," Phyllis said. "That doesn't mean I'd be working for you. And it would only be for this case."

Tess held up both hands. "I know, I know. Sometimes I try to be funny, but I don't have the greatest sense of humor in the world." Her expression grew more solemn. "But here's what rubs me the wrong way. Sure, I should've been more discreet about what I told those ladies. But that doesn't excuse one of them killing the guy, if that's what happened. You're right, Mr. Fletcher, I want the truth. I guess that's why I became a detective in the first place."

"I figured as much," Sam said. "Just like I figured the two of you ladies ought to be workin' together instead of against each other."

"Oh, I'm not totally altruistic. I'll stand a better chance of not losing my license if I can pinpoint Roy Porter's killer."

"I guess we should start by sharing information," Phyllis said. She paused, then took the plunge. "I think there's a chance either Jan or Pete Delaney could have killed Roy."

Tess's eyes widened in surprise. "The people who run the bed-and-breakfast? Why, other than the fact that they were on the scene?"

Phyllis went through the scenario she had developed in her head after she and Sam had visited the bed-and-breakfast that morning. Tess listened intently, nodding every now and then as if agreeing with one of Phyllis's points.

"It certainly sounds plausible," she said when Phyllis was finished. "But it's the sort of thing that Mrs. Porter's attorney could use during the trial. If she could get Mrs. Delaney on the stand and press her about this pass Porter supposedly made at her, there's no telling what might come out."

"Maybe not," Phyllis said, "but I don't want to wait that long. I don't want the case to ever get to the trial stage. Eve needs to be cleared before it goes that far."

"Ideally, yes. But so far, all we're talking about is material to create reasonable doubt."

"That's what it keeps coming back to," Phyllis said with a sigh. "We need something more concrete."

Tess smiled. "Hey, we're just getting started here. There's plenty for us to look into. Who knows what we'll find?"

"Here's something that Sam brought up earlier. Ingrid Pitt

was staying at the bed-and-breakfast. Roy must have seen her. Why didn't he recognize her?"

"That one I can answer," Tess said. "Have you ever seen Ingrid, or a photo of her?"

"I saw the wedding photo from when she married Frank Pitt."

"Ten years ago she looked a lot different. Her hair was longer, all the way down her back, in fact, when she wasn't wearing it in a braid. She looked like one of those Norse Valkyries."

"The choosers of the slain," Sam murmured.

"Exactly. Also, she looked a good ten years younger than she really was. I didn't know her then, of course, but I've seen pictures of her. Now her hair is short and gray and she looks ten years older than she really is."

"But if Roy was introduced to her, he would have heard her name . . ." Phyllis's voice trailed off for a second before she went on, "Which is Ingrid Pitt now, of course. That's the only name he would know her by."

"And while Ingrid isn't the most common name in the world, by any means, it's not so unusual that he would automatically think an Ingrid he ran into in Texas was the same person as the woman he'd married and conned ten years ago in Minneapolis."

"You're right," Sam said. "Still, she was runnin' quite a risk by stalkin' him like that."

Phyllis said, "Not really. She hadn't done anything illegal then. Even if Roy recognized her, he wouldn't be very likely to blurt out that he'd married her and stolen that money from her."

"No, he would have kept quiet," Tess said, "and hoped that *she* didn't recognize *him*, and that her being there was just a wild coincidence."

"Wouldn't he have gotten a mite suspicious if she came to his room while Eve wasn't there?" Sam asked.

"Probably, but what could he do but talk to her?" Phyllis said. "He had to try to talk her out of reporting him to the police." She shook her head. "Let's face it. He'd been talking women into doing what he wanted for at least twenty years. He had to be confident enough to at least try to smooth things over with Ingrid."

"That's assumin' she even came to his room," Sam pointed out.

"And we don't know that she's the one who did," Tess said. "It could have been one of the others, someone who wasn't bold enough to actually stay there at the bed-and-breakfast with him but finally got up the nerve to confront him."

Phyllis nodded. "That's right. Who were the other three women?"

Tess hesitated. She took a sip of the margarita that had been on the table when Phyllis and Sam got there, then said, "I really would be breaking confidentiality if I told you that. You knew Ingrid Pitt's connection to Porter already."

"Yes, but we're working together now, remember? And our goal is the same, to find out what really happened."

"What if what really happened is that your friend killed him when she found out what he was planning to do?"

"No," Phyllis said flatly. "That's impossible. Eve would have left him, but she wouldn't hurt him."

"I know that's what you want to believe, but if we dig into

this, the facts are going to lead us where they lead us. And if they prove that Eve Porter is the only one who could have killed him, then so be it. I'm not whitewashing anything." Tess took another drink. "Now, are you sure you want to work together?"

Phyllis looked at Sam, then back at Tess. She gave the younger woman an emphatic nod. "Eve is innocent, and I'll prove it with or without your help, Ms. Coburn."

"All right. But if we're going to be working together . . . you really ought to call me Tess."

"I suppose I can do that," Phyllis allowed. "Now, what about those other three women?"

"Let's finish our food," Tess suggested. "Then I'll fill you in on everything I know."

Chapter 26

The three of them had barely finished their food when the server showed up to ask them if they wanted anything else. Phyllis and Tess shook their heads, and Sam said, "I think we're fine."

The young woman laid the leather folder containing their bill on the table. "I'll be your cashier whenever you're ready," she said. "Let me get those empty plates out of your way."

When the server was gone, Sam said, "She's not gonna come right out and ask us to leave, but I think they want the table."

"Of course they do, as busy as they are tonight," Tess said. She started to reach for the bill. "I'll get this—"

Sam laid his hand on top of the folder first. "Nope. I got it. When a fella has dinner with two charmin' ladies, it's only right that he pays."

Tess shrugged. "I never argue when somebody wants to buy me a meal. But we'll have to go somewhere else to talk about the case. My hotel is close by."

Phyllis nodded and said, "That's all right. We'll follow you there."

Sam put enough cash to cover the bill and a decent tip in the folder and left it on the table. He slid out of the booth and held out an arm to indicate that Phyllis and Tess should go first.

When they reached the parking lot after being in the warm, crowded restaurant, the cold air felt chillier than it really was. Tess pointed to a car and said, "That's mine."

"Lead the way," Sam said. "We'll be right behind you."

Like the restaurant, the hotel was part of a chain and offered only suites. It was located just half a mile from the restaurant along the highway's frontage road, so it didn't take long to get there.

"Have a seat," Tess said as she led them into the suite's sitting room. "Can I get you something to drink?"

Phyllis shook her head and said, "No, I think we should get right down to work."

"I agree." Tess went to the desk where her laptop computer sat closed. As she opened the computer, she said, "Let me call up my files."

Phyllis and Sam sat on the room's love seat. It took only moments for Tess to have several windows open on the laptop's screen.

"I can e-mail these files to you if you want," she offered, "but for now, here's the information you wanted. The other women I told about Roy Porter were Becky Tuttle, Samantha Hogan, and Mary McLaren."

Phyllis took a small notebook and a pen from her purse and made a note of the names. "Those three and Ingrid Pitt, right?"

Tess nodded. "Right."

"Any of them married?" Sam asked.

"Becky and Samantha are. Like Ingrid, they were able to get their marriages to Roy annulled on the grounds that the unions were fraudulent. Mary did, too, but she never married again."

Phyllis said, "So that's two more husbands who might have wanted revenge for what happened to their wives, even though they never met Roy."

"Yes, I suppose we have to include them as potential suspects, too," Tess agreed.

"I assume you know where they are?"

"Roy—I guess we might as well call him that—worked a lot in the South and Midwest. Mary lives in Arkansas, Becky in Iowa, and Samantha in Illinois."

"We'll need to check alibis for all of them, find out if they took a trip to Texas recently."

"That may not be easy to do," Tess said. "I can try checking with the airlines. I have some sources that might be able to get me that information. It won't be cheap, though."

"I'll cover your time and expenses," Phyllis said.

Tess smiled. "Maybe it would be better if I was working for Mrs. Porter. Do you think she'd be agreeable to that?"

"I can't speak for Eve," Phyllis said. "But you go ahead and do whatever you need to, and I'll make sure you don't lose any money on the deal."

"I don't really care that much," Tess muttered. "Like I said before, I just want to get to the truth."

"Why don't you tell us about the scams Roy pulled on those women?"

"You can take my word for it that they were pretty bad." Tess shrugged. "But since I've gone this far, it won't hurt to give you a few of the details, I guess."

The stories all had a depressingly similar ring to them: Charming, handsome man meets, romances, and marries wealthy, successful woman and manages, in one way or another, to get his hands on all of her money (or at least a significant chunk of it) before vanishing. The mechanics of the scams ranged from the simple—cleaning out joint bank accounts— to the more convoluted—setting up business deals with dummy companies that wound up funneling the loot into the con man's pockets. Clearly, the man they had known as Roy Porter was smart, ruthless, and cruel, Phyllis thought.

When Tess was finished, Sam said, "Well, I can see why somebody would want the fella dead. And what you've told us is just the tip of the iceberg, right?"

Tess nodded. "Yes, there's really no way of knowing how many times he pulled off variations of the same scheme. Like I told you, I've identified seventeen cases where I'm pretty sure the same man was behind them. There are bound to be more."

"If that's not reasonable doubt, I don't know what is," Phyllis said. "Unfortunately, that's all it is. We need to be able to do more than just point fingers and say, well, this woman or her husband *could* have done it."

"Let me work on that this weekend," Tess suggested. "I'll try to find out if any of those other three women have solid alibis. If they do, we can cross them off the list." She shook her head sympathetically. "I know you wanted to spare Mrs. Porter another court appearance, but it doesn't seem likely to me that we'll be able to come up with anything concrete before the arraignment Monday morning."

Phyllis sighed. "I know. Just do your best, and if there's anything Sam and I can do to help you, let us know."

"Actually, I'm very intrigued by what you told me about Jan and Pete Delaney," Tess said. "I have to say, I'm not surprised that the man we're calling Roy made advances toward Mrs. Delaney. He's used to getting what he wants from women with impunity, you know."

"Maybe I should go back out there and talk to Jan again," Phyllis suggested. "And while I'm doing that, I can find out if Frank and Ingrid Pitt are still staying there, or if they've gone back to Dallas."

"Good idea," Tess agreed with a nod. "You can probably handle that better than I can, since she already knows you."

Phyllis laughed. "I know you can handle all that computer work better than I can."

"Just be careful," Tess said. "From what I've read about you, you've been in some pretty risky situations when you started closing in on a killer."

"It's nothing I can't handle," Phyllis said.

"And I'm usually with her," Sam added.

Of course, that was one of the things Phyllis worried about. She didn't like the way Sam had wound up in danger on more than one occasion because of her investigations.

But as long as she knew going in that she might be dealing with a killer, she could take the proper precautions.

"We'll stay in touch," Tess said. "You've got my cell phone number. You might want to give me yours."

Phyllis did, and Sam gave Tess his number as well. She entered them into her phone.

"Here's to finding the truth," she said as Phyllis and Sam were about to leave. "Whatever it may be."

Phyllis nodded, although she knew what Tess meant. But there was no way Eve might be guilty, and Phyllis knew that, too.

"Seems like a pretty smart young woman," Sam commented as they drove away from the hotel. They would have to loop around to get to the other side of the highway and head back to Phyllis's house.

"She appears to know what she's doing," Phyllis agreed. "I don't think I could do all those things on the computer that she does."

"We weren't born to it, like she was. It's harder to learn things when you're older. We're set in our ways, as the sayin' goes." Sam chuckled as he peered through the pickup's windshield at the cones of light ahead of the vehicle. "Although you seem to have done a good job of learnin' how to be a detective."

"I taught history all those years," Phyllis said. "That's nothing but cause and effect. Something happens and causes something else, and then you can look back on the effect and see how events reached that point."

As she said that, a frown formed on her forehead. She had seen the effect—Roy Porter's murder—and so far they had uncovered a number of different things that could have caused it. What was missing were the links between those causes and the end result.

And there was something else missing as well, an unanswered question that would tie everything together if she could just figure out what it was. An insistent feeling nagged at her that she already knew what the question was. She just didn't see its importance yet, and so she couldn't answer it.

But sooner or later she would, and then the picture would be complete, revealing Roy's killer. Phyllis had to believe that, or else the weight of this case might be too much for her to go forward.

"You goin' back out to the bed-and-breakfast tomorrow?" Sam asked, breaking into her thoughts.

"Yes, I think I will. Are you coming along?"

"You bet. I don't have anywhere else I need to be, or anywhere else I'd rather be, for that matter."

Phyllis leaned her head against his shoulder as he drove. "Thank you for dinner," she said.

"It was my pleasure. The company was good."

"You know, I couldn't stand Tess when we first met her. But I'm starting to like her. I think that she really does hope Eve turns out to be innocent."

"Yeah, I got the feelin' you two are gonna make a good team." Sam laughed again. "Somewhere out there in the night there's a murderer who thinks that he or she got away with it. But they don't know who they've got on their trail, and sooner or later they're gonna have a big surprise waitin' for 'em."

Chapter 27

After more than a week of cloudy weather, the overcast finally broke during the night, and Saturday morning dawned cold and clear. Phyllis was glad to see the sun again. She hoped it boded well for the visit she and Sam were going to pay to the Delaneys.

First, though, because the sunshine had put her in better spirits, she fixed a big breakfast. The delicious aromas of coffee, bacon, and crumbled-pecan-topped banana muffins soon filled the house and inevitably drew the other inhabitants down from upstairs, including Eve.

"Somethin' smells mighty good," Sam said as he was the first into the kitchen in his pajamas and robe.

"Well, you're certainly full of enthusiasm this morning, Phyllis," Carolyn added as she followed Sam into the room.

Eve was right behind her, saying, "My, I haven't been this hungry in days."

"I'm glad to hear it," Phyllis told her, "because I feel like cooking this morning. The coffee's ready. Everyone help yourself. I think I'm going to scramble some eggs to go with this bacon."

Soon all four of them were sitting at the kitchen table, eating and talking . . . and not about murder, either. For those few minutes, it was as if nothing had changed, and it felt wonderful to Phyllis.

But everything *had* changed, or at least it would if Eve was convicted of killing Roy. If that happened, there would never be any more moments like this one.

Phyllis had to prevent that. At almost any cost, she had to stop it.

They lingered over coffee, and when they were done, Eve said, "I feel so good this morning, I might go out and do a little shopping."

"I'll come with you," Carolyn volunteered immediately. "We've been cooped up in this house for too long." She glanced at Phyllis and Sam and added, "Some of us didn't go out on the town last night."

Phyllis wouldn't have called trying to solve Roy's murder going out on the town, but let Carolyn believe whatever she wanted to, she thought. Right now that was easier than trying to explain the theories they had come up with by talking to Tess Coburn.

"Sam and I have some errands to do, too," she said. "So it looks like we'll all be busy today."

"Busy is good," Sam said.

Before she got dressed, Phyllis looked out the front window at the thermometer on the porch. Twenty-two degrees, she thought with a little shiver. But the wind wasn't blowing very hard, and in the sun it would feel warmer, whether it really was or not. Her thick jacket and blue jeans would feel good anyway.

Sam offered to drive, and Phyllis agreed. The pickup's heater quickly warmed its cab as Sam piloted the vehicle west out of town on the interstate, then cut to the southwest on a smaller road that led through the rolling hills. It didn't take long to reach the drive of the Delaneys' bed-and-breakfast.

The gravel parking area was full, so Sam steered the pickup onto a grassy area next to it. Marks in the grass made it obvious that cars had been parked there in the past.

"Looks like they've got a full house," Sam commented. "Folks either don't know or don't care what happened here. They want their time off."

"I don't blame them," Phyllis said. "Back when we were working, I enjoyed every bit of vacation I could get."

Sam grinned. "Now we got vacation full-time, don't we?"

Phyllis supposed that, technically, he was right. They had no jobs, no real responsibilities other than those of day-to-day life. At times like this, though, she sure didn't feel like she was on vacation.

Quietly, she said, "If Pete is here, do you think you could distract him so that I can talk to Jan alone?"

"I can sure give it a try," Sam said with a nod.

They went onto the porch, and Phyllis knocked on the door. When it opened a moment later, Jan Delaney greeted them with a smile.

"Well, hey there," she said. "I didn't expect to see you two again. Certainly not this soon anyway." Her smile disappeared and she looked concerned instead. "Has something else happened with Eve?"

Phyllis shook her head and said, "No, other than the fact that her arraignment is scheduled for Monday morning."

Pete appeared behind Jan in time to hear what Phyllis said. He looked at her and Sam over Jan's shoulder and asked, "Then what brings you back out here?" He added, "Jan told me you already came to get those things we boxed up."

"Eve asked us to come." Phyllis didn't think they would bother to check up on that and find out she was lying. "She wanted to make sure there was no outstanding balance on her bill."

"Oh, goodness gracious," Jan said. "She could have just called about that if she was worried about it. But there was no reason to even be concerned. Roy paid for everything in advance. In fact, we probably ought to refund her some of what he paid, since they didn't stay here the whole time they had booked."

"I don't think that's necessary," Phyllis said. She was beginning to worry that the Delaneys were going to keep them standing on the porch for so long that they wouldn't have any excuse to stay.

Jan settled that, however, by saying, "You came all the way out here on a cold morning, so you at least ought to get a cup of coffee out of it. There's still some in the pot from breakfast. I have some apple fritters, too. Come on inside and warm up."

Pete didn't look particularly happy about that, but he wasn't going to uninvite them. He grunted and moved back as Jan held the door open for Phyllis and Sam to come in.

"Thank you," Phyllis said as they stepped into the warmth of the bed-and-breakfast.

"Come on out to the kitchen," Jan said. "We don't stand on ceremony here."

If she was a killer, she was one of the friendliest, sweetest murderers Phyllis had ever encountered. And of course, that was entirely possible, Phyllis reminded herself.

No one was in the parlor. As they went into the big kitchen, Phyllis said, "It looks like you have quite a few guests again."

"Yes, everyone's had breakfast and gone back upstairs, except for one couple. They're young and on their honeymoon, so they'll probably drag down later for coffee." Jan laughed. "They have to keep their strength up, you know."

"Are the Pitts and the Mitchums still here?"

Jan shook her head as she got cups and saucers from a cabinet. "No, they left yesterday. So did Alice Jessup. Everyone who's here came in yesterday evening. I guess that means everyone who was here when . . . when . . ."

"When Roy Porter was killed," Pete finished for her. "They're all gone now."

"Except for Pete and me, of course," Jan added.

"Yeah, but we don't count."

Phyllis wasn't completely convinced of that. Pete didn't seem nearly as friendly this morning. Was that because he was afraid that Phyllis was investigating Roy's murder? Did he have something to hide?

Jan poured the coffee for Phyllis and Sam and moved a plate of fritters from the counter to the table. "Sit down," she said. "Tell me how Eve's doing today."

"She's starting to get her appetite back and seem more like herself," Phyllis said. There was a glass container on the table with packets of sugar and artificial sweetener in it, along with a bowl full of individual creamers. She started fixing her coffee the way she liked it as she went on, "It's just a matter of time."

"Of course," Jan said with a nod from the chair where she'd sat down on the other side of the table. "She's had a lot of shocks. I just hope she doesn't have too many more."

"So do I," Phyllis said.

Sam took a sip of his coffee and picked up one of the fritters to take a bite. When he had swallowed, he said to Pete, "Your wife mentioned the other day that you'd been havin' some trouble with your water well."

"Yeah, the pressure switch has been acting up," Pete said. He seemed relieved to be talking about something other than Roy Porter's murder. "I've had to go out there and reset it several times lately. I just hope the pump's not fixing to go out."

"You know, I had a well where I used to live in Poolville, and I had to work on it quite a bit over the years." Sam chuckled. "Once, I was convinced that the pump needed to be replaced, so I set up an old metal swing set over the wellhead, put a block and tackle on it, and pulled the whole hundred and fifty feet of pipe out of the ground."

"By yourself?" Pete asked.

Sam shook his head. "No, I had a friend help me. Took most of a day to get that pump up, and when we did, it turned out there was nothin' wrong with it. Problem was actually in the wirin' in the well house. Fire ants had got into it. For some reason, those little varmints really like electricity."

"You know, I haven't checked the wiring," Pete said with a frown. "I was going to call the well-repair people the next time it gave trouble."

"No need to do that," Sam said as he waved a hand. "Let's go out there and take a look at it. They say you learn by foulin' things up, so I'd be glad to give you the benefit of my vast experience."

"Are you sure you don't mind? It's pretty cold out. Although I've got a heat bulb burning in the well house to keep it warm enough the pipes won't freeze on these nights the temperature gets so low."

"It'll be fine," Sam said. "Especially if I can take this coffee and fritter with me."

"Sure, come on," Pete said as he got to his feet. He led Sam out the back door.

When they were gone, Jan said, "Men are all alike, aren't they? They just love to piddle with things."

"Sam's pretty good with his hands," Phyllis said.

"That, too," Jan said.

Phyllis felt her face warming and tried to ignore it. Jan had given her an opportunity, though, so she took it.

With what she hoped was a serious, solemn expression on her face, she said, "I'm really sorry about what you had to go through with Roy. It must have really taken you by surprise and upset you when he . . . when he . . ."

"Put his hand on my butt and asked me to go upstairs with him when Eve wasn't here?" Jan nodded. "Oh, yeah. Not taken by surprise that much, really, because like I told you, I've had guests make passes at me before. But it did bother me, because I like Eve and I didn't want to think that she'd gone and married an old lech." She shrugged. "But hey, it wasn't really any of my business. I just moved his hand and told him as politely as I could that I didn't think it would be a good idea."

"How did he take that?"

"He kept flirting at first, saying that nobody would know and that I'd be surprised how much I would enjoy myself. I told him I had other things to do. He got the idea, and he didn't keep pushing, I'll give him a little bit of credit for that. He laughed it off and said I didn't know what I was missing."

"So he gave up?"

"For the time being," Jan said. "I remember thinking, though, that I wouldn't be surprised if he tried again." She shook her head. "But of course he never got the chance."

"Did you tell Pete what he'd done?"

"Why would I do that?" Jan asked with what appeared to be genuine puzzlement. "Nothing happened. Not really. Roy got a quick feel; that's all. Nothing to cause a big ruckus about."

Phyllis wondered if that meant Pete would have caused a big ruckus if he had known what Roy had done. And was it possible that Pete knew, even though Jan wasn't aware that he did? Phyllis decided that she couldn't rule that out.

"Well, you're more tolerant than I would be," she said.

"One thing you learn pretty quickly in this business," Jan said, "is that everybody has their own little eccentricities when it comes to romance. You learn not to pay attention to some of the things you hear . . . and some of the things that happen." The back door opened as she added, "So I didn't worry about Roy making a pass at me—"

Pete stepped inside in time to hear that, and when he did, his face instantly darkened with anger.

"Blast it, Jan!" he burst out. "She's interrogating you again! Didn't I warn you about this?"

Chapter 28

*J*an stood up, and so did Phyllis. "Pete, take it easy," Jan said. "We were just talking—"

"No, you weren't," he said. "She was asking you all sorts of questions, wasn't she? Just like the other day when they came out here snooping!"

"We just came out here that day to get Eve's things—," Phyllis began.

Pete took a step toward her. "And you took advantage of me not being here to meddle in things that are none of your business. The men from the sheriff's department warned us not to talk to anybody about what happened, but my wife just can't keep her big mouth shut!"

"Pete!" Jan said. "Stop it!"

"No, I won't. This old woman's just trying to play detective and get us in trouble. She'll do anything to help her friend, even if it means blaming somebody else for that murder, somebody who didn't have anything to do with it!"

Sam had followed Pete into the kitchen. He put a hand on Pete's shoulder and said, "Hey, amigo, you'd better settle down there—"

Pete jerked away from him and turned quickly, and for a second Phyllis thought he was going to throw a punch at Sam. From the way Sam tensed and got ready to meet the attack, he thought the same thing.

But Pete kept his clenched fists at his sides and went on, "And you, trying to act like my friend! Helping me out by taking a look at my well, when all you really wanted to do was get me out of here so this old biddy could ask her meddling questions!"

"Pete, that's enough!" Jan said. "I won't have you talking to our guests that way."

"They're not guests," he said. "They're detectives! Or at least in their deluded minds they think they are."

"Sam, I think we should go," Phyllis said.

Pete sneered at her. "I think you should go, too. In fact, get the hell out of here!"

"By God, mister—," Sam said. He moved toward Pete, and now he was the one who looked like he was going to start swinging.

Phyllis stepped quickly around Pete to intercept Sam. She grasped his arm and said, "Let's go."

She steered him around Pete, who stood there with his feet planted and an angry glare on his face. Jan stood by looking embarrassed and upset. She wasn't wringing her hands, but she might as well have been.

She started to follow Phyllis and Sam toward the front of the house as she said, "I'm so sorry about this—"

Pete grabbed her arm and jerked her to a halt, startling a little cry from her. "Just let them go," he said. "You've done enough damage already."

Sam opened the door and let them out. Phyllis glanced back over her shoulder and saw Jan's stricken face staring after them. Then Pete stomped up and slammed the door behind them.

They didn't say anything until they were back in the pickup. Then Phyllis said, "Well, he's certainly not as nice a man as I thought he was the first time I met him."

"Sometimes it's hard to tell about folks from the first impression they make," Sam said. "I think it's safe to say, though, that ol' Pete's the sort who flies off the handle pretty easy."

"You think he could lose his temper enough to stab somebody with a letter opener?"

"I wouldn't rule it out," Sam said as he sent the pickup back along the driveway toward the county road.

"The problem is that Jan claimed he didn't know Roy made that pass at her."

"Maybe he knew and she just didn't know it."

Phyllis nodded. "I thought about that. It's certainly possible. Not to change the subject, but Ingrid Pitt is gone."

"Yeah. If she came here to kill Roy, there was no reason for her to stay, was there?"

"But she didn't want to leave right after the murder because she was afraid that might make her look guilty. Assuming, of course, that she is guilty, which we don't know at all."

"We don't know she's not," Sam said. "If she did kill him, I think she missed a bet. She could've left right away, and I don't reckon anybody would have ever thought anything about it. After all, who wants to stay in a house where a murder's been committed?"

Phyllis nodded. "You're right. No one would have been suspicious of that." She paused. "I wonder if Tess has come up with anything on those other three women."

"Roy's previous victims, you mean?"

"That's right."

"You can call her and ask her."

"I will, later," Phyllis said. "If I haven't heard from her by then."

Eve and Carolyn were still gone when they got back to the house, so Sam went out to the garage to do some work while Phyllis got on the computer and searched for any record of Pete Delaney being in trouble for losing his temper in the past. Bar fights, assaults, anything along those lines.

There was nothing, of course. She had searched for such things before, with no luck. Pete might be the type to lose his temper easily, but evidently he had kept it under control enough that he'd never landed in the newspapers because of it.

If things were different, she thought, she could ask Mike to check and find out if Pete had ever been arrested. Under the current circumstances, that wasn't going to happen.

Tess Coburn called a little before noon. "I've spoken to Becky Tuttle, Samantha Hogan, and Mary McLaren," she said. "All three of them claim they haven't been anywhere near Texas."

"Can they prove that?" Phyllis asked.

Tess hesitated, then said, "I'm not really in a position where I can ask them for alibis, Phyllis. They were clients, and now the job is over, and they don't even have to talk to me if they don't want to."

"I know that. But I thought maybe you'd be able to work around to the subject . . ."

Tess laughed and said, "Give me a little credit. That's exactly what I did. Becky and Samantha talked about the things they'd been doing with their families, so I think we can be pretty sure they weren't flying down here to murder Roy Porter. The things they told me would be too easy to check. It's a little more difficult with Mary, since she's not married and lives alone. I just had to take her word for it."

"Did any of them seem suspicious that you were calling?" Phyllis asked. "Like you said, they're not really your clients anymore . . ."

"No, they're not, but we became friends, too, while I was working for them. It's hard not to form some sort of bond when these women are telling you everything they went through because of that man, all the emotional turmoil."

Phyllis heard Tess pause and take a deep breath.

"You know, one of my clients was actually the daughter of one of Roy's marks. The victim herself couldn't hire me because she was dead. She'd been a widow for a number of years when she met Roy. According to her daughter, it wasn't really the money he stole from her that was so devastating; it was the broken heart. The poor woman thought she'd never fall in love again, and then she did, and it all turned out to be a lie. She took a bottle of sleeping pills and killed herself." Tess sighed. "If you ask me, that's almost the same thing as murder right there. Roy Porter killed that poor woman, just as surely as if he'd poured those pills down her throat."

232 · LIVIA J. WASHBURN

"I agree," Phyllis said, shaken a little by what Tess had just told her. But shaken or not, her brain was still working. "What about the daughter?"

"What?"

"The daughter of the woman who killed herself. Is it possible *she* could have wanted revenge on Roy?"

"Well, sure. Wouldn't you? But it's a long way from, say, wishing somebody would drop dead to actually making it happen. The other problem with considering her a suspect is that I never told her where Roy was."

"Oh." Phyllis tried not to feel too deflated. For a moment there, she'd thought they might be on the trail of another lead. It was looking more and more like they weren't going to be able to find the real killer. They had plenty of theories but absolutely no proof. The only real evidence was still the murder weapon itself, and that pointed only to Eve.

"Don't get too discouraged," Tess said. "We still have several suspects, and I'm not through digging. I'm just sorry this isn't going fast enough to keep Eve from having to go through the arraignment."

"You're doing your best," Phyllis said. "I know that. And at least we have something for Juliette to work with during the trial, if it comes down to that."

With a note of heartiness in her voice, Tess said, "We won't let it come to that. Hey, we're like Miss Marple and Kinsey Millhone. We'll find the truth."

"I hope you're right," Phyllis said.

After she was off the phone with Tess, she started making tuna sandwiches for lunch. Since she didn't know exactly when Carolyn and Eve would be back, those would be good to put in the refrigerator so there would be something for them to eat whenever they got there.

Sam came into the kitchen from the garage. "I heard the phone ring a while ago," he said. "Good news?"

"Not really. It was Tess, all right, but she didn't have anything to report except that we can probably cross off two of those other women from our list of suspects."

"What about the third one?"

"She claims not to have been down here in Texas, but she's not married and she lives alone, so Tess was less inclined to accept what she said at face value. It would have been easier for her to lie."

"So we're left with Eve, Ingrid Pitt, and the Delaneys as viable suspects?"

Phyllis nodded. "That's the way it seems to me."

"Well, maybe that'll be enough for an acquittal."

"I don't *want* an acquittal," Phyllis said.

Sam nodded. "I know. You want Eve's name cleared, once and for all. But this may be one case where we have to take what we can get, and havin' her not be in prison is a whole heck of a lot better than the alternative."

"She might not go to prison even if she was convicted," Phyllis said. "When you consider her age and the fact that Roy was planning to swindle her, a jury might easily decide to give her probation . . ."

Phyllis's voice trailed off as she realized what she was saying. She shouldn't even be considering the possibility that Eve would be found guilty, she told herself, let alone trying to figure out what a jury might do when it came time for passing sentence.

But Sam was right. It might come to that. And if it did, they would just have to hope for the best.

Right now, though, Phyllis felt as helpless as she ever had in her life.

And she didn't like that feeling. Not one bit.

Chapter 29

*T*he rest of the day passed quietly on Saturday. Carolyn and Eve came back to the house in the early afternoon after their shopping trip. Eve had quite a few bags with her, while Carolyn didn't have any. That wasn't unusual. Eve had always been the most extravagant shopper among them. Phyllis supposed that was natural enough, since Eve had all those millions in the bank that none of them had known about. Right now, though, Phyllis considered it a good sign that Eve felt like going out and spending money again.

Sunday was equally uneventful. The only thing that really changed was that the wind turned around to the south and the cold snap broke. The temperature warmed well above freezing, and the forecast predicted that Monday would be even nicer . . . at least where the weather was concerned.

Phyllis didn't think there was anything nice about Eve having to go to court.

Juliette called that evening to remind them to be at the

courthouse at eight thirty the next morning, as if they would forget anything that important, Phyllis thought. Maybe after the arraignment she could sit down with the lawyer and fill her in on everything that she and Tess had found out. Juliette needed the information about the other possible suspects in order to start formulating a defense for Eve.

Even though the weather had improved, there was still a chilly wind blowing as the four of them climbed the court-house steps the next morning shortly before eight thirty. Juliette was waiting for them just inside the lobby, looking as trim and efficient as ever.

"Let's sit down," she said as she nodded toward a couple of benches along one wall. "I'll go over everything that's going to happen this morning."

Eve sat next to Juliette, with Carolyn on her other side. Phyllis and Sam took the other bench, which was close enough for them to hear everything Juliette said.

"There are a number of cases being arraigned this morning, but yours should be one of the first. It wouldn't surprise me if Sullivan managed to get it first in line. He won't want the press sitting around getting bored with the tedium of going through other cases. And trust me, it *is* tedious."

Carolyn said, "I still don't understand how the man thinks that persecuting someone like Eve will help him get reelected."

"A murder conviction is a murder conviction, no matter who the defendant is," Juliette said. "And by next November, a lot of the voters won't remember the details of the case. They'll just remember that Sullivan won. That's what he's counting on, anyway."

It would certainly be nice to mess up those plans of District Attorney Sullivan's, Phyllis thought.

"The proceedings this morning shouldn't take long," Juliette went on. "The clerk will read the charge, and the judge will ask how you plead."

"Not guilty, of course," Eve said.

Juliette nodded. "That's right. The clerk will enter your plea, and the judge will bind the case over for a grand jury hearing next month. Sullivan will want to get to this one as soon as he can." She paused. "There's one more thing. It's possible he'll ask the judge to revoke bail. I think the odds of him doing that are small, and even if he does, the odds of the judge granting the request are even smaller. But I don't want you to be surprised if it does happen."

"I haven't gone on the lam so far," Eve said. "I don't think I'm likely to now."

Juliette smiled. "If it comes up, I may ask you to repeat that for the judge."

"Will it be the same one who did the bail hearing?"

"No, we'll be in Judge Schumacher's court this morning. She can be pretty tough, but she follows the law."

"She?" Carolyn said.

"Don't think that'll make any difference in how she rules," Juliette warned.

"But being a woman, she might understand what sort of man Roy really was," Carolyn persisted.

Juliette shook her head. "I wouldn't even play the gender card. Trust me on this."

"I do, dear," Eve said. "My fate is in your hands."

"No pressure there," Sam said.

"It's going to be all right," Juliette said. "We'll just take everything one step at a time."

It was close enough now to nine o'clock to go upstairs. They took the elevator to the second floor this time, and Juliette led them down the hall to the courtroom. The corridor was fairly crowded. For the most part, it was easy to separate the lawyers in their conservative suits from the more casually dressed defendants they were there to represent.

There were also several reporters on hand. When they started toward Eve, Juliette shook her head, held up a hand, and said, "No comment." She ushered Eve past them through the doors of the courtroom.

When they went inside, Phyllis saw that Timothy Sullivan was already at the prosecution table with one of his assistants. There was no way he was going to let an underling handle any of this case, she thought. That was an indication that Eve's case would be the first on the docket.

Phyllis would have been willing to bet that Sullivan hadn't told the reporters, "No comment," when they asked him about the case.

Phyllis, Sam, and Carolyn took seats in the second row of spectator benches while Eve and Juliette went to the defense table. Juliette gave Sullivan a polite smile and a perfunctory nod. He returned the nod but not the smile. Eve didn't look at him.

Phyllis expected Judge Schumacher to be a few minutes late, as Judge Hemmerson had been at the bail hearing. However, when the clock on the wall indicated that it was exactly nine o'clock, a door at the side of the room opened and the clerk came in, followed by the bailiff. The bailiff looked back over his shoulder as if checking to make sure he should go ahead, then told those in the courtroom, "All rise."

The judge was a middle-aged woman with graying blond hair. When she had taken her seat behind the bench, the bailiff told everyone else to be seated, too. When the hubbub from that had quieted down, Judge Schumacher said, "Good morning. The clerk will read the first case."

From her desk, the clerk gave a case number, then said, "The State of Texas versus Eve Porter."

"Is Eve Porter here?" the judge asked . . . even though she probably knew good and well who Eve was and could see her there at the defense table a dozen feet away, Phyllis thought.

Eve and Juliette both stood up. "Juliette Yorke representing Mrs. Porter, Your Honor."

Judge Schumacher nodded to the clerk and said, "Read the charge."

The clerk said, "In the matter of the State of Texas versus Eve Porter, the defendant is charged with murder in the second degree, a felony."

"How do you plead to this charge, Mrs. Porter?" the judge asked.

Phyllis saw that Eve's hands were trembling just a little. It must have been quite an ordeal for her, having to stand up there and listen to the clerk read the charge. Juliette must have noticed the trembling, too. She put a hand lightly on Eve's arm.

Then Eve lifted her head, squared her shoulders, and said in the same sort of loud, clear voice she had used for years in her classroom, "Not guilty, Your Honor."

At that moment, Phyllis was extremely proud of her.

"Very well," the judge said. "Your plea will be entered, and your case will go before the grand jury in its next scheduled session. Mr. Sullivan, do you have anything?"

This was the moment where things might take a bad turn, Phyllis recalled. The district attorney could ask that Eve's bail be revoked, and even though Juliette thought that was unlikely, the mere possibility of it was enough to make Phyllis worry. The way Carolyn had her hands clasped tightly together in her lap told Phyllis that she was worried, too. Even Sam's customary nonchalant demeanor had vanished as he sat stiff and straight on the hard wooden bench.

Sullivan took his time getting to his feet. He had to know that all eyes in the room were on him, and he probably enjoyed the feeling. He leaned slightly forward, rested his fingertips on the table, and shook his head.

"Nothing, Your Honor."

Schumacher nodded. "Very well. We'll move on to the next case."

Phyllis managed not to heave an audible sigh of relief. Eve was still free on bail, and that wasn't going to change. She could continue living at the house while Phyllis, Sam, and Tess Coburn continued working to clear her name. Even though this court appearance hadn't been pleasant, it hadn't been too bad, either, and now some of the pressure was off for a while.

As much as the pressure could be off while Eve was still facing a murder charge, Phyllis reminded herself.

Eve and Juliette left the defense table and came through the gate in the railing to join them as Phyllis, Sam, and Carolyn got to their feet.

"Is that it?" Carolyn asked.

"That's it," Juliette said. "We can all go now."

They left the courtroom and stepped out into the crowded hallway. "Now what?" Eve asked.

"Now we keep working on your defense," Juliette said. "There's a chance the grand jury will decline to indict you on the charge, but I seriously doubt that's going to happen unless we can come up with some new evidence between now and then."

That was where she came in, Phyllis told herself, because the authorities certainly weren't going to continue investigating. They had already done their job, at least to their way of thinking.

Once again telling the reporters that she and her client had no comment, Juliette began leading the way through the crowd. It thinned out the farther away they got from the courtroom. They headed for the elevators, which were beyond the landing where the staircase with its brass banisters led up from the first floor.

A couple of sheriff's deputies stood near that landing, blocking their path, and as the group approached, Timothy Sullivan appeared from somewhere and joined the deputies. Phyllis frowned as she saw Sullivan speak to the deputies and nod toward them.

Neither of the uniformed men looked happy about being here, and that made the concern Phyllis suddenly felt increase even more. Then Sullivan stepped out in front of the deputies to confront Phyllis and the others as they came to a stop.

"What's going on here?" Juliette asked.

Sullivan ignored her. He said, "Mrs. Newsom, I have to ask you to go with these officers."

Phyllis's heart thudded heavily in her chest, and she seemed to hear the blood roaring in her head. Despite that, she was able to maintain a calm tone as she asked, "Why should I do that?"

The district attorney couldn't keep a smile off his face as he said, "Because you're under arrest."

Chapter 30

Even though Phyllis had a pretty good idea, in those brief few seconds before Sullivan spoke, of what the district attorney was going to say, his words still came as a shock to her. She stood there in silence while Carolyn exclaimed, "Under arrest!" loudly enough to make everyone in the hallway stop talking and turn to look at them.

Juliette moved in front of Phyllis, shielding her from Sullivan and the deputies, and asked sharply, "What are the charges?"

"Obstruction of justice and interfering with an investigation, to start with," Sullivan said. "More charges may be forthcoming once we've looked further into the matter."

"Into what matter?"

Sullivan turned his narrow-eyed gaze on her. "Are you representing Mrs. Newsom, counselor?"

Juliette looked back at Phyllis, who gave her a curt nod. Phyllis didn't really trust herself to speak right now, so she was very glad Juliette was here.

"I am," Juliette told Sullivan.

"Then I suggest when you have a chance to talk to your client again, you ask her what she's been doing to get herself arrested." Sullivan motioned to the deputies. "Take her into custody."

Both men looked like they would rather be anywhere else in the world right now, but they had no choice except to do as the district attorney ordered them. One of them, a beefy young man who looked vaguely familiar, said, "I'm sorry, ma'am, but you'll have to come along with us."

"Chuck Murphy?" Phyllis asked. The name had popped into her head.

The deputy winced. "Yes, ma'am."

"You were in my class, what, fifteen years ago?"

"Seventeen, ma'am."

"That's enough," Sullivan said. "This isn't a junior high re-union. Arrest her."

"We're trying to, . . . sir," Chuck said.

"This is crazy," Sam said. "Phyllis hasn't broken any laws."

Sullivan sniffed in disdain. "That'll be up to a judge and jury to decide."

Eve said, "And it'll be up to the public to decide whether you're a decent district attorney, dear, or just a bully who likes to terrorize innocent old ladies."

Sullivan's face darkened. "You can't—"

"A citizen still has a right to express an opinion," Juliette interrupted him. She nodded toward the reporters who stood nearby, writing furiously in their notebooks. "And the public has a right to know what their elected officials are doing."

"You must've wanted a spectacle, mister," Sam said in a hard voice. "Well, you've got one."

"Get her out of here," Sullivan snapped at Chuck Murphy and the other deputy.

From somewhere, Phyllis mustered up the strength to put a smile on her face as she told the deputies, loud enough for the reporters to hear every word, "Don't worry, gentlemen. I won't put up a fight."

Sam let out a bray of laughter. Most of the other people looking on in the hallway joined in. That made Sullivan flush even more. He turned on his heel and stalked away.

"Go with the deputies, Mrs. Newsom," Juliette said. "I'll be there as soon as I can."

"Go ahead now, dear," Eve told her. "We're done here, aren't we?"

Juliette nodded. "I'll be at the jail before you are," she promised Phyllis.

"And we'll be right behind her," Carolyn added. "We'll have you bailed out in no time."

Phyllis hoped that was the case. She had no desire to spend any more time behind bars than necessary.

Chuck gestured toward the stairs. "If you'll come with us . . . or we can use the elevator . . ."

"The stairs are fine," Phyllis said. "Aren't you supposed to handcuff me?"

Chuck winced again. "I think we can dispense with that." He looked at the other deputy. "Don't you agree, Carl?"

Carl shrugged his acceptance of the decision.

"Are you sure?" Phyllis asked. "I wouldn't want you to get in trouble."

"You didn't seem to feel that way when you were sending me to the principal's office every other week," Chuck said, but the grin on his face told Phyllis that he didn't hold a grudge against her for that.

"That's because you were only capable of behaving yourself for a week at a time," she told him. "You were too fond of making the other students in class laugh and not interested enough in your schoolwork."

"Yeah, that's the truth. I've, uh, gotten to be less of a troublemaker since then."

"I should hope so."

"And your son, Mike, is a buddy of mine, so I wish they'd given this job to somebody else!"

"I don't," Phyllis said. "I'm glad that if someone had to arrest me, it was you, Deputy Murphy."

They had reached the bottom of the stairs. The reporters were following them. District Attorney Sullivan had disappeared somewhere, probably to his office, until the hullabaloo of Phyllis's arrest died down. She wasn't sure how he had expected everything to play out, but obviously it hadn't gone exactly the way he'd intended.

Now that she'd had a chance to calm down and think it over, Phyllis had a pretty good idea why Sullivan had had her arrested. Pete Delaney must have contacted the district attorney and told him that she and Sam had been out at the bed-and-breakfast asking questions about Roy's murder. Sullivan had passed the word through Sheriff Haney and Mike that he wasn't going to stand for any more amateur investigations.

Phyllis doubted that he could make the charges against her stick. He might even drop them before things went any further. He'd just wanted this arrest to send a message to her.

Well, she had gotten that message loud and clear, she

thought as the two deputies took her outside, put her in the backseat of a sheriff's department car, and started toward the jail with Carl behind the wheel and Chuck in the passenger seat. But she wasn't scared anymore, as she instinctively had been at first, and she wasn't intimidated, either.

Instead she was angry for the most part, and a little relieved that Sullivan hadn't had Sam arrested, too. After all, he had been with her at the bed-and-breakfast, and Sullivan could have brought the same charges against him.

But she was the one the district attorney wanted to teach a lesson to. Sam didn't really mean anything to him.

As she was being booked, fingerprinted, and photographed, Chuck said, "You're sure taking this well, Mrs. Newsom."

"It's nothing to worry about," she assured him. "I'm going to be fine. This is all a misunderstanding, and I'm sure my lawyer will straighten it all out very quickly."

"I hope so. Because you know, Mrs. N., being locked up in jail . . . it's not quite the same as being in detention, you know."

"It's all right," Phyllis told him.

She clung to that belief . . . until the door of her cell clanged shut and the electronic lock slammed into place with a loud *thunk!* Her heart started to pound again, and the anxious feeling inside her grew stronger, and as the long minutes passed, the crazy thought came to her that she ought to be singing that song convicts always sang in the movies . . .

Nobody knows . . . the trouble I've seen . . .

"Mom?" Mike said.

Phyllis gave a little shake of her head. "What?"

"You looked like you drifted off there for a second. You were saying that you couldn't let Eve go to prison for a murder she didn't commit, and then you seemed like you were somewhere else a million miles away."

"I was just thinking about everything that's happened," she said. "You know there's no real reason for me to be here, don't you? Other than the fact that I annoyed the district attorney, that is."

"You did exactly what we all told you not to. You got in the middle of an official investigation—"

"No, I didn't," Phyllis broke in. "How could I? The investigation was over. Eve had already been charged with murder. No one was even asking questions anymore except me, so how could I have interfered with anyone?"

Mike scrubbed a hand wearily over his face and sighed before he admitted, "You've got a point there. I'm not sure the district attorney intends to go forward with those charges—"

"He'd be foolish if he did. He can't make them stick," Phyllis said, giving voice to the thought she'd had earlier. "He just wanted to scare me off. To teach me a lesson."

The scathing contempt that came into Phyllis's voice made Mike grin. "Yeah, that was kind of a dumb move on his part, wasn't it?" he said. "Anyway, Sam, Carolyn, Eve, and Juliette Yorke are all out there looking like they're ready to storm the Bastille—"

"You remembered what we studied about the French Revolution," Phyllis said, unexpectedly pleased by that.

"Yeah, well, it's not like you took it easy on me when it came to grading. Anyway, there's about to be a bail hearing, and I asked if I could come get you for it. It's pretty irregular, but the sheriff agreed." Mike paused. "I'm not sure he thought Eve should have been charged, at least at this point, but he's not going to come right out and say that."

"I don't imagine deputies' mothers get arrested and have to be bailed out very often."

"It's not real common," Mike said. "Let's go."

As they stepped out into the corridor, he added, "Have they treated you all right?"

"Oh, yes, everyone's been very nice. Chuck Murphy was one of the deputies who brought me in. Do you remember him? He's a few years older than you, but I think you dated his little sister a few times in high school."

"Yeah, I know Chuck," Mike said.

"That's right, he mentioned that you were friends," Phyllis said. "I have to say, he turned out better than I expected. He was always the class clown, you know."

"Yeah, Chuck's a good guy." Mike's voice was starting to sound a little strained again, so Phyllis decided this probably wasn't a good time for reminiscing.

There were a couple of courtrooms in the jail building that could be used for bail hearings and other proceedings, and that was where he took her. As Mike had said, Sam and the others were all waiting there for her.

Sam started to reach out and put a hand on Phyllis's arm, but Mike gave him a little shake of the head, indicating that he shouldn't do that.

"No touchin' the prisoner, eh?" Sam said. "Are you all right, Phyllis?"

"I'm fine," she assured him. "I'm ready to get out of here, though."

"Can't blame you for that."

Juliette said, "This shouldn't take long. The bail should be very manageable." She looked at Mike. "Can I take custody of my client now?"

"Of course, Counselor," he told her. Juliette took Phyllis's arm and led her to the defense table, which was smaller than the one in the courtroom where Eve's arraignment had been held. There was barely enough room for both of them to sit there.

A few minutes later, a man came into the courtroom and went to the prosecution's side. Phyllis looked over and recognized him as one of Sullivan's assistant district attorneys. She wondered if the presence of the ADA, instead of Sullivan himself, meant anything.

There was only one row of seats for spectators. Sam, Carolyn, and Eve sat there, while Mike stood to one side. After a few more minutes, the clerk, bailiff, and judge came in, one right after the other. The judge didn't have a bench like in the other courtroom, just a table of his own. He wore a suit instead of a robe.

As soon as the judge, a tall, horse-faced man in his forties, had called the court to order, the ADA got to his feet and said, "If I may, Your Honor?"

"Go ahead, Mr. Fisher," the judge said.

"The State waives reading and moves to dismiss the charges against Mrs. Newsom."

"You're sure?"

"Yes, Your Honor."

"Motion granted," the judge said. He banged his gavel and added, "You're free to go, Mrs. Newsom."

Juliette stood up and said, "Thank you, Your Honor."

Phyllis noticed that she didn't thank the ADA, Fisher.

Since there were no other bails to set, the judge adjourned the court and left the room, taking the clerk and bailiff with him. Mike came over to the defense table, where Sam, Carolyn, and Eve were already gathering around Phyllis.

Juliette smiled and said, "When I told you it wouldn't take long, I didn't know it would go quite that fast. That was the best scenario we could hope for."

"That varmint, Sullivan, didn't have the nerve to show his face after what happened at the courthouse," Sam said. "That's why he sent that other fella to take care of it."

"Having Phyllis arrested backfired on him; that's for sure," Carolyn said. "It just made him look foolish."

"Yes, and it's liable to make him madder than ever," Mike warned. "Mom, I think it would be a good idea for you to be very careful until all this is over."

Phyllis said, "By all this, you mean Eve's murder trial?"

"Well . . ."

"I'm not going to stand by—"

Eve interrupted her. "What you're not going to do is get yourself in trouble again because of me. You were lucky this time, Phyllis. Juliette's taking care of everything, and I have confidence in her."

"I appreciate that, Mrs. Porter," Juliette said, "but if Mrs. Newsom has found out anything that might help with your defense . . ."

"Let's all go back to the house," Phyllis suggested. "I don't have much that might help, but I'll tell you everything that I've found out. All that time I spent behind bars might as well be worth it!"

Chapter 31

When they got back to the house, Phyllis was surprised to see a strange car parked at the curb. After a second, though, she recognized the vehicle. It belonged to Tess Coburn.

She would have known that a second later, because Tess got out and came toward them. Phyllis had driven her Lincoln to the courthouse square, and Sam had taken his pickup. Juliette parked her SUV in the driveway behind the pickup. Everyone converged in the garage, since the doors were still open.

"Tess, it's good to see you," Phyllis greeted the private investigator. "What are you doing here?"

"I knew that Mrs. Porter's arraignment was this morning," Tess said with a nod toward Eve. "I wanted to find out how everything went."

In a voice edged with chilly dislike, Eve said, "Phyllis, you act like you're friends with this woman. I assumed she'd left town by now."

Phyllis took a deep breath. "There are things you don't know, Eve. Tess has been working with me, trying to help clear your name."

"Why would she do that?" Eve asked with a frown.

"Because I want the truth to come out," Tess said. "I know my part of the case is over, but I'm not going to be satisfied until I'm sure we know what happened. I think I owe that much to my former clients."

Juliette said, "Excuse me, but what's going on here? Who is this woman?"

"I planned to explain all of that to you when we got back here," Phyllis said. "Now that Tess is here, that'll make it easier. Let's all go inside."

Eve still didn't look happy that Tess was there, and Juliette seemed to be both confused and annoyed that things had been kept from her until now, but the way to solve both those problems was to get everything out into the open, Phyllis thought.

It was the middle of the day, so as they went inside, Phyllis said to Carolyn, "Let's get some coffee going and make some sandwiches. Then we can all sit down in the living room and discuss the case."

She could tell that Carolyn didn't like having Tess there, either, but hospitality won out over irritation, as Phyllis had known that it would. Carolyn nodded and said, "All right."

"Sam, if you'd get everyone settled . . ."

"Sure," he said.

Once Phyllis and Carolyn were alone in the kitchen, Carolyn asked, "What's going on here?" Before Phyllis could answer, Carolyn's eyes suddenly widened. "Oh, goodness! Have you solved the case?"

Phyllis shook her head. "I wish I had. I'm no closer to knowing who killed Roy than I was when I started looking into this."

And yet she had the oddest feeling that wasn't true. A persistent voice in the back of her head told her that she did know—she just couldn't prove it. Some of the things she had seen and heard fit together in a certain way to point in the direction of the killer, but Phyllis just couldn't quite grasp them. When she tried, they slipped away like smoke.

"Phyllis?"

Carolyn's voice brought her out of her momentary reverie. "I'm sorry. I was trying to think . . . Sandwiches. We need sandwiches."

She busied herself getting lunch ready, thinking that if she distracted her mind from the problem plaguing it, she might be more likely to come up with a solution. Unfortunately, that didn't work. By the time she had plates of Cobb wraps made, she still hadn't figured out what it was she was missing.

The atmosphere in the living room was a little strained when Phyllis and Carolyn came in with the food and coffee. Eve and Juliette were on the sofa, while Sam and Tess sat in armchairs. Phyllis put the plates on the coffee table and told everyone to help themselves.

When they all had food and were sitting down, Tess said, "I've explained to Ms. Yorke who I am and what my connection to the case is, but I haven't told her about the things we've found out over the past few days, Phyllis. I thought maybe you'd want to do that."

Phyllis nodded. "All right. What we've been trying to do, Juliette, is to come up with other possible suspects who had a reason to want Roy Porter dead." She saw Eve wince slightly and hurried on, "I'm sorry to have to be so blunt about all this, Eve, but it's your freedom we're talking about, not to mention your reputation."

"I'm too old to give a hoot about my reputation, dear," Eve said. "I'll admit, though, that I'd hate to be locked up in prison. Those outfits they make convicts wear . . ."

Phyllis knew that Eve was trying to mask her own worry with humor. She nodded and went on, "Before she ever came to Weatherford, Tess found out a lot about the things Roy did in the past."

Juliette said, "I know about some of that. Eve told me. She had a hard time believing it."

"I still do," Eve said with a sigh. "But the evidence seems incontrovertible."

"It is," Tess said. "The man you knew as Roy did all those things, Eve. I wish it could be different, but it isn't."

Eve said, "All right, let's agree that Roy was . . . the sort of man he was. But doesn't that just make it seem more likely that I killed him?"

"Only if you found out what he was planning," Phyllis said. "I think we all know from your reaction when you first met Tess at the cemetery that that wasn't the case."

"I had no idea, and I'll swear to that in court."

"You may have to," Juliette said. "Unfortunately, we just have your word for it." She looked over at Phyllis. "I suppose you've been thinking that some of the women Roy scammed in the past are possible suspects? You're trying to establish reasonable doubt?"

"Won't that help?" Phyllis asked.

"It certainly won't hurt anything. All we have to convince is one juror for a mistrial, and if we can get that, Sullivan might not push for a retrial. If we can convince all of them, we might get an outright acquittal, but that's going to be hard. Those women might have had a motive, but what about opportunity?"

Phyllis and Tess exchanged a glance before Tess said, "That's where we have something. One of the women was at the bed-and-breakfast at the same time Roy and Eve were."

Eve looked shocked as she said, "Oh, dear. Who?"

"Ingrid Pitt," Tess said. She explained who Ingrid was and how Roy had swindled her years earlier.

"I spoke to that woman several times while we were there," Eve said. Her eyes were wide with amazement. "I can't believe she was one of . . . one of Roy's . . . victims."

Tess nodded. "I'm afraid so."

"It does seem like she'd be a viable suspect," Juliette said, "but that's only one. It's suspicious, her being there, I'll grant you that, but I'm not sure it establishes reasonable doubt."

"There were other women who could have been there," Tess said. She went on to tell them about Becky Tuttle, Samantha Hogan, and Mary McLaren. "It really reflects badly on me as a professional investigator that I let it slip to them about Roy's location, especially since I hadn't gotten here and made sure it was really him yet," she concluded, "but I can't worry about that now. I'm trying to establish if any of them could have been in this area at the time of Roy's murder."

Juliette nodded slowly. "This is starting to sound more promising," she said.

"And that's not all," Phyllis said. "There's also the matter of Jan and Pete Delaney."

"They're such sweet people," Eve said. "Wait a minute. You don't mean . . .?"

"Let me explain what Jan told me. And I'm sorry, Eve, but this is going to be unpleasant for you, too."

Eve took a deep breath and lifted her chin. "Go ahead, dear," she told Phyllis. "I think I'm getting used to these shocks."

Feeling uncomfortable despite what Eve had said, Phyllis launched into an account of what Jan Delaney had told her about Roy making a pass at her. Eve's lips tightened a little in hurt and anger, even though Phyllis tried to phrase things discreetly.

"So what it comes down to," Eve said when Phyllis was finished, "is that my husband was a wolf as well as a rat."

"I wouldn't put it that way—"

"I would," Carolyn said. "Or worse."

Tess said to Juliette, "You'll be able to cross-examine both the Delaneys. If you can manage to raise the subject without the district attorney objecting and the judge shutting down that line of questioning, there's no telling what you might be able to get out of them."

Juliette nodded. "I can try. I can always call them as hostile witnesses, too, but I'd rather bring out the information on cross so there's no chance of Sullivan getting wind of what I'm trying to do."

"That's what I thought, too."

They had been eating and sipping coffee as they talked. Now the conversation died down as everyone concentrated on lunch. When they were finished, after Carolyn had freshened everyone's coffee, Juliette said, "This has certainly been helpful. I think it would be a good idea, though, if I officially hired you as an investigator, Ms. Coburn. That is, if both you and Eve agree."

"Yes, I suppose so," Eve said. She summoned up a weak smile for Tess. "I'm sorry, dear. I suppose I fell prey to blaming the messenger, and that's not fair to you."

"That's all right, Mrs. Porter, I understand," Tess told her. "You've been through so much, of course you'd be thrown for a loop." She turned to Juliette and went on, "I'd be fine with making it official."

"Good. I'll draw up a simple contract retaining your investigative services, unless you have one you'd prefer to use."

"No, that's fine, you go ahead," Tess said. She took another sip of coffee and went on, "If you'll all excuse me, I think I need to visit the ladies' room."

Carolyn started to stand up, saying, "I'll show you—"

"Oh, that's all right. I've been here before."

Carolyn settled back in her chair. "That's right," she said with a note of disapproval in her voice. "Phyllis snuck you in while Eve and I were upstairs."

"It wasn't exactly like that," Phyllis said, letting her own irritation show. She loved Carolyn, but the woman was as stubborn as a mule and quick to hold a grudge.

Tess smiled and held up her hands as she stood. "Let's just call a truce," she suggested. "After all, we're all working toward the same goal, aren't we? We want to uncover the truth and clear Mrs. Porter's name."

"Well, I can't argue with that," Carolyn said grudgingly.

"I'll be right back," Tess said. She left the living room and went upstairs.

When Tess was gone, Carolyn said quietly, "I'm sorry, I just don't like that woman, and I never will." She looked at Eve. "But she's right about all of us needing to work together."

"It's good that everything's out in the open now," Juliette said. She looked at Phyllis. "Everything *is* out in the open, isn't it?"

"I don't know anything else to tell you," Phyllis said. "I wish I did."

"Like I said, this is a good start. And we've got some time. It'll be a couple of months, anyway, before the case comes to trial. We'll have time to dig out everything we can about Roy's background." Juliette put a hand on Eve's arm. "I know it'll be uncomfortable for you . . ."

"Do what you have to do," Eve told her with a decisive nod.

"I always do," Juliette said.

A moment of silence passed, and Carolyn broke it by saying, "Can you believe that it's only been a little over a month since Christmas? So much has happened since then!"

"And only a little more than a month since the shower," Eve said with a wistful note in her voice as she remembered that afternoon. "That was such a wonderful day, even with that huge crowd here." She smiled at Phyllis. "I'm sorry about that, dear. I really wouldn't have invited so many people if I'd had any idea all of them would show up like that!"

"It was no problem," Phyllis assured her.

Carolyn snorted. "It almost was when it looked like Loretta Harbor and Velma Nickson were going to get in a catfight right in the middle of the living room!"

"Oh, that was scandalous, wasn't it?" Eve said with a laugh.

"Not to be indelicate, but it probably put a strain on the plumbing, too," Carolyn went on, "that many ladies trooping in and out of the bathrooms. And this is an old house."

Phyllis remembered. She'd had to point out both the upstairs and downstairs bathrooms a number of times . . .

Her breath froze in her throat. She looked over at Sam, who had been quiet during the lengthy conversation about possible suspects. She knew from the intent expression on his face what he was thinking, too, and so she wasn't all that surprised when both of them exclaimed at the same instant, "The letter opener!"

"What?" Carolyn asked.

A smile began to spread across Sam's rugged face. He said to Phyllis, "You just solved the case, didn't you?"

She returned the smile, even though she was upset by what she had figured out, and said, "I think we both just did."

Chapter 32

"What in the world are you talking about?" Carolyn asked.

Juliette leaned forward intently. "You're onto something, Mrs. Newsom?"

Phyllis held up a hand to stop them from asking any more questions as she heard footsteps coming down the stairs. "Wait a minute," she said. "Tess needs to be here for this."

A moment later, Tess came into the living room, and she must have sensed that something had changed, because she looked around, frowned, and asked, "What is it? Is something going on?"

"Sit down," Phyllis told her. "There's something else we need to talk about. Something we haven't even considered."

Tess sank into the armchair she had occupied before. "What is it?" she asked.

"The letter opener," Phyllis said.

"The murder weapon?" Tess frowned. "It belongs to Mrs.

Porter, doesn't it? Without it, there's no physical evidence against her."

Juliette said, "And without any physical evidence, there's no case. At least, not one strong enough to take to a jury."

Phyllis leaned forward and said, "So if we accept the fact that Eve's innocent, we also have to accept the fact that she has no reason to lie about how the letter opener got to the bed-and-breakfast."

"I don't know how it got there," Eve said. "I didn't take it with me. I swear I didn't."

Phyllis smiled. "I believe you. That's because the murderer brought it to the bed-and-breakfast."

"Wait just a minute," Carolyn said. "The last time any of us saw that letter opener, it was upstairs in Eve's room. At least, that's the last place *I* remember seeing it."

"That's right," Phyllis said. "That means the killer must have taken it from Eve's room at some point before Roy's murder."

"You're right," Juliette said, excitement growing in her voice. "But how could the murderer have gotten hold of it?"

"That's been the key all along," Phyllis said. "I just didn't realize it. Someone who was in this house took the letter opener."

Carolyn said, "Well, it certainly wasn't any of us! Although I might have felt like killing Roy if I'd known what sort of scoundrel he really was."

"I'd advise you not to say things like that in public, Mrs. Wilbarger," Juliette said.

Carolyn snorted.

"Now, hold on a minute," Tess said. "I'm getting confused

here. You just said somebody who lives here took the letter opener and killed Roy Porter."

Phyllis shook her head. "No, I said someone who has been in this house did that."

"Well, who could that be?"

"Only one person I can think of," Phyllis said as she looked straight across the living room at Tess. "You."

All the others except Sam turned to look at Tess, who stared at Phyllis in evident disbelief. Sounding stunned, Tess said, "Me? How is that possible? I didn't even get to Weatherford until after Roy Porter was dead. I arrived on the day of his funeral, remember?"

"And what proof do we have of that?" Phyllis asked. "Your word; that's all. You could have been in town for a week or a month or even a year, and none of us would know any different. But you *told* us that's when you got here, and you even showed up at the cemetery to reinforce that in our minds. None of us ever thought to question it until now. So it never occurred to us that you might have killed Roy."

"Why in the world would I do that?" Tess demanded.

Phyllis shook her head. "I don't know, exactly, but I suspect it has something to do with that story you told us about the woman who committed suicide after Roy broke her heart. Was she your mother? Your aunt? Maybe an older sister?"

Tess blew out a breath of laughter. "I think you've let your reputation as a detective go to your head, Mrs. Newsom. You're grasping at straws here. I have no motive, no means, no opportunity! I wasn't in town, and I never set foot in your house until a few days ago. I couldn't have gotten my hands on that letter opener."

"Oh, you were here before," Phyllis said, and confidence made her voice strong and clear. "You were here on the day of Eve's bridal shower. When I first saw you at the cemetery, for a second I thought you were one of the teachers from Eve's last couple of years at the high school. I don't know all of them, you see, so it was an easy mistake to make. Even then, I must have recognized you, even though I wasn't aware of it at the time. You probably looked considerably different at the shower. Maybe you were wearing your hair different, or you wore a wig, or maybe even a more elaborate disguise. But you were here." Phyllis paused. "Otherwise how would you have known just now where the upstairs bathroom is?"

"That's *it*?" Tess asked. "You came up with this crazy idea because I needed to go to the *bathroom*?"

"When you came here on the day of the funeral, you didn't use the bathroom, upstairs or down." Phyllis nodded toward Sam. "Sam can confirm that."

"While I don't usually concern myself with ladies' bathroom habits," he said, "yeah, I can testify that you didn't go while you were here. You sat in the living room and talked to us for a while, and then you left when Eve came downstairs. You gave me your card right there in the foyer."

Tess shook her head. "This is so far-fetched—"

"But it seems to fit together," Juliette said. "Go on, Mrs. Newsom. How did she plan the whole thing?"

Before Phyllis could answer, Tess burst out, "You can forget about me working for you!"

"Oh, yes, I think so," Juliette said with a nod.

"I don't know what her plan was," Phyllis said. "Maybe she just came here to get a look at the woman who was going to marry the man she hated so much. Maybe she planned all along to kill Roy and frame Eve for the murder. I just don't know. But I'm convinced she waited until the downstairs bathroom was occupied so she'd have a good excuse to go upstairs. I sent a number of ladies up there myself, including some I didn't know."

"So did I," Carolyn said. She studied Tess's face. "She could have been one of them."

"You're just going along with what your delusional friend says," Tess practically spat at her.

Juliette said, "How did she know about the shower? How would she know she could get away with pretending to know Eve?"

"Like I said, we have no idea how long she's really been in town," Phyllis replied. "She could've been investigating Eve for a long time, long enough that she already knew all of our names at the funeral. She's a real private investigator, you know. That doesn't mean she can't be a murderer, too."

Tess heaved a sigh of apparent exasperation and said, "You've gone off the deep end."

"Maybe she didn't even mean to come in that day," Phyllis went on as if she hadn't heard Tess's comment. "Maybe she was just watching the house, trying to get a look at Eve. But then when she saw so many people arriving for the shower, she realized she could blend in with them and get an even closer look. I'm sure that as a private investigator, she's had some experience at pretending to be people she's not. And then she went upstairs to look at Eve's room and saw the letter opener and realized that if she bided her time, she could kill Roy and put the blame on Eve."

"That's premeditation, whether she planned it all along or just came up with that when she stole the letter opener," Juliette said. "But why even show up in Weatherford at all after he was dead?"

"So she could make sure the authorities knew that Eve had a motive for killing Roy," Phyllis said. "And I think she probably wanted to keep an eye on the case, too, and make sure things were going the way she wanted them to. She dragged in those other suspects to muddy the waters, just in case Eve was cleared somehow. I'm sure that's why she told those other women where they could find Roy. It wasn't a mistake at all. But all of them except Ingrid Pitt failed to cooperate. They didn't come to Weatherford, so they couldn't serve as alternate suspects in case she needed them." Phyllis nodded slowly. "The more I think about it, the more I'm convinced she'd been planning to kill Roy for a long time."

Tess stood up. "I've listened to enough of this garbage," she said. "Even if there was anything to it, you can't prove anything that you've said. You're just some crazy old woman who thinks she's a detective."

"I'm not," Juliette said as she came to her feet, too. "I'm not a detective, but I know how to dig out the facts once somebody has pointed me in the right direction. And I think you'd better stay right here, Ms. Coburn, while someone calls the sheriff's department."

"Go to hell," Tess muttered as she swung toward the door.

Sam started to get up, but Juliette reached Tess first and put a hand on her shoulder. Tess turned sharply, slashing out at Juliette with a savage expression on her face. Carolyn and

Eve both cried out in alarm. Phyllis and Sam bolted to their feet. In Tess's job, she had probably learned how to handle herself in a violent situation.

But Juliette was in no danger. She ducked under the blow that Tess aimed at her head, drove a stiffened hand into Tess's midsection, and then swung her leg in a roundhouse kick that sent Tess crashing against the wall so hard a couple of framed pictures leaped off their hooks and fell to the floor. Tess collapsed, stunned.

"Good Lord!" Carolyn said.

Juliette was breathing a little hard. "Somebody better call 911," she said.

Sam had already beaten her to it. He was punching in the three digits on the phone.

Eve was staring at the stunned Tess Coburn. "Oh, dear," she said. "I guess I was right not to like her all along, wasn't I?"

"I'd say so," Phyllis told her with a smile.

"She didn't change her appearance to go to the shower," Juliette told them that evening when they had all gathered in the living room of Phyllis's house again. Mike was there, too.

Juliette took a printout of a photograph from her briefcase and went on, "This is what she normally looked like. I got it from her Louisiana driver's license. It was when she showed up later that she looked different than she usually did, just to make sure none of you remembered her from Christmas Eve."

The picture showed a woman with dark brown hair pulled back away from her face. Phyllis and Carolyn both nodded, and Carolyn said, "I'm pretty sure I recall her being here on the day of the shower."

"I do, too," Phyllis said. "I'm not sure I could testify to that in court, though."

"You shouldn't have to," Mike said. "According to the sheriff, the woman's probably going to reach some kind of plea deal with Sullivan."

"Oh, so he's going to let *her* get away with it, after all the misery he put poor Eve through," Carolyn said.

"You know, it would be all right with me if I never heard the expression 'poor Eve' again," Eve said.

"She's not going to get away with it," Mike said. "But she might only spend a few years behind bars. After all, what Roy did drove her mother to suicide, so I'm sure her lawyer will play up the sympathy angle."

"So it was her mother who died," Phyllis said.

"Yep," Mike replied with a nod. "Tess had been looking for him for years. She sought out all those other victims and made them think *she* was trying to help *them*, and they wound up hiring her and funding her search for revenge. It's a shame. From what I can tell, she was actually a pretty good PI."

"As well as a ruthless murderer," Carolyn said.

"Well, yeah. I don't think there's much doubt about that."

"It is a shame," Phyllis agreed. "I can't blame her for hating Roy. But when she tried to make it look like Eve killed him . . . well, that crossed a line."

Juliette said, "If you hadn't figured it out, Mrs. Newsom, she would have continued pretending to work with you, and she would have tried to steer you away if you started coming too close to the truth. It was a pretty bold game she was playing, all the way through." She replaced the photograph in her briefcase and snapped the latches closed.

"What happens now?" Carolyn asked.

Mike said, "The sheriff's department has reopened the investigation. Burton and Conley are pretty ticked off that they bought into the frame. They'll keep digging until they have everything there is to find about Ms. Coburn."

"But what about Eve? She's still charged with murder!"

"District Attorney Sullivan has already called me," Juliette said, smiling. "He informed me that he'll move for a dismissal of the charges first thing tomorrow morning."

"Can't it be done any sooner?" Carolyn asked. "Eve shouldn't have to spend one more night like this!"

"It's all right," Eve said. "Everyone knows the truth now. That's the most important thing."

"What I'd like to know," Sam said, "is where you learned to handle yourself in a ruckus like that, Ms. Yorke."

"Martial arts training," Juliette said. "It's a good workout."

"Well, it certainly came in handy today," Phyllis said.

Eve asked, "Will I need to go into court in the morning?"

Juliette shook her head as she stood up. "No, I can take care of it. From now on, you can just go ahead and live your life, Eve."

Eve got to her feet and hugged her. "Thank you," she said, her voice catching a little. She looked around at the others. "Thank you so much, all of you. You never lost faith in me."

"We certainly didn't," Carolyn said.

"And you, Phyllis," Eve went on. "I don't know how you do it."

"She's had to develop those detective abilities," Carolyn

said, "because it seems like the police around here think she lives in a house full of serial killers!" She pointed at Sam. "They'll arrest you next. Mark my words!"

Sam grinned and lifted his hands in surrender. "Not me. I'm walkin' the straight and narrow from here on out!"

Phyllis wasn't sure what made her come downstairs late that night, after the house was quiet and dark. She turned the light on in the hall, and in the glow it cast into the living room, she saw Eve sitting and looking out the window.

"Eve . . . ," Phyllis said as she stepped into the room.

"Go on and live my life," Eve said quietly. "That's what Juliette told me to do. But I can't really do that, can I? Because my life . . . the life I believed I'd lead from now on . . . was going to be with Roy."

Phyllis knelt beside Eve's chair. "That wasn't meant to be," she said, making her voice as comforting as she could. "It's not your fault. You were honest and sincere—"

"I loved him, you know." Eve turned her head to look at Phyllis in the dim light from the hallway. "I really loved him. Even after . . . even after that woman told us the truth about him, about what he did in the past, I might have forgiven him if he'd just . . . stayed with me."

"I know," Phyllis whispered. "But that was never what he intended."

"I know that . . . in my brain. But in my heart . . ."

Phyllis clasped Eve's hand and leaned her head against her shoulder as Eve began to cry. In the morning, Phyllis thought,

Eve would be all right. She would put all this behind her and move on, just as Juliette had told her.

But the scars on her heart would remain. Those scars always did. They might heal over, but they never went away.

The two of them stayed together for a long time into the night.

Recipes

Sweet Bacon Crackers

Ingredients
32 Club crackers
8 slices bacon, cut into fourths
Cayenne pepper (optional)
¼ cup brown sugar

Directions
Preheat the oven to 275°F.

Arrange the crackers in a single layer on a large, ungreased baking sheet. Top each cracker with ¼ slice of bacon, add a light dash of cayenne, and sprinkle brown sugar over all.

Bake for 1 hour, or until bacon is browned and brown sugar is caramelized. Serve warm.

These sweet and spicy bites are better warm than cold, but they reheat easily.

Makes 32.

Nutty Caramel Pretzels

Ingredients

15 ounces mini twist pretzels

4 cups mixed nuts

1 cup (2 sticks) unsalted butter

2 cups packed dark brown sugar

½ cup light corn syrup

Pinch of salt

Directions

Preheat the oven to 250°F.

In a 9 x 13-inch baking dish, combine the pretzels and nuts. Set aside.

In a large saucepan, combine the butter, brown sugar, corn syrup, and salt. Stir together over medium heat until the brown sugar dissolves. Bring to a boil and cook until the mixture is very thick and reaches the firm-ball stage (260°F on a candy thermometer). Remove from heat, pour over pretzel-nut mixture, and mix.

Bake for 20 minutes, stirring once after 10 minutes.

Remove from the oven and spread on parchment paper to cool.

Serves 25–30.

Cheddar Garlic Palmiers

Ingredients

1¼ cups (3½ ounces) finely grated sharp Cheddar cheese
¼ cup finely grated Parmigiano-Reggiano cheese
2 teaspoons minced garlic
1 teaspoon garlic salt
2 puff pastry sheets (from a 17.3-ounce package),
thawed if frozen

Directions

Toss the Cheddar, Parmigiano-Reggiano, minced garlic and garlic salt in a bowl.

Sprinkle ¼ cup cheese mixture onto a work surface. Unfold 1 pastry sheet and place it over the cheese. With a rolling pin, roll the pastry into a 10-inch square. Sprinkle ½ cup cheese mixture all over the top of the pastry, pressing lightly to adhere. Fold the sides of 2 ends to meet in center. Fold once more, lengthwise, into the center, and press the ends together. Wrap tightly in plastic wrap and chill until firm, about 1 hour (or freeze 15–30 minutes). Repeat with remaining cheese and second sheet of pastry.

While the dough chills, preheat the oven to 400°F with racks in the upper and lower parts of the oven. Line 2 large baking sheets with parchment paper.

Working with 1 piece at a time (keep remaining chilled until ready to use), unwrap the pastry and cut, seam side up, into ¼-inch-thick slices, arranging them 1 inch apart on the baking sheets. Bake, turn-

ing the palmiers over and switching the positions of the pans half-
way through, until the pastry is golden and cooked through, 18–22
minutes total. Transfer the palmiers to a rack to cool. Cut and bake
the remaining pastry on the cooled baking sheets.

Makes 6–7 dozen.

Stuffed Mushrooms

Ingredients

12 whole fresh mushrooms

1 tablespoon extra-virgin olive oil

1 tablespoon minced garlic

1 (8-ounce) package cream cheese, softened

¼ cup grated Parmesan cheese

¼ teaspoon ground black pepper

¼ teaspoon onion powder

⅛–¼ teaspoon ground cayenne pepper

Directions

Preheat the oven to 350°F. Spray a baking sheet with cooking spray. Clean the mushrooms with a damp paper towel. Carefully break off the stems. Chop the stems extremely fine, discarding the tough ends.

Heat the oil in a large skillet over medium heat. Add the garlic and chopped mushroom stems to the skillet. Saute until any moisture has disappeared, taking care not to burn the garlic. Set aside to cool.

When the garlic-mushroom mixture is no longer hot, stir in the cream cheese, Parmesan cheese, black pepper, onion powder, and cayenne pepper to taste. The mixture should be very thick. Using a small spoon, fill each mushroom cap with a generous amount of stuffing. Arrange the mushroom caps on the prepared cookie sheet.

Bake for 20 minutes, or until the mushrooms are piping hot and liquid starts to appear under the caps.

Makes 12.

Zesty Cheeseball

Ingredients

1 (8-ounce) package cream cheese, softened

1 (8-ounce) container Philadelphia Garden Vegetable
cream cheese

1 cup shredded Cheddar cheese

¼ cup shredded pepper jack cheese

½ green bell pepper, minced

1 jalapeño pepper, seeded and minced

1 teaspoon Worcestershire sauce

½ teaspoon hot sauce

½ teaspoon garlic salt

Directions

In a medium bowl combine the cream cheeses, ¾ cup of the Cheddar cheese, and the pepper jack cheese, green bell pepper, jalapeño pepper, Worcestershire sauce, hot sauce, and garlic salt. Mix together and form the mixture into a ball. Roll the ball in the remaining ¼ cup shredded Cheddar cheese and serve with your favorite crackers.

Serves 20–25.

Mini Curried Turkey Croissant Sandwiches

Ingredients

2 cups cubed cooked turkey

1 medium unpeeled red apple, chopped

¾ cup dried cranberries

½ cup thinly sliced celery

¼ cup chopped pecans

2 tablespoons thinly sliced green onions

½ cup fat-free mayonnaise

¼ cup fat-free yogurt

2 teaspoons lime juice

½ teaspoon curry powder

12 mini croissants

Lettuce leaves

Directions

In a medium bowl, combine the turkey, apple, cranberries, celery, pecans, and green onions. In a small bowl, combine the mayonnaise, yogurt, lime juice, and curry powder; add to the turkey mixture and stir to coat. Split croissants, spread on mixture, and top with lettuce leaf. Cover and refrigerate until ready to serve.

Makes 12 mini sandwiches.

Blue Punch

Ingredients
Blue Hawaiian Punch
Lemon-lime soda
Pineapple juice
Pineapple sherbet

Directions
Combine equal parts punch, lemon-lime soda, and pineapple juice. Taste and adjust quantities as desired. Add scoops of sherbet (about ½ gallon per punch bowl). Float an ice ring in the middle if desired.

Chocolate Chocolate Chip Cupcakes

Ingredients

2 cups (12 ounces) milk chocolate chips

¾ cup (1½ sticks) butter or margarine

1½ cups granulated sugar

3 eggs

2 teaspoons vanilla extract

2½ cups all-purpose flour

1 teaspoon baking soda

½ teaspoon salt

1½ cups water

Directions

Preheat the oven to 350°F. Place 24 cupcake liners in muffin pans.

Melt 1 cup of the chocolate chips and the butter together in a microwave oven or on the range over low heat. Stir until the chocolate is completely melted. Pour the mixture into a large bowl. Add the sugar and beat with an electric mixer on low until well blended. Beat in the eggs, one at time. Add the vanilla and stir until incorporated. Stir in ½ cup of the flour and the baking soda and salt; mix well. Add the remaining flour and the water and mix until smooth. Pour the batter into the cupcake liners.

Bake for 3 minutes; then add the remaining cup of chocolate chips, sprinkling the chips evenly on the cupcakes. (This keeps the chocolate chips from dropping to the bottom.) Return to the oven and bake for 18–24 minutes more, or until a toothpick inserted in the center comes out clean. Make sure you don't stick the toothpick through a chocolate chip. Cool completely before frosting.

Makes 24 cupcakes.

Buttercream Frosting

Ingredients
½ cup vegetable shortening

½ cup (1 stick) butter or margarine, softened

1 teaspoon vanilla extract (for a cream color;
use clear vanilla for white)

4 cups (approximately 1 pound) sifted confectioners' sugar

¼ cup coconut milk

Directions
In a large bowl, cream the shortening and butter with an electric mixer. Add the vanilla. Gradually add the sugar, one cup at a time, beating well on medium speed after each addition. Scrape the sides and bottom of the bowl often. When all the sugar has been mixed in, the icing will appear dry. Add the coconut milk a little at a time and beat at medium speed until light and fluffy. Keep the bowl covered with a damp cloth until ready to use.

For best results, keep the icing bowl in the refrigerator when not in use. Refrigerated in an airtight container, this icing can be stored for 2 weeks. Rewhip before using.

Chocolate Buttercream Frosting

Ingredients
½ cup vegetable shortening
½ cup (1 stick) butter or margarine, softened
1 teaspoon vanilla extract
1 cup cocoa powder
4 cups (approximately 1 pound) sifted confectioners' sugar
¼ cup coconut milk

Directions
In a large bowl, cream the shortening and butter with an electric mixer. Add the vanilla and cocoa powder. Gradually add the sugar, one cup at a time, beating well on medium speed after each addition. Scrape the sides and bottom of the bowl often. When all the sugar has been mixed in, the icing will appear dry. Add the coconut milk a little at a time and beat at medium speed until light and fluffy. Keep the bowl covered with a damp cloth until ready to use.

For best results, keep the icing bowl in the refrigerator when not in use. Refrigerated in an airtight container, this icing can be stored for 2 weeks. Rewhip before using.

Fruit Dip

Ingredients
1 (8-ounce) package cream cheese, softened
1 (7-ounce) jar marshmallow creme
½ teaspoon vanilla extract

Directions
Using an electric mixer, blend the cream cheese, marshmallow creme, and vanilla extract until mixed thoroughly. Serve with a fruit tray.

Veggie Dip

Ingredients

1 (8-ounce) package cream cheese, softened

1 tablespoon salad dressing or mayonnaise

1 teaspoon yellow mustard

1 tablespoon sweet relish

2 tablespoons chopped green onion

1 teaspoon ketchup

1–2 tablespoons milk

Directions

Using an electric mixer, blend the cream cheese, salad dressing, mustard, relish, onion, and ketchup. Add milk until the dip is the thickness you desire. Serve with a vegetable tray or chips.

Coconut Wedding Cake

Ingredients

½ cup (1 stick) butter, softened

½ cup coconut oil

3 cups granulated sugar

7 eggs (for a white cake, use 10 egg whites)

1 tablespoon vanilla extract (for a white cake, use clear vanilla extract)

1 teaspoon coconut extract

3 cups all-purpose flour

¼ teaspoon baking powder

¼ teaspoon baking soda

½ teaspoon salt

1 cup sour cream

Directions

Preheat the oven to 325°F. Grease and flour two 8-inch cake pans, a 9 x 13-inch pan, or a 10-inch Bundt pan.

In a large bowl, cream together the butter, coconut oil, and sugar. Beat in the eggs, one at a time, mixing well after each. Stir in the vanilla and coconut extract.

In a large bowl, combine the flour, baking powder, baking soda, and salt. Add the flour mixture to the creamed mixture and mix until all of the flour is incorporated. Finally, stir in the sour cream. Mix for 2 minutes to be sure there are no lumps. Pour the batter into the prepared pans.

Bake for 45–60 minutes, or until a toothpick inserted into the center of the cake comes out clean. Allow the cake to cool in the pan for 10 minutes before inverting onto a wire rack.

White Coconut Buttercream Icing

Ingredients

½ cup coconut oil

½ cup (1 stick) butter, softened

1½ teaspoons coconut extract

1 teaspoon clear vanilla extract

6 cups (1½ pounds) confectioners' sugar, sifted

¼ cup coconut milk

Directions

In a large bowl, cream the coconut oil and butter with an electric mixer. Add the coconut and vanilla extracts. Gradually add the sugar, one cup at a time, beating well on medium speed. Scrape sides and bottom of bowl often. When all sugar has been mixed in, icing will appear dry. Add the coconut milk a little at a time and beat at medium speed until light and fluffy. Keep the bowl covered with a damp cloth until ready to use.

For best results, keep the icing bowl in the refrigerator when not in use. Refrigerated in an airtight container, this icing can be stored for 2 weeks. Rewhip before using.

Alcohol-free Piña Colada Punch

Ingredients

1 (20-ounce) can crushed pineapple

½ gallon vanilla ice cream, softened

1 (8-ounce) can coconut cream

1 (46-ounce) can pineapple juice

1 (2-liter) bottle lemon-lime soda

Directions

Put the crushed pineapple in a blender and pulse a few times so there won't be large chunks of pineapple floating in the glasses.

In a large plastic container, combine the ice cream, blended crushed pineapple, coconut cream, and pineapple juice. Mix well, and slowly stir in the lemon-lime soda. Freeze for 4 hours or until slushy.

Serves 25–30.

S'more Pie

Ingredients

1½ cups finely ground graham cracker crumbs

⅓ cup granulated sugar

6 tablespoons (¾ stick) butter, melted

1 (10.5-ounce) snack-sized brownie mix

½ cup milk chocolate chips

1 (7-ounce) jar marshmallow creme

Directions

Preheat the oven to 350°F.

To make the graham cracker crust, mix the graham cracker crumbs, sugar, and melted butter until well blended. (An easy way to do this is to put one package of graham crackers in a 1-gallon resealable plastic bag. Roll a rolling pin over the graham crackers until they are fine crumbs, add the sugar to the bag, and close and shake. Add the butter to the bag and use your fingers outside of the bag to work the butter into the mixture.) Press the mixture into the bottom and sides of a 9-inch pie plate.

Make the brownies per the instructions on the box and pour the batter evenly over the crust.

Bake for 5 minutes, remove from the oven, and add the chocolate chips. Bake for 20–25 minutes, or until a toothpick inserted 1 inch from the edge comes out clean. Make sure you don't hit a chocolate chip.

Spread the marshmallow creme on top while the pie is still warm.

Grilled Ham and Pepper Sandwich

Ingredients
2 teaspoons Philadelphia Garden Vegetable cream cheese

2 slices sourdough bread

2 slices provolone cheese

2 thin slices ham

½ roasted red pepper packed in oil, drained and sliced

2 teaspoons butter

2 teaspoons grated Parmesan or Romano cheese

Dash of garlic salt

Directions

Spread cream cheese on one side of each slice of bread. On 1 slice of bread, place 1 slice of provolone cheese, then the ham, the red pepper, and the other slice of cheese. Top with the other slice of bread with the cream cheese facing the filling. Lightly butter the outsides of the sandwich, and sprinkle a little bit of Parmesan cheese and garlic salt onto the butter.

Heat a skillet over medium heat until warm. Fry the sandwich on both sides, until the bread is golden brown and the cheese is melted.

Serve warm.

Banana Oatmeal Crumb Muffins

Ingredients

Muffins
1 cup all-purpose flour
½ cup oatmeal
1 teaspoon baking soda
1 teaspoon baking powder
½ teaspoon salt
3 bananas, mashed
½ cup granulated sugar
¼ cup brown sugar
1 egg, lightly beaten
¼ cup (½ stick) butter, melted

Topping
¼ cup packed brown sugar
¼ cup chopped pecans or walnuts
2 tablespoons all-purpose flour
⅛ teaspoon ground cinnamon
1 tablespoon butter

Directions

Preheat the oven to 375°F. Lightly grease 12 muffin cups, or line with muffin papers.

To make the muffins, in a large bowl, mix together the flour, oatmeal, baking soda, baking powder, and salt. In another bowl, beat together the bananas, sugars, egg, and butter. Stir the banana mixture into the flour mixture just until moistened. Spoon the batter into the prepared muffin cups.

To make the topping, in a small bowl, mix together the brown sugar, chopped pecans, flour, and cinnamon. Cut in the butter until the mixture resembles coarse cornmeal. Sprinkle the topping over the muffins.

Bake for 18–20 minutes, or until a toothpick inserted into the center of a muffin comes out clean.

Makes 12 muffins.

Tuna Salad Sandwich

Ingredients

½ cup salad dressing or mayonnaise

2 tablespoons sweet pickle relish

2 tablespoons chopped green onion

1 small apple, diced

1 hard-boiled egg, chopped (see recipe, next page)

2 (7-ounce) cans solid white tuna packed in water, drained

8 slices whole wheat bread

1 cup spinach leaves, stems removed

Directions

Mix the salad dressing, relish to taste, green onion, and apple together in a medium bowl. Add the egg and tuna and stir with a fork until well mixed. Spread the tuna mixture equally on 4 slices of bread, and top with spinach leaves. Spread a small amount of salad dressing on the remaining bread slices and place each on top of the spinach. The dressing helps hold the sandwich together.

Serves 4.

Hard-Boiled Eggs

Ingredients
Eggs
Water
½ teaspoon salt

Directions
Put the eggs in a single layer in a saucepan, and cover with at least 1 inch of cold water. Add the salt to the water to make the eggs easier to peel. Heat on high to bring the eggs to a boil. As soon as the water starts to boil, reduce the heat to low. Let simmer for 1 minute. Remove the pan from the heat, cover, and let sit for 15 minutes.

Drain the water from the eggs and run cold water over them. Repeat until the eggs are cool. Once the eggs are cooled, strain the water. Cooling the eggs will prevent them from cooking any more. Overcooking will cause the yolk to turn green or gray, which isn't bad to eat but can be distasteful to the eye.

Cobb Wraps

Ingredients

¼ cup salad dressing or mayonnaise

1 teaspoon Dijon-style mustard

2 eggs, hard-boiled and chopped (see previous recipe)

½ small avocado, chopped

1 tomato, seeded and chopped

2 ounces blue cheese, crumbled

2 slices bacon, cooked until crisp, drained, and crumbled

4 (10-inch) flour tortillas

8 thin slices ham

Leaf or romaine lettuce

Directions

Combine the salad dressing and mustard in a medium bowl. Add the eggs, avocado, tomato, blue cheese, and bacon and stir until combined.

Layer each tortilla with 2 ham slices and some of the lettuce. Place a heaping tablespoon of the egg mixture at one side of each tortilla. Starting at the side with the filling, roll up each tortilla.

Makes 4 servings.

Don't miss the next Fresh-Baked Mystery!
Christmastime has come again to
Weatherford, Texas, and Phyllis has cookies
to bake—and a killer to catch.
Read on for an excerpt from

The Gingerbread Bump-off

by
Livia J. Washburn

*P*hyllis Newsom lifted her head and frowned as she heard the unmistakable strains of "Grandma Got Run Over by a Reindeer" drifting through the house.

A baking sheet full of German chocolate cookies ready to go into the oven sat on the kitchen counter in front of her, but she left them sitting there as she walked out to the living room, wiping her hands on a towel as she went.

Sam Fletcher stood in front of the stereo system, which rested on a shelf next to the television. His hands were tucked in the hip pockets of his jeans, and his head moved slightly in time with the music. He was tall and slender, in keeping with his background as a basketball player and coach, and although his rumpled thatch of hair had a lot more white in it now than gray, he still didn't really look his age.

"Sam," Phyllis said, "you know I don't really like that song. It just doesn't seem very . . . *Christmasy* to me."

He looked back over his shoulder at her. "Sorry," he said.

"I thought with you out in the kitchen it might not bother you." A smile spread across his rugged face. "I got 'Jingle Bells' by the Singin' Dogs if that'd be better."

She was about to tell him that it wouldn't be, when she realized that he was joking. She wasn't going to give him the satisfaction of seeing that he had almost fooled her, so she just waved a hand casually and said, "Play whatever you want. I really don't care."

With that, she went back to the kitchen. By the time she got there, the music had stopped as Sam ejected the CD. A moment later, Nat King Cole started singing about chestnuts roasting on an open fire. Phyllis smiled. That was one of her favorites.

She looked down at the cookies on the baking sheet. The base was a dark chocolate cookie, each with a thumb-sized depression in the middle that Phyllis had filled with a mixture of German chocolate, grated coconut, and crushed pecans. The oven was ready, so she opened the door and slid the baking sheet onto the rack. If these cookies turned out well, she would make another batch. With any luck, this recipe would be her entry in the local newspaper's annual Christmas cookie recipe contest.

The past two years Carolyn Wilbarger, who also lived in the big house in one of Weatherford's tree-shaded old residential neighborhoods, had won that contest, with Phyllis finishing as a runner-up both times. That was fine with Phyllis—she just enjoyed coming up with recipes and sharing them with people—but it might be nice to really give Carolyn a run for her money this year. Not that there was any money at stake, Phyllis reminded herself, only prestige, and she didn't really care all that much about *that*, either. She had a good life here, with a lovely son, daughter-in-law, and grandson, and three good friends who were retired teachers like her to share this house with her.

But that comfortable, well-ordered life was about to be shaken up, and although she knew she ought to be happy about the circumstances, she still wasn't sure how she felt about it.

"Everyone, meet Roy Porter," Eve Turner had said when she brought the silver-haired stranger to the house on Thanksgiving. "Roy and I are engaged. Do you believe it? We're going to be married!"

That news had been a bolt out of the blue. None of Eve's housemates had had any idea she was seeing anyone. It shouldn't have been that surprising. Eve had been married several times before, and she always had her eye out for an eligible bachelor of the proper age. She had even pursued Sam for a while after he moved into the house to rent one of the vacant rooms. But she certainly had been more discreet about her courtship this time.

"We met on the Facebook," Eve had explained. "It turns out we have mutual friends. We started writing on each other's door—"

"Wall, dear," Roy had corrected gently.

"On each other's wall," Eve went on, "and, well, one thing led to another."

With Eve it usually did, given half a chance.

Thanksgiving hadn't necessarily been the best time to break the news of an engagement, but to be fair, when Eve and Roy came in, Eve didn't know that Phyllis had just solved one murder and prevented several more from occurring. That had turned out to be a very busy Thanksgiving indeed.

Now Christmas was coming up, but before then, a bridal shower on Christmas Eve, to be followed by the wedding itself on New Year's Eve. An abundance of Eves, including the bride, Phyllis thought as she stood there in front of the oven for a long moment, thinking about everything that was going on this holiday season.

"Well," she said aloud, "at least nothing else—"

"Don't say it," Sam interrupted sharply from behind her.

She turned her head to look at him. "Don't say what?"

"You were about to say that with all you've got goin' already this year, at least nothin' else can happen," Sam said in a warning tone. "Don't you know that's the surest way to jinx things?"

"Oh, goodness gracious. I'm not superstitious. Anyway, *you* just said it."

"Yeah, but that's all right. I can say things like that without all heck breakin' loose. You're the one who can't."

"That's not fair."

Sam shook his head. "Fair's got nothin' to do with it," he said with a solemn expression on his face. "It's just the way the cosmos is. Some folks seem to attract trouble to start with. You don't want to go makin' the odds even worse."

"Well, that's just silly."

But despite what she said, Phyllis had to wonder if there might not be something to Sam's idea. There had to be some explanation why she seemed to keep getting mixed up in murder cases these past few years.

That thought was going through her head when the doorbell rang.

Sam spread his hands. "See? There you go. Trouble at the door."

"Oh, hush," Phyllis said. She took her apron off and thrust it into his hands as she went past him. "Keep an eye on those cookies. Don't let them burn."

"Wait a minute. I don't know anything about bakin' cookies—"

"Take them out if they start to burn," Phyllis told him over her shoulder.

"But . . . they're chocolate. How will I know?" Sam asked as Phyllis went out of the kitchen and up the hall to the living room.

She patted her graying brown hair to make sure it was in place as she went to the front door. It was the middle of the afternoon, and she wasn't expecting anyone. Her son, Mike, who was a Parker County deputy sheriff, dropped by unexpectedly sometimes, and so did Mike's wife, Sarah. Carolyn was out somewhere, and so was Eve. Neither of them would have rung the doorbell, anyway. This big old house was home to them now.

When Phyllis looked out one of the narrow windows that flanked the door, she saw that the visitor wasn't family or one of her housemates. Definitely a friend, though. She opened the door, smiled, and said, "Hello, Georgia. Please, come in. What brings you here?"

December weather in this part of Texas could range anywhere from summerlike heat to snowstorms and wind chills well below zero. Today was on the warm side, but the air still had a pleasant crispness to it that came into the house with Georgia Hallerbee.

Georgia was what people once called "a handsome woman." She was about Phyllis's height and well shaped despite her age. Her hair was dark brown, and she insisted she didn't color it. Phyllis believed her. Georgia wore a dark blue skirt and a matching blazer over a white blouse. She was an accountant and tax consultant, and she was also very active in civic affairs.

"How are you, Phyllis?" she asked as Phyllis closed the door behind her.

"I'm fine. How are you?" They had known each other for at least ten years, and while they had never been close friends, Phyllis was always glad to see Georgia.

"Busy as always," Georgia replied with a smile and a sweet drawl in her voice. She wasn't a native Texan, having grown up somewhere in the deep South, possibly even the state that bore the same name as she did. Phyllis didn't know about that.

She ushered the visitor into the living room and said, "Have a seat." As Georgia sat down on the sofa, Phyllis stepped over to the stereo to turn off the CD.

"Oh, let it play," Georgia said. "Don't turn it off on my account. I love Christmas music."

"So do I." Phyllis settled for turning down the music to a level that wouldn't interfere with their conversation. She sank into one of the armchairs and went on. "What can I do for you?"

"Maybe I just came by to visit," Georgia said.

Phyllis shook her head. "You said it yourself. You're one of the busiest women I know. You're always up to your elbows in some project or other."

Georgia smiled and tilted her head. "You know me too

well," she said. "I've come to ask a favor of you. You may know that I'm in charge of the Jingle Bell Tour this year."

The Christmas Jingle Bell Tour of Homes was an annual tradition in Weatherford, and in many other Texas towns, for that matter. Each holiday season, a dozen or so homes would be selected and beautifully decorated. Some might even say extravagantly decorated, both inside and out. Then, on one night a few weeks before Christmas, people could pay a small fee to go on a tour of those houses, with the proceeds going to one of the local civic organizations. There would be caroling, hot cider, and snacks at the homes on the tour, and it was a gala evening for everyone concerned . . . except perhaps the homeowners, who had to go to the trouble of decorating and then opening their homes to the public.

"I did know that," Phyllis said. "I'm looking forward to it, like always. There are such beautiful decorations every year."

"Yes, there are," Georgia agreed. "And I'm hoping you can give me a hand this year."

"You mean in organizing the tour? I assumed all that was done already—"

"It was. Or at least, it was supposed to be. But this year we have a . . . situation."

Phyllis frowned slightly. "Whenever someone says 'situation' like that, they're usually not talking about anything good."

"I'm afraid you're right," Georgia said with a sigh. "One of the homeowners had to drop out. Doris Treadwell was diagnosed with cancer yesterday."

"Oh, no." Phyllis recognized the name but didn't actually know Doris Treadwell. Still, it was a terrible thing to hear about anyone, especially at this time of year when everything was supposed to be festive.

Georgia nodded. "She'll be starting chemo right away and then radiation, of course. And naturally she's not going to feel like participating in the tour."

"Of course not," Phyllis said. An uneasy suspicion stirred in the back of her mind. "But you're not asking *me* to—"

"To take her place, yes," Georgia said, nodding. "We'd like for this lovely old house of yours to be part of the Christmas Jingle Bell Tour of Homes this year."

Phyllis sat back, surprised and unsure what to say. Georgia was asking her to take on a big responsibility on short notice. Plus there was the notion of allowing strangers to troop through her house, and the bridal shower to get ready for . . .

"Excuse me, ladies," Sam said from the door between the living room and the foyer. "I hate to interrupt, Phyllis, but those cookies are startin' to smell a little like they might be gettin' done. . . ."

Phyllis got to her feet. "I'm sorry, Georgia. I really need to check on that."

"Of course, go right ahead. I wouldn't want to be to blame for ruining a batch of Phyllis Newsom's cookies."

On her way out of the living room, Phyllis fluttered a hand in Sam's direction and said, "I don't know if you two have met. . . . Georgia, this is my friend Sam Fletcher. . . . Sam, Georgia Hallerbee."

Sam nodded, smiled, and said, "Pleased to meet you." Then he followed Phyllis down the hall to the kitchen.

Phyllis picked up a potholder, opened the stove, and leaned down to check the cookies. She reached in and took hold of the muffin pan, pulled it out, and set it on top of the stove.

"They're not burned," she said.

Sam heaved a sigh of relief.

"But they are done," Phyllis went on. "You did the right thing to come and get me." She lowered her voice. "Now, tell *me* the right thing to do about what Georgia wants."

"What's that?" Sam asked, equally quietly.

"She wants me to help her with the Jingle Bell Tour."

"You mean that thing where folks go around and look at all the fancy-decorated houses? That doesn't sound so bad."

Phyllis pointed at the floor under their feet. "She wants *this* house to be one of the stops."

Sam's eyes widened a little. "Oh. Well, it's kinda late to be askin' something like that, isn't it?"

"They had an emergency. Someone had to drop out of the tour."

Sam nodded and said, "Yeah, I guess that could happen, all right. What're you gonna tell her?"

"I don't know. It would be a lot of work . . . and we already have this business with Eve's shower and wedding coming up. . . ."

"It's gonna be a busy month, all right," Sam agreed.

"On the other hand, it's for a good cause. And I *do* like to decorate for Christmas. . . ."

"Yeah, but you'd almost have to go overboard for something like that, wouldn't you?"

"You can have a lot of decorations and still be tasteful."

"I don't know. I've seen some places so lit up with Christmas lights, I wouldn't be surprised if you could see 'em from space. But you know whatever you decide, I'll be glad to give you a hand."

"I know." Phyllis nodded her head as she came to a decision. "I may regret it, but I'm going to do it."

"I'm sure it'll be fine," Sam told her. "You want me to, uh, sample one of these cookies for you and tell you how it tastes?"

"Keep your hands off of them. They have to cool first. With that topping, you'll burn your mouth if you eat one now."

"I'll try, but they smell mighty good."

He wasn't the only one who thought so. As Phyllis came back into the living room, Georgia Hallerbee said, "My goodness, those cookies smell delicious, Phyllis. Nothing smells much better than cookies right out of the oven."

"I know. They're cooling now. If you can wait a few minutes, you can try one."

"I'd like that, but I really do have to be going soon." Georgia paused. "So, have you thought about what I asked you?"

"I have, and . . . I'm going to do it."

A smile lit up Georgia's face. "That's wonderful! Thank you so much, Phyllis. I can't tell you how much it means to me, knowing that you'll step in and do a good job, like you always do at everything."

"I don't know about that. I'm not going to have as much time to prepare as the others. But I'll do the best I can."

"I'm sure the place will be beautiful," Georgia said as she stood up and started for the front door. "Thanks again. I'll be in touch with all the information you need, like which stop you'll be on the tour and when you can expect people to start showing up. And if there's anything I can do to help you get ready, just let me know."

"An extra six or eight hours in the day would be nice."

Georgia laughed. "Don't I know it! I've been wishing for that for a long time now, but it hasn't come true yet."

Phyllis opened the door and followed Georgia out onto the small front porch. Georgia's stylish crossover SUV was parked in the driveway.

She paused and looked down at the pair of large ceramic gingerbread men that sat on the porch, one on each side of the doorway. "These are new, aren't they? They're adorable."

Phyllis nodded. "Yes, Sam and I were out driving around one afternoon, and we stopped at that place between Azle and Springtown that has all the ceramic things. These gingerbread men were cute, and I thought they'd look good up here."

"You were right." Georgia gave Phyllis a look. "You and Sam . . . are the two of you . . . ?"

"Goodness, no, we're just friends," Phyllis said. That wasn't *strictly* true, but she had been raised to believe that it was best to be discreet about some things.

"You know what you should do?" Georgia said, looking down at the gingerbread men again. "You should dress them up for the tour. You could make, I don't know, elves or something out of them."

"Or Mr. and Mrs. Claus," Phyllis said, getting caught up in the spirit of the thing. "I've thought from the start that one of them was male and the other female."

"Well, there you go. You see, I knew you'd be good at this." Georgia lifted a hand in farewell as she started toward her SUV. "I'll be in touch. Enjoy those cookies!"

"We will," Sam said from behind Phyllis, then added, "You think they've cooled off enough to eat yet?"

Photo by James Reasoner

Livia J. Washburn has been a professional writer for more than twenty years. She received the Private Eye Writers of America Award and the American Mystery Award for her first mystery, *Wild Night*, written under the name L.J. Washburn, and she was nominated for a Spur Award by the Western Writers of America for a novel written with her husband, James Reasoner. Her short story "Panhandle Freight" was nominated for a Peacemaker Award by the Western Fictioneers. She lives with her husband in a small Texas town, where she is constantly experimenting with new recipes. Her two grown daughters are both teachers in her hometown, and she is very proud of them.

CONNECT ONLINE

www.liviajwashburn.com